THE HERESY OF RAIN

Zac Mooney

Publisher's Cataloguing-in-Publication Data

Mooney, Zac
    The heresy of rain / written by Zac Mooney
ISBN: 978-1-953932-08-2

1. Fiction - General I. Title II. Author

Library of Congress Control Number: 2021950075

For Olivia

Prologue

The blues is a language unique and irrespective. It is a foreign tongue but also familiar, a dialect whose roots reach depths unimaginable. It does not ask anything of its devotees. It does not require perfection. And it does not require technical precision. What it requires is soul. It floats and slides about in the darkness, and it smooths the rough places. It rounds the angles. The blues is a prayer. It is an offering of one's sadness and misery to all who can hear and all who might answer. The blues is a confession. It is sin and redemption. It is salvation. It is a belltoll of loss and an offering of tears. It is forgiveness. It is an invocation to darkness and a benediction to the same. It is a celebration of melancholy as rain is a celebration of misery. The blues is a universal call to worship.

The blues is a soulstorm of spirit.

Part I

"I would gather wildflowers, wild violets, honeysuckle, yellow jas-
mine, snakeflowers, and waterlilies, and with wire grass we'd weave them
into necklaces and crowns. We'd bedeck ourselves with our handiwork
and loll about thus beautified, beyond the touch of the everyday world.
Then when the slanted rays of the sun burned orange in the tops of the
pines, we'd drop our jewels into the stream and watch them float away
toward the sea."

—James Hurst

The Heresy of Rain

THE AIR IN THE RESTAURANT WAS THICK with smoke and dust and heat and wetness. This was no matter to the young man because his eyes were closed against the night, against the world and all that could be seen. And he could not have seen if he had wanted to, by and by, the room so foggy with the miasma of two o'clock Sunday morning. A dense and pungent cloud, palpable and knowable and comforting to all it shrouds. There was the pulsing of two hundred feet tapping and tapping and tapping in time, stomping to the ragged beat of a young bluesman. When he opened his eyes he could barely see the keys through the restaurant's haze, but no one ever needed to see to hear music. No one ever needed to see. And so he played. Black keys and white keys and adjacent keys and tri-tones and octaves, sevenths diminished and fifths augmented. Arpeggios and syncopated rags. Blues real enough to make a man cry. Dirty and grimy in-between sounds of the soul. The club patrons echoed their approval like the devoted congregants they were. Men and women would say yes sir, yes sir, or they would hum and nod. The pianist Henry King knew how to play the piano. And he knew what kind of music these folks wanted to hear. He knew how to play the blues.

The club was Sammie's Restaurant, near the seawall at the Texas coast of the Gulf of Mexico, in Galveston. The piano was on an elevated dais in the dining area. It was a fine grand piano. A black Baldwin, whose timbre was rich and resonant and earthy and magical. The restaurant was done up in opulent shades of burgundy, with wainscoting and art and photographs in black frames with gold flecks. Some of the photographs were black and white pictures of musicians who had once played at Sammie's, all of them inscribed to the proprietor and his staff. And all about the place was crystal: chandeliers, wine glasses, candleholders on tables. The crystal and dinnerware concerted in an everpresent din of chiming and clinking. The tables were round with cream-colored linen to match the ivory in the wainscoting. Some tables sat two diners; others sat four. Waiters ran the dining area like a cadre of insects, darting deftly through the room in curving aisles like burrows and then disappearing into the kitchen or behind the bar as if reporting to the colony's queen. No one had ever seen a Sammie's waiter spill, drop, or trip. The boss required precision. With the lush carpet and high ceilings and paneled walls, the acoustics were perfect, ideal for a solo pianist. How often people would ask the boy where did you learn to play like that? And he would shrug and mumble something sheepish, not for coyness but shyness. Or if not shyness exactly then something like it, for he did not always like attention, and his voice was the music. He required no accompaniment. His voice was hammers on string, and everyone was fine with that. Also: he never did learn the way people learn to read or drive or ride a bicycle. His music was the product of listening and repeating, hours of cacophonic and clanging and dissonant experiments on his grandmother's upright until one day, there it was.

It was a typical Saturday evening or Sunday morning crowd, and he saved his best for the last set, the one-thirty set. Maybe he would play "Ain't Nobody's Business" or "Dust My Broom," or if he wanted to play something modern he might do "It Hurts Me Too" in B-flat. But it really didn't matter. They all just wanted to hear the boy play. If he was feeling brave he might even trot out something he composed. There were no dancers, for this was not dancing music. No, something else is what it was, something that affected people the way a preacher affects people. Henry's blues was a sermon and a call to God, perhaps, if you believed in God. And sometimes Henry's blues would make people believe in God once again because what else could explain the music? If this wasn't religious then nothing was religious.

He finally stood and straightened his back and nodded humbly to those in attendance, for perhaps he was shy after all. He recognized most of the faces in the dining area; these were mostly weekend regulars. Revelers and diners who delighted in the aristocracy of a night out. Having gathered the bills from his glass jar he smiled and shook a man's hand and then another and then looked a woman in the eye as she sloshed about. She was pretty with almond eyes and dark skin, and her hair was done up and her dress revealing. She'd had too much to drink and had to be helped to her feet. She started to say something but fell from drunkenness and required assistance out the door. Henry was relieved. He tipped out to the waiters and barmen and left quickly before his devotees could call for an encore.

The Heresy of Rain

He walked home the usual way, traveling the two miles over parking lots, half-lit streets, alleys, and sidewalks. Some nights he would come across a dozen nightcrawlers and late revelers. And some nights he didn't come across a soul. Three minutes into his walk, he heard his name called in the salty and breezy night and turned around to find the police chief in his patrol car easing up alongside him.

"Evening, Henry."

"Evening, Chief Wisdom."

"Call me Grant, son. I've told you a hundred times. Just call me Grant."

"Seems too informal."

"I'm police chief, not the king."

"Well, all right."

Wisdom said: "How was work tonight?"

"Pretty much like any other night."

"Everybody behave in there?"

"Sure." He paused and then looked down and up again. "When are you going to get over to our place and have supper with Grace and me? You haven't been over since last Christmas. It's been too long."

The chief sighed and nodded. "It sure has. Most nights I'm on patrol. My officers can't handle a goddamn thing without me explaining it to them or doing it for them. Christ almighty. Maybe next week?"

"You got it."

"You need a ride home?"

"No, it's only a few minutes. I like the walk. I can clear my head a little in the quiet."

"All right. Be safe."

"Good night, Chief."

Henry had turned toward his route home before Wisdom could chastise him again for formality. So the police chief watched Henry walk for a few seconds and then rolled up the window of his patrol car and continued on his way.

WHEN HENRY ARRIVED HOME it was after two, almost two-thirty. Their house was a small wooden cottage on 4th street. There were only two small bedrooms, one of which was a catchall, a room with coats and keepsakes and photographs and albums and china and old toys. Too, they had tried upon a time to do some gardening but could never stay with it, so the landscaping seemed to be in a kind of perpetual transition. Half-tended hedges and flowerboxes with a mishmash of perennials. The house needed paint, but all the houses on the island needed paint. Even the Victorian mansions on Broadway with their resplendence and money. Those houses were the sentries of the island, with their majesty and high porches with swings and wooden rockers and ceiling fans and glasses of sweet iced tea. They lined the main road like hulking soldiers ever-awaiting commands. Even those houses needed paint. He took off his shoes and hat in the kitchen after closing the screen door and the heavy wooden door against a light rain. He hung his jacket on a chairback. He did not switch on the light.

"Henry?"

He cursed himself silently for waking her.

She said again: "Henry?"

"It's me, Grace. I'm sorry for waking you. I didn't mean to make so much noise."

"You didn't wake me. I was worried is all."

"You worry too much."

She appeared as a shadow at the mouth of the dark hallway, then as his eyes adjusted to the darkness she was lovely, gowned in a simple white slip and her soft, round face framed by long brown hair that fell all about her bare shoulders. He was again reminded of her simple beauty, and he was glad she was not asleep. She moved surely but braced herself with one hand on the doorframe.

She said: "You are somebody who needs to be worried about." Even in the shadows her mouth was beautiful and red and expressive.

He smiled because she was so easy to love.

"Maybe you're right," he said, "but I'm home now."

"Was work all right?"

"It was crowded and smoky. People were loud and drunk, and most of them smelled bad. But everyone seemed to like the music."

"Everyone always likes the music."

"Maybe not everyone."

"Anyhow, I like the music."

"I should hope so on account of you're married to the musician."

He strode across the chipped and spotted linoleum floor and took her in his arms and held her tight. Together they listened to the rain as it fell harder, and they did not move, for there was nowhere to go. Her hair and skin were soft, and she smelled clean and fresh. They stood for a time, paired perfectly against the night, for their bodies fit together and held one another and matched seamlessly. He closed his eyes and swayed with his young wife in his arms. A sweet dance to the sound of early autumn rain. Some nights there was the sound of the surf. The ocean's rhythm, so patterned and cadenced. But rain or any other nighttime noise muted the surf. On this night it was only the rain they heard.

After some time she reached up and touched his cheek and asked if he would play for her.

"It's late, Grace."

"You know it helps me sleep. Play softly so you don't wake the neighbors. The Daleys wouldn't mind to be woken, but the Albans are cranky."

"The Albans are always cranky. But you can't blame them for being woken up at three in the morning."

"Then don't wake them." She held out her hand, and he took it and led her to the old sofa in their small den or living room. They had a radio along with the sofa, and the old and faded and scuffed upright piano that Henry doted on and loved and cherished as though it were a child.

He often played for Grace. After all, it was how they met. Not in a restaurant or a club but at a funeral. When he was eighteen a woman offered him ten dollars to play at her mother's funeral. Her mother had loved the Southern spirituals, and the woman asked Henry to play four spirituals and a few hymns. That day Grace had been visiting her parents' graves with her older sister, Diana, and she heard Henry playing inside the small church and told her sister to please find out who the pianist is. They waited until the service was over, and Diana approached Henry and introduced Grace. Within a year they were married. And now she often asked him to play so she could sleep. So he led her to the sofa where she sat and folded her legs beneath her and smoothed out her gown and rested her head on the sofa's arm. She closed her eyes and parted her lips in a kind of halfsmile.

He was tired after working so late but played very softly some simple lullabies he'd composed for her years before. He would give them names like "Sweet Grace" or "A Rose for Grace" or "Moonlit Grace." So he played for her but not so loud for fear of the Albans, whose bedroom was only just twelve or fifteen feet from the piano. The houses in their neighborhood were packed close. Perhaps on this night the neighbors would not be bothered because of the steady rain, which muffles all sounds. He knew he would only have to play for a few minutes. She would soon be asleep, her lips still slightly parted in that dream smile. And he would carry her to bed, careful not to wake her. She loved his music, the same way she loved his voice and his touch and even his smell. Her senses alighted at his presence. She cherished him and all of his palpable qualities devoutly.

For Grace King was blind.

The Heresy of Rain

IT WAS THE NEXT EVENING, and Henry took Grace to the seawall to feel the breeze that wafted from the Gulf of Mexico and blanketed Galveston with salt air. It was a night off for Henry. Occasionally the restaurant's day-to-day operator—a man who was Sammie's only son—would bring in a guitarist or saxophonist and give Henry a break. Anyhow this night was Sunday, and there was no live music on Sunday evenings. On the seawall they sat on a bench overlooking the water and listened to the ocean. The sun had set, and now there were stars and a moon that was nearly full. The moon hung so low in the sky, Henry told her, it seemed you could almost reach out and touch it. Grace asked him to describe the things he saw, as she often did. A childhood sufferer of German measles, Grace had been completely blind by the age of five. Now at twenty-one, she had forgotten almost everything she'd seen as a child. She vaguely remembered some colors and shapes.

"Tell me about the sky." She leaned her head on Henry's shoulder as he cradled her. Cars passed occasionally behind them along Seawall Boulevard. Couples jaunted quietly along the way. At this hour there were no swimmers or fishermen in the water.

"It's unlike anything else," he said. "Tonight there are a million stars."

"Stars." Grace had the cuteness of a child and often in her wistfulness parroted Henry's words, not for immaturity or even silliness but for devotion.

"And the moon is just in front of us."

"Tell me what the moon looks like." She had asked him a hundred times before. She said: "I remember it a little. But it's so far back. I don't know if I'm remembering the moon. Or if the thing I am thinking of is something else, like someone's face or a cloud or a loaf of bread. You have to tell me. Please."

"It's a circle or ball. I guess a sphere is what you would call it. Almost like a plum or marble. Mostly it's white, and sometimes you can see the whole thing, right in the middle of the sky at night. Some parts of the moon are darker, like shadows or shades of gray. No one really knows how it got there, a giant round rock that sits in the sky. If you look long enough and closely enough the gray spots might look like shapes or pictures or even a face. Sometimes the moon is hidden in a shadow and appears as just a sliver or a halfcircle."

"Is it full tonight?"

"It's almost full tonight. And people say someday we'll land on the moon, on a spaceship or airplane of some kind."

"What do you think?"

"I don't know anything about space. It doesn't seem likely, I suppose. We can only just now fly around our own world in an airplane. How can we expect to fly to another world? I don't know."

"What about the stars?"

"There are so many of them. Countless, I guess."

"You said a million."

"That's just the highest number I could think of. Maybe thousands or hundreds or more than a million. I don't know of any numbers larger than that. They are little dots of bright light all about the sky." Henry stared at the dotted and nebulous sky and wished for an instant that he and his bride might be transported at once into the night so that they may be angels of ablution and that they may be absolved and made whole again. The clouds were black and the sky black but the clouds very few. The clouds drifted about the mooned sky both a lifetime away and inches from the admirers. If Grace and Henry willed it perhaps they could indeed thrust themselves into the night or pull the sky to them and be not mere admirers but participants in the magic of the universe. The wind was cool and comforting, and they closed their eyes like mendicants of the night, awaiting the sky's alms and supplicating that the cosmos may sanctify them as faithful adherents of the evening.

Grace sighed but not of sadness so much as her own longing.

She said: "I know it's silly, but I wish I could see them. The stars."

"It's not silly. And I would give you my sight a thousand times if I could."

"I know you would."

The Heresy of Rain

SOMETIMES HENRY AND GRACE would stay awake all night talking. Maybe it would be the rare night when Henry was home before one or two. Grace would be up, and perhaps the two of them would sit in their bedroom or go into the kitchen or living room with coffee or walk to the sea's edge. The things they discussed were variable. Often they spoke of music, and sometimes they talked about the sky. Sometimes Henry would just let Grace talk, for she had so much to say. He was often intimidated by her ideas though enthralled and driven on by her enthusiasm for history or politics or philosophy. Henry's heart burst for love, but he knew little of such things. So he was content to listen to her speak of notions beyond his learning or even beyond his understanding. He would not stop her because to him the sound of her voice was home.

Sometimes they would speak of family.

One evening she asked: "Do you ever think about us having a baby?"

"Sometimes I guess."

"What do you think about it?"

"About a baby?"

"Yes, a baby."

"Well, I don't know."

"You are stalling."

"No, I just, I don't know. I don't know. Sometimes I do."

"You think about us with babies?"

"I think about us having a family."

"I'm glad," she said.

"Well. All right."

"Do you ever think about starting a family soon? Having a baby soon?" She turned toward him and smiled sweetly and reached up and touched his cheek.

"How soon?"

"I don't know. I would like to have a baby before I'm old."

"You're twenty-one."

"I'll be old before we know it."

"Then I'll be old too."

"Stop teasing. I'm serious."

"All right."

"Listen to me, Henry. Listen. I want a baby. I want us to have a family. Promise me we will have a baby soon."

"I don't know if that's the sort of thing a person can promise."

"Well promise me you'll think about a baby."

He was silent for a long time, and she leaned her head on his shoulder. They sat on their sofa listening to soft music on their radio.

After some time she said again: "Promise me, Henry."

"It's hard for me to imagine a baby in our life right now."

"Of course it is. Because there's no baby."

"I mean I work most nights. And what if you needed help?"

"Henry, I'm blind. Not crippled."

"I know. I know."

"Are you really worried about me being able to handle a baby by myself?"

"A little I guess."

"Well don't."

"All right."

"You know I can do anything any other woman can do."

He reached over and tucked a loose strand of hair behind her ear and touched her shoulder which was soft but also like fine china and rested his cheek on the top of her head.

"I know it."

"Good."

"It's also the world, Grace."

"What do you mean?"

"I mean is this the kind of world to bring a baby into? Is Galveston the kind of city to bring a baby into?"

"No time is ever just right. No city is ever just right. Nor any home. Nothing is ever perfect, Henry. If people waited for the right time and place to start a family there wouldn't be any families. People get married, and their lives are busy and unpredictable. It's always been that way. Babies have a way of forcing people to adjust. People find room for babies, for family. Galveston is not perfect, but it's home. This house isn't perfect. It's small and too close to the other houses and needs repairs and sometimes we get in each other's way." She laughed lightly, and so did he. "But it's home. It's home. And a baby would make it even better."

"Maybe you're right."

"I'm always right."

"You're always right."

"So you'll promise?"

"To think about having a baby?"

"Yes."

"I promise. I like the name Elizabeth."

"So you *have* thought about it."

"Maybe a little."

"I like Elizabeth too. And Camille, Claire. And Olivia. I really love Olivia."

"Olivia's nice too. What about Rebecca?"

"I like them all. What if we have a boy?"

"A boy? I haven't thought any about boy names."

"It's a possibility, you know."

"For some reason girl names are more fun, more interesting to talk about. Why is that?"

"I don't know. I guess we can name a boy Rebecca or Claire and then tell him it's his fault for being a boy, and we'd only thought about girl names."

He said: "I love you."

"I know you do."

GALVESTON HAD EXISTED as a politically or geographically important island since the early 1800s when it was named for a man named Galvez, who was an early magistrate or count. A few miles off the Texas mainland, it was a thin barrier island that had served as a strategic point for several different nations or factions over the course of the nineteenth century. Because of this it bore a rich history, one that would have seen the island become the hub of the whole of the United States South had it not been devastated by a hurricane in 1900. Galveston had been poised to be a greater cultural and financial boomtown than Houston, Atlanta, Little Rock, or even New Orleans. A failure to act urgently in the face of a coming storm, or perhaps a weatherman's hubris, had eight thousand Galvestonians lose their lives in just a few hours. The city's growth was stunted, and it never reached its potential. Never. It was a mishmash of architecturally-unrelated neighborhoods and a garish conglomeration of bars and clubs and restaurants. In this way it was unique. Some might say the island's hodgepodge was the island's character. Others might say it was an unsightly haven for criminals and lowlifes. Still others might say it was both.

Prohibition had seen the island become an important link in the burgeoning rum-running trade during which Cuba and other places supplied the entire southern half of the United States with rum. Organized crime added another layer of complexity and intrigue to the island, and though it would never rival New Orleans or Mobile or Nashville it managed to establish a niche for itself. Interesting and beautiful people arrived on Galveston and called it home, and the island's old and white oligarchy built mansions and churches and hotels. Music made its way to the island sometime between the world wars, and Henry found himself caught up in this new wave, one in which black music became everyone's music. He found during his teenage years that people would pay to hear him play the blues, so he quit school and played the blues.

The Heresy of Rain

Prohibition also brought with it to Galveston much of the debauchery associated with this era across the United States. Racketeering, money laundering, and prostitution all gained footholds in the area. And then there were the illegal card rooms. Hundreds of these dark and out-of-the-way speakeasies existed at the time. Henry King stumbled upon the poker room at Sammie's when he was seventeen, in the face of a high school dropout's boredom. He and Grace had not yet met, but they soon would. He kept his gambling habit from Grace, who never knew how much money to expect from week to week. Some weeks Henry made twenty-five dollars in tips, and the next week he would bring home more than a hundred. After some time, the game's host allowed Henry to play on credit, which worked fine for a while, until Henry ran up a debt that, with interest, became unmanageable.

LATER THAT WEEK he walked from the restaurant toward his neighborhood. The night was cloudless and sharp, and the sounds of the island were audible and crisp and palpable. The night offered him clarity. The sounds echoed and darted about. He put his hands in his trouser pockets and kept his head low and tried to ignore the sounds for fear of distraction. It is true that sometimes the world conspires against us. The sights and sounds and other sensations draw us into snares that we should have known were there. So he stayed focused on the road before him. Because he knew of the world and its many conspirators. Sirens of the night who with their song lure men into jagged rocks.

So this night was calm and clear; there were no clouds about. Henry walked quickly and silently the way a cat moves, or a burglar. When he was within a half-mile of his house he eased up his pace and allowed himself to absorb the night. And that's when he heard footsteps. He came to a stop. To continue was useless, and he especially didn't want a scene near his home. He was in an area that offered little light beyond the moon that hung low over the sea. There were two gas lamps at the intersection. And there were stars. No cars at this hour.

He turned. There were three men, like shades of the underworld, only barely lifelike and not walking so much as gliding. Soundless shadows in the night. He knew only one man would speak. They stopped several feet short of him, and the middle shade stepped forward a few feet more. Then that man paused and stood for a short moment and then turned and waved off the other two men. They retreated to a place out of earshot.

The man said: "Have you got it, Henry? Please tell me you've got it."

"I have some, Maddock. I have some."

"Some?"

"I can give you one hundred right now."

"One hundred." The man was not a large man. He was slight with a sneering but harmless countenance. But he bore a stare intense and unnerving. He had a dark complexion, was of some undeterminable ethnicity. His voice was raspy. A half-whisper.

Henry swallowed hard and searched for his voice. "Yes. Right now. I can give it to you if you'll let me."

"What is one hundred?"

"I'm sorry. What is one hundred? It's a hundred. I have it now."

"What is one hundred when you owe five thousand?"

"Five thousand? It was only four—"

"It was four thousand until it was forty-five hundred. And then it was forty-seven hundred. And now it is five thousand. You think businessmen don't charge interest? You are lucky our rates are low. So I'll repeat what I said: what is one hundred when you owe five thousand?" The man's voice had risen. It was pitched and tense, and he seemed to be aware of it, for his voice swelled and ebbed. He half-turned as if to signal to the other men he was all right, and they should remain at a distance.

"You know I don't have five thousand, Maddock. If I had five thousand dollars I would have paid you when I owed you three thousand."

"Well. That's the balance. That is your debt. There's nothing I can do about it."

"I need more time."

"There isn't any more time, Henry. Don't you understand? You've had weeks and even months. And that's it. I can't give you any more time."

"Look, let me get home and grab a few hundred more. I can pay the points."

"Pay the points. What are you talking about, pay the points?"

"The interest."

"That's not how this works, Henry. Come on, you know that. Jesus."

Henry had never seen the man so tense. Maddock's eyes twitched with some sort of fury that was just below the surface. A rage unescaped. The man seemed desperate, pleading.

Maddock continued: "Goddamn it, Henry. Goddamn it. Don't you understand what is happening? Do you think I am answerable to no one? Do you not realize the consequences of ignoring your debts? You think I like chasing people around in the middle of the night?"

"I haven't ignored my debts. I just need more time. But let me get you a few hundred more, like I said."

"Stop, Henry. Just stop. I know you. I've known you a long time. I know you mean well."

"We were friends once, Maddock."

"Maybe, maybe. Who knows, really. But that was grade school. We ran around together. Played baseball in the street. We're adults now."

"Get your boss to give me more—"

Then Maddock's very physiognomy shifted, changed, and he barked. No longer was he contemplative and prodding. No, now he was authoritarian. The time for sentimentality was over.

"You have until tomorrow, Henry, and that is all. You have hours to produce the five thousand my boss is owed. All of it. Not one hundred goddamn dollars. Not four thousand. Five thousand."

"I can't—"

"You have a wife to take care of."

Maddock said it quietly. You have a wife. A wife. He looked at Henry through the night. This was his final plea. His final play. If this wasn't it then what was there?

Henry's shoulders and neck tensed. He opened his mouth to speak but could not say anything. He only nodded slowly with dumb confirmation.

Maddock repeated: "You have a wife. You love your wife." Not questions. Statements of confirmation. Of fact.

Henry said yes but softly. His ethos had been wrenched from him. He had neither power nor authority in this exchange. He could not protect her here. This meeting was a thing whose framework and thrust and tone he could not control. Nor could he protect his home. He was powerless and helpless, and he could not even speak.

Maddock said, "I work for a man who will be paid. He will be paid. He must be paid, Henry. He must. I work for a man who does not forgive. He will make this very clear if you test him."

"I don't have five thousand, and I won't have five thousand tomorrow."

"I can't help you then. You have to try."

The Heresy of Rain

THAT NIGHT GRACE WAS ASLEEP when Henry arrived home. He went quietly about the house and took bills from the few places he had hidden them, places into which he knew Grace would not stumble. High in a kitchen cabinet behind boxes of oatmeal and cans of broth. Tucked beneath the piano's topboard near the hinge. In a paper envelope taped shut behind the quilts in the closet of the small second bedroom. He quietly laid out the bills and counted four hundred seventy dollars plus the hundred from the bar that evening. He gathered it all into one stack and rolled it and fetched a rubber band from a drawer and kept it rolled tightly and then stuck it in one of his shoes.

In the morning he told Grace he needed to take care of some business and would be home in the early evening. It was nine o'clock. Grace was uneasy. She possessed a keenness of the mind; she was sharp and perceptive and could detect small variations in Henry's voice easily when something was awry. A barometer of truth. A human polygraph. She guided herself to the small kitchen table and sat in her normal chair, and Henry poured her another cup of coffee and placed the mug in front of her and stroked her soft brown hair and kissed her forehead. She would not be so easily mollified.

She said: "You don't usually have business. And so early? What kind of business?"

Henry was prepared but knew he would sound unconvincing. He knew Grace could detect the slightest oddity in his speech. He could only hope to stumble about and leave the house quickly.

He said: "The piano at the restaurant needs tuning and a few other small repairs. And they're bringing in a drummer and a bass player to try it out and see how it sounds."

"A drummer and a bass player?"

"Yeah, sure, to see how it sounds. It's not a bad idea."

"Why would they do that? You play to a full house every night by yourself. And you'd share your pay?" She sipped her coffee.

"Also, there's a guy up on Broadway who might have some work for me during the week. Some weeks he could use an extra pair of hands to paint or haul lumber."

"Haul lumber? You can't afford splinters and jammed thumbs and broken fingers, Henry. What do you mean haul lumber? Who is this person on Broadway?"

Henry could feel the lies slipping dangerously to a place from which he'd not be able to navigate. He understood more than most men the slippery slope of trying to pass a lie by a woman.

"It's just to talk to him. I wouldn't do it if it wasn't safe."

Grace sat silently for a moment and then took her coffee and walked into the living room where she turned on the radio and sat on the sofa. Henry fingered the roll of bills he'd taken from his shoe and put in his pocket and then took his hat from the peg on the wall. He passed through the living room on his way out, stopping to kiss her on the top of her head. Then he went through the front door but turned and went back inside and strode quickly to Grace where she was sitting on the sofa, and he said I love you and kissed her tenderly on the mouth. She smiled just so and stroked his cheek and said she loved him too.

Then as he turned to leave again she said: "I thought I heard thunder earlier. Will there be rain today?"

"Looks like it. The sky is gray and a little angry-looking. You can almost hear the waves crashing if you listen close enough. I heard thunder too."

"Good, I like the rain."

"I've never heard you say that before. I thought you liked nice weather. Sunshine."

"I like sunshine, too, of course. But it's awfully disrespectful of the rain to say it's not nice weather."

"You know what I meant."

She smiled. "I know what you meant. The rain, though, it's nice too. The rain is a promise paid off by the sky. The heavens are reminding us that there will be growth. Plants and flowers and animals and trees and people, they all grow stronger and healthier with the rain. The rain softens the world a bit, makes things cleaner. And you know what I always notice about the rain?"

"What's that?"

The Heresy of Rain

"It makes everything smell nicer."

"I guess I've never thought of it that way."

"It's true. The next time it rains close your eyes for a while. Stand outside with your eyes closed. I promise you'll notice it. The world smells better, fresher. It's like everything just got a big bath, and the world is renewed. There's promise and hope. The rain makes everything possible again."

"I'll do that."

"Good. I'll see you later today."

Then he added, an afterthought: "You have your usual lunch at the church today?"

"Yes, but we're starting a little later than usual. I won't be late getting home, though."

"All right. Enjoy your day."

He left through the front door.

Grace

SHE SMILED SWEETLY AND LISTENED for the front door to close and then stopped smiling and bowed her head slightly. She drew in a deep breath and exhaled slowly and steadily. Then she closed her eyes. And she listened. She heard the clock in the living room where she sat. She listened to the ticking, and she smoothed her dress with her hands, her eyes still closed. And she timed her breathing to the clock. The predictability of the clock and its ticking. It was her metronome, her guide.

For some while longer she listened. She tried to pray but didn't know what to pray for, so she closed her eyes and leaned back into the familiarity of the old sofa. It smelled familiar as well. Not a scent she could identify, other than the scent of the sofa. It may have been vanilla or honeysuckle or biscuits or some perfume or aftershave. To Grace it was just the sofa, how the sofa smelled. Familiar, like the closing door and the clock and Henry's touch.

She stood and stepped away from the sofa and toward the front door. She turned the lock and checked to make sure the door was secure and then walked slowly to the kitchen where she checked the back door. It was locked already. Then she felt along the kitchen wall for the light switch and shut off the light and then walked down the hall toward the back of the house and drew a bath. She felt a certain unease. A feeling or some intuition. Warm baths always helped soothe her. She would take a bath and be ready around lunch time when one of the church volunteers was scheduled to pick her up for the weekly wives' luncheon.

Less than an hour later Grace stood from the bathtub and toweled her hair until it was only damp and slipped into her robe. She'd relaxed in the bath, with the rain calming her unusually frayed nerves. The robe was like the sofa. It was soft and familiar. She wrapped the robe around her body and cinched it and tied it in the front at her waist. She stepped to the sink and reached and reached for her small assortment of creams and lotions.

Then she froze.

The sound of breaking glass.

Someone else was in the house.

Henry

HE SPENT THE NEXT HOUR walking the island. He had no contacts. He had lied to Grace. There was no extra job hauling lumber and no other musicians. He had no prospects. Only the cash rolled and tucked into his pocket. Five hundred seventy dollars. Just a few minutes after leaving the house the rain started. But it was only a short shower. Quick and loud but then gone. He stepped under a rusted corrugated bus stop awning while the weather was bad; then he began walking again. He inhaled deeply. The air was fresh, clean. Just as Grace had promised.

But there was no new outlook, no fresh perspective. He was still a poor blues pianist with a gambling debt he couldn't pay. He walked on until he reached a small bookshop at the corner of Texas and Pecan. He had seen the store many times during his life but had never been inside. The sun shone brilliantly after the shower, and the shop's windows and even the wooden sign were iridescent in the morning light. He stood peering in through one of the windows. Shelves and shelves, rows and rows of books bound in cloth and paper and leather. He cupped his hands on his brow, above his eyes, so he could better see. Globes and telescopes lining the shelftops. Maps unscrolled and tacked to the walls, some framed.

Then the door swung open with a jangle. An older man with glasses and a pencil tucked behind his right ear said good morning, and they were open for business.

Henry shrugged and entered the shop.

Grace

SHE STOOD MOTIONLESS IN THE BATHROOM, burning with fear, her heart pounding and her head thundering a thousand thoughts. A drop of water fell from her hair, and water slid down her body beneath the robe. She no longer felt fresh and clean. Now she felt clammy and breathless and shaky. Weak and vulnerable.

She placed a palm on the vanity top to steady herself, and she turned toward the door to better hear. She again heard the sound of breaking glass. She heard too the clock. And the last of the bathwater draining. And then nothing again, just silence. She breathed deeply but silently, realizing only then that she had been holding her breath for some time.

Then she heard the rattling of the doorknob, the back door in the kitchen. The door opened with the creaky groan; Grace hadn't realized until then that the door creaked at all. What else hadn't she noticed? Had she missed over these months and years any other sounds spoken by the house? She tucked a strand of damp hair behind her right ear and listened. Footsteps. Feet shuffling over broken glass. Scraping and more broken glass. Then the door was closed with a loud click. She thought about the Albans and the Dalcys. The men were at work. She couldn't remember if this was the day the wives volunteered at the library. She couldn't remember, but she always remembered. Was it Tuesday or Wednesday? And when would the kind church volunteer—Dorothy—arrive to take her to the luncheon?

"Goddamnit, I think I have a piece of goddamn broken glass in my hand. Jesus Christ." The voice was gruff and harsh and unfamiliar.

"Keep your voice down. Jesus."

"Shit, it just hurts is all."

There were two voices. Two men. Two intruders. Grace's lips quavered. She couldn't swallow. Her knees were weak. Her face burned.

"Look everywhere. The boss ain't gonna be happy if we leave empty-handed. He's got to have some cash stashed here somewhere. You seen what he makes in tips."

"All right. You look around the kitchen. I'll check over in the living room. Maddock said not to take too long. He's waiting."

"Hell, I know he's waiting."

"Fine. When is the wife supposed to be home?"

"She has a church lunch on Tuesdays. Maddock said she'll be gone till about three."

"All right."

Then the sound of cabinet doors opening and closing. Furniture being pushed across the floor. The piano's various sections and compartments being searched. Drawers. Photographs and art moved or taken from the wall and rehung. Grace began to cry softly. She mouthed the Lord's Prayer and clasped her hands under her chin, still leaning on the door.

Henry

"LOOKING FOR ANYTHING IN PARTICULAR, young man?" It was the book-shop owner.

"No, I don't reckon I am. It's just I've never been in here. I don't know why. I guess I'll look around for a while if that's all right with you."

"Of course; stay as long as you like. Let me know if you have any questions."

"Sure. Thanks." Henry smiled slightly and touched the brim of his hat.

The shop had a particular smell. The sweet pungency of old paper, dust, leather. The shop wasn't large. He walked slowly about for a moment before seeing a small card marking the music section. He walked slowly toward this shelf of volumes, many books dealing with Southern music and slave spirituals and ragtime and classical music, and there were several biographies of famous composers, American and European alike. It was a dizzying collection of works whose existence he had never considered.

Near the top of the music section was a dusty cardboard box. Henry pulled down the box and coughed away the dust and set the box on the floor and squatted down to have a look at its contents. There were several bundles of old sheet music along with some vinyls. He flipped through the vinyls until he came to an Octavian Pace record, an older one he didn't already own. He took the LP out of the box and replaced the box on the shelf and carried the LP toward the front of the store.

"How much for this Octavian Pace record?"

The shop owner smiled. "I forgot about those records." He put his finger to his chin in an act Henry could neither discern as serious contemplation nor a caricature.

Henry smiled in spite of his dark mood.

"Would you give me a dollar for it?"

"Of course."

"Are you a musician?" The shopkeeper took the dollar from Henry and slid it into his apron pocket.

"I play the piano. Octavian Pace is one of the best around."

"If I recall correctly, he's played on the island before, though I can't rightly remember when."

"It would be a treat if he came back some day."

"That it would. Is there anything else I can help you find?"

"No, I don't think so. I really appreciate the record, though. I think my wife will like it."

"Is she a musician as well?"

Henry smiled shyly and lowered his eyes. "No, but she loves music."

The shopkeeper took off his glasses and wiped the lenses with his apron and returned the smile. "You ought to bring her by here someday. Maybe we could find a book for her."

Henry nodded and began to turn toward the door but stopped himself.

"Actually—" He didn't know how to reinvent the conversation.

"Something else?"

"Yeah. My wife, she's blind—"

"Ah, I see." The shopkeeper returned his glasses to his nose and stepped around the front counter and grabbed Henry's elbow—not in an aggressive manner; more like an excited grandfather leading his grandchild to a favorite fishing spot or some such thing—and led Henry back toward the darker and dustier rear of the store, a different aisle than the music selection.

"I have a few braille titles back here."

"That's what I was wondering."

"I know; it's not an easy thing to ask. For some reason—" now the man stopped and turned and looked Henry directly square: "for some reason there are things in life that are difficult to talk about, to ask about, even though they shouldn't be."

Henry nodded.

The shopkeeper took a few more steps and pointed to a stack of volumes that appeared to have been there for years.

"These have been here for years!" The man blew the dust away from the books and patted them with pride.

"Grace reads sometimes, but she doesn't talk much about books."

"Do you talk much about books?"

"No. No, I guess I don't."

"Well, maybe you should. Pick out a few of these."

"I really don't have much money—"

"Nonsense!" The man laughed lightly. "I don't remember when I got these or how long I've had them. Search through them and take however many you think she'd like. No charge. But on one condition."

"What's that?"

"You bring your bride to the store and introduce her to me. Sound good?"

"Yes sir."

The man grasped Henry's shoulder for a second and then smiled and walked back toward the front of the shop. He turned before disappearing around an aisle of shelving.

He said: "By the way, I'm Martin. Martin Adams."

"Good to meet you, Mr. Adams. I'm Henry."

Several minutes later Henry was back on the drying sidewalk. He held his Octavian Pace record and three books for Grace: one Jane Austen novel, a book on Galveston history, and a small collection of Poe stories.

He smiled to himself—proud and somehow revitalized—and walked toward Sammie's. He'd get a cold soda from the club before taking his bookstore haul back to the house.

Grace

"JESUS CHRIST, STU. There ain't shit here."

"Keep looking, Darryl. And keep your goddamn voice down, for Christ's sake."

Grace leaned her forehead against the door and placed her left palm flush on it and slid her right hand to the knob. She very quietly unlocked the door and tried to breathe steadily and silently.

The intruders—there were two—rummaged for a few more moments and then shuffled together toward the rear of the house, toward the bathroom.

"Look," said one of the men, "there's two rooms back here. One guest bedroom and the master bedroom. That son of a bitch sure as shit has some cash stashed here somewhere. He told Maddock last night. He said he had hundreds holed up here. Maybe he's got thousands. That son of a bitch. We still have plenty of time before anyone gets home. We'll check the bathroom before we leave."

The men shuffled past the bathroom. She heard one man enter the very small extra bedroom and the other pad his way into the room she shared with Henry.

Grace closed her eyes and pulled close and tight the collar of her robe and then pulled the sash snug. She tried to swallow but still could not and willed herself not to cry or scream and then opened the bathroom door as quietly as she could and ran for the kitchen. Her only hope was getting through the back door and screaming for help.

As she tried to hurry through the hallway her knee hit the bathroom door, and the door swung around and hit the wall loudly. She kept going.

"What the hell was that?"

"Is someone home? Jesus Christ!"

The intruders both left their stations and hurried back to the hallway. They saw a white-robed figure making for the kitchen. They hurried after her.

She ran, saying "please, please, please" for the back door. She knew exactly how many steps it would take, knew exactly where every piece of furniture should have been situated. But the burglars had moved the chairs; they had upset the furniture slightly during their looting. With the men just a few feet behind her, Grace tripped as her foot was tangled with a chair leg. She yelped as her robe was caught on the chair backing and screamed in pain as she fell onto a floor covered in broken glass and slid headfirst into the door. Searing pain.

The last sounds she would hear were the horrible men closing in on her.

"Goddamnit, she heard us say our names."

"Are you sure? Should we get Maddock?"

"Yeah, I'm sure. Aw, hell. Just damn it all to hell. Shit."

"We got to do this?"

"Shit, I don't see no other way."

She tried to scream but could not. All she could do was retreat within herself and pray it would end quickly.

There were the sounds of footsteps and crunching glass. There was the whitehot pain.

A few moments.

Then blackness.

Then nothing.

Henry

He walked through the side door into the club and went for the bar.

"Trav," he said. "Could you get me—"

Trav looked up and nodded toward the phone. "Henry, Chief Wisdom has called here twice looking for you. Something important."

"Important?"

"An emergency, he said. He needs you to get home immediately."

"He called here?" Henry couldn't process what was happening. He didn't understand Trav, didn't understand why Wisdom would need to see him.

Trav said: "Let's go. I'll take you." He tossed a white bar towel toward the sink and grabbed his keys from under the cash register.

Henry said stupidly: "Did something happen? What does he mean there's been an emergency? Grace is at the church today. What happened?"

"Goddamnit, I don't know. Let's go."

They hurried to the small parking lot behind the restaurant.

"I was just at the bookshop."

"Jesus, Henry. Get in the car."

Henry knew something was very wrong when he and Trav drove up to the house. There were three Galveston Police patrol cars parked along the street at odd angles, as if driven and left in haste. He left Trav and ran toward the front door, still clutching his Octavian Pace record and the three braille books for Grace. Just as he reached the door Grant Wisdom appeared and caught Henry in his arms and held Henry and shook his head, and Henry could tell the chief had been crying.

Henry screamed: "What's happening, Chief Wisdom? Grant, where's Grace? Where's Grace?"

Wisdom only shook his head and said "I'm sorry, son. She was gone when we got here. Already gone. I'm sorry. We don't know who. I'm so sorry, Henry."

Henry pushed the chief aside and ran into the house and threw the record and the books onto the sofa and then saw Grace splayed on the kitchen floor, motionless and half-covered in her bathrobe and broken glass all about and her head blue and red and crushed with blood all about, so much blood. He cried no, no, no and knelt to the floor and gathered her in his arms and wailed into the afternoon. There was so much blood. He said he was sorry and held her head tightly to his chest and rocked back and forth and kissed her head and stroked her hair.

As Henry cried loudly that he was sorry and he loved her his neighbors began arriving, first the Albans then the Daleys with their gossipy curiosity that so quickly turned to real horror upon this terrible scene of lamentation. Of death.

The Heresy of Rain

HENRY SAT AT THE KITCHEN TABLE. It was the following day, and Grace's body had been carted to the morgue where it was awaiting a close examination. But no examination was truly necessary. An autopsy would reveal nothing that wasn't already obvious to all involved. So Henry was in the kitchen, his head heavy with no sleep and his eyes heavy with crying and sadness and disbelief in the face of such a dreadful discovery the previous evening. The books and the record he had acquired at the bookshop sat still splayed on the sofa. There was no sound, save the occasional scratch of a pen on paper, for Galveston Police Chief Grant Wisdom sat in the other chair. The living room clock chimed ten. What had once been Grace's audible standard of a passed hour was now a garish and clanging reminder that she was gone, a knell of sorrow and a dirge for the living.

"Henry."

Henry did not move nor look at his questioner nor even hear the question.

Wisdom said once more but louder: "Henry."

Henry jolted slightly and looked fuzzily at the chief who was also his godfather.

"Henry, are you listening?"

"Yeah."

"You have to tell me."

"Tell you?"

"Son, you've got to tell me, tell me whatever it is."

"What do you mean whatever it is?"

Henry could see the chief was growing frustrated. But the chief's frustration was no concern of his.

"Jesus, Henry. I sat with you two hours last night but agreed to come back over here this morning on account of you could get some sleep. I know this is difficult. It would be difficult for anyone, but you, so young, no other family. I'll help you whatever way I can, but you have to let me do my job. And I can do my job if you'll just talk to me."

"What is there to say?"

"Plenty, I think."

"About what?"

Wisdom sighed, said quietly and almost with apology: "About who murdered your wife."

Henry shrugged and looked past the chief into the living room and stared at the piano, which now sat like a mute relic from a distant time gone by. A barren and cold and foreign thing.

"I don't know. I told you."

Wisdom sat silently for a moment and then sighed again.

"Henry, I know about the gambling."

Henry's gaze darted from the piano to his godfather, and he opened his mouth to protest but stopped and couldn't even stammer something in his own defense. So he looked down at the table and sighed as his eyes welled up at the thought of his wife being attacked by some cowardly goon and her not knowing what was happening and finally suffering if even for seconds.

"I know, Henry. The police department, we know about this."

"Then why are you talking to me?"

"We've only had our eye on the gambling outfit for a few months. We have an idea of the regular players, the locations, even the dealers. But we don't yet know who runs the show. We have an idea but nothing concrete yet. You can help us with that, and it'll put us a step closer to finding Grace's killer."

"What does it matter? She'll still be gone."

"I know it doesn't seem like it now, but this is all very important."

Henry just looked at his godfather and then looked about the kitchen and could not reconcile what was happening with what ought to be happening. The terrible and heartbreaking reality of the world against the happy simplicity of the way the world should be. And he looked again at the books that had been for Grace and thought about those rare and cherished nights when he and Grace could sit on the seawall, and he could be her eyes and tell her of everything he saw in the sky.

"I guess I don't have anything to tell you other that what you already know."

"Henry, I know you can help us. You can give us a name. Tell me who runs the poker games, and I can protect you."

"Protect me?"

"Well—"

"I don't deserve protecting. Grace, she needed protecting. She deserved..." Henry's thought trailed into the air.

"You don't have to go about this alone."

"I am alone."

"You aren't alone. I'm here with you. I'm not going anywhere."

"That's not what I meant."

"I know, but it needed saying anyway."

"Maybe I just need to be alone a few days."

"I can't leave this for long, Henry. It's not just the poker rooms. It's my job to find Grace's killer. Or killers. And I think you have an idea but won't tell me."

"I don't know anything. I told you that already."

"I figure you were in a hole against those guys. I figure you might have been in deep."

"Maybe."

"When? How much? Henry. Come on, son."

Henry could not even look at the chief now. He sighed heavily and put is head in his hands, and Wisdom put his hand on top of his hat, which was on the small dining table with the formica surface and the aluminum ridges. He put his hat on his head and took the pen and the small pad and slid them into his shirt pocket and pushed his chair from the table.

He said: "Henry. I've known you your whole life. I've not always been an attentive and thoughtful godfather, but I haven't stopped loving you, ever. My heart hurts for you right now, and I wish I could take away your pain. I wish I could, but I can't. What I can do is listen to you anytime you'd like to talk. And I can do my best to serve justice and bring in the man who did this. And I think you can help. I'm going to leave you alone for a day or two, let you get your wife buried. Then I'm going to bring you in to the office if I have to. I ask that you don't make me do that."

"I'll do my best."

Chief Wisdom put his hand on Henry's shoulder and let it remain there for a time before exiting through the back door and leaving Henry to his misery.

Henry walked slowly to the piano that had for so long served as a conduit that linked his wife and him. He sat down and stared at the cold white keys, and then he began to play in her honor. He did not care if his playing could be heard in other houses or whether it bothered anyone, for who could possibly ask him to stop? He played all of the lullabies he had written for her. His eyes wet and his heart aching, he couldn't bring himself to stop.

For hours that day he sat at his grandmother's old upright, and with his lullabies and his blues and his hymns of lamentation he tried to exalt Grace to the heavens, for he alone could. And when the sky opened sometime that afternoon and flooded the island with torrents, he played louder and dared the rain to choke him out. Finally, he stopped playing and crossed to the window, where he parted the thin curtains and watched the storm and thought about Grace's notion that rain is a cleansing force of renewal and hope. But the rain was a requiem. The rain was a requiem for the dead and the living. A requiem for the blind and the seeing. A requiem for the loved and the loathed. A requiem for the innocent and the guilty. A requiem for the saved and the damned. A requiem for eternity. A requiem for nothing, for nothingness.

He finally gave up staring at the rain that evening and walked slowly to the bedroom and fell onto the bed exhausted and sad. He thought of Grace and resolved to think about her as much as possible from this point on for fear of forgetting her face. So he lay there in the bed he had just the day before shared with his wife, and willed himself not to forget.

GRACE'S FUNERAL WAS A QUIET CEREMONY on the central part of the island, a graveside service attended by only a few mourners. The morning was bright and cheery, which seemed to Henry to be a mockery of grief, a reminder of life and motion in this time of sorrow and stillness, like when a child misses a day of school and returns the next day to find that everything went on without him, that the world did not stop and honor his absence. No, it churns on and on with little regard for anyone's troubles. Other than the pastor and Henry and Grant Wisdom there was Grace's sister Diana, who at this point was Grace's only surviving close family member. There were three of Grace's classmates—who attended the school for the blind with her—and their small cadre of handlers. There was the gravedigger and one other graveyard attendant. There was a teacher from Grace's school, a stern older woman with a shock of white hair and cheeks purpled with rouge, a woman who at any other time might have been strict and intimidating but who now was softened and sad. There were Trav and Joe, both barmen at Sammie's. And there was a young married couple from the Lutheran church where Grace had often volunteered to work with the children. Lastly there were Grace and Henry's neighbors. Two middle-aged couples with their genuine empathy but also their awkwardness and stiffness and unfamiliarity.

Grace's body would be borne to the earth in a simple white casket only lightly adorned. It was lacquered and shiny and had pewter handles and trim. On the casket's lid there was a kind of relief sculpture of two hands joined in prayer. Diana had helped Henry by paying for the casket, and now at the service she appeared numb and miserable, a tired woman staring at her sister's coffin with a cruel understanding of life's misfortune. Her husband could not attend because he was on a job off the Louisiana coast. So this small company of grievers peered unblinking in the sun at Grace's white coffin as the pastor spoke of God's plan and salvation and heaven. He declared victory on Grace's behalf on account of her essential goodness. He declared she was meeting her maker and her savior, and those left on earth who grieve should not be sad but rather should be overjoyed in the face of her ascent to paradise. The pastor spoke of angels and heaven's gate, of our covenant with God and of sadness and pain. He spoke of redemption. He spoke of God's mercy and how even though it was difficult to see at a time like this we can be sure God is a loving and compassionate creator, as seen most clearly in his son, Jesus of Nazareth. There was a soft breeze, by and by, and Henry could hear the distant sounds of life: birds tittered about, and children squealed their delight in games of tag or kickball or jumprope. Cars passed loudly in the distance. That the world carried on with such nonchalance seemed disrespectful to the dead. But it is a fact that the living must press on. The world at large does not grieve. It does not. So we press on.

After the short ceremony the mourners filed away one by one, peeling from the gravesite after touching Henry's shoulder or placing a solitary flower on the casket that so gleamed in the midmorning sun. Grace's former teacher placed such a flower on the casket and then turned and glared at Henry with sudden bitterness and hatred. Diana was there with Henry when the pastor backed away slowly and nodded his solemn condolences to Henry and finally turned and walked away with his head bowed slightly and his hands clasping a worn black bible behind his back. The chief had peeled off with the others but stood at the churchyard's periphery to give Henry some space. Diana stood next to Henry as the cemetery workers began to lower the casket into the grave. Henry's shoulders slumped, and he began to cry silently in the morning's bright glory, and Diana touched Henry's back and cried too.

Diana said quietly: "I know it doesn't seem fair."

"That's because it isn't fair."

"I know. I know."

"I'm sorry, Diana."

"You don't have anything to be sorry for, Henry. You loved her more than anything. Anyone could see that. Everyone knows you did."

"I keep thinking of her in those last seconds. The terror—"

"Henry, don't. What good does that do?"

"Goddamn. I'm sorry."

"You loved her. I don't know what happened. I don't know who killed her, and these past few days have seen me go about the scenario in my head. I suppose you know who killed her or who ordered her killed.

Maybe not. I can't possibly know. I have thought about whether it was a robbery. But this was no robbery. I have thought about other things, more heinous and sinister things. But this was no rape. I believe she was killed by someone evil and terrible. I know she didn't do anything to provoke her killer. Perhaps you did, I don't know. But I believe you loved her more than anything, and I believe that there's nothing you could have done once her murder was decided."

"I could have been there."

She dabbed her cheeks below her eyes with a handkerchief. "A person can't always be there."

"She said she wouldn't let me die."

"What do you mean she wouldn't let you die?"

"When we got engaged. She said she would protect me."

Diana smiled sadly. "That sounds like Grace."

"But it was I who should have been protecting her."

Diana rubbed Henry's back and stood on her toes to kiss Henry's cheek, and she and Henry watched as the cemetery keepers began to shovel dirt into the grave, like two ancient shamans performing some sacred and rhythmic rite.

Diana said softly that Grace was surely in a place free of pain, a place absent of suffering.

"Why do we say things like that?"

"Like what?"

"Like she's in a better place."

"To comfort the living, I guess."

"I guess so. Do you really suppose she's in a better place?"

"Could she possibly be in a worse place? Worse than this place where beautiful young and defenseless blind women are bludgeoned in their own homes?"

Henry had no response. He only shook his head and watched the shoveling.

Diana touched Henry's cheek and offered another sad smile before walking away and disappearing onto the mainland and out of Henry's life.

When the casket was at last covered and when the workers had left, Henry crouched near the ground and apologized to Grace again and again. He offered to God or something like God his own soul in exchange for her life. He then cursed the same God for allowing such an injustice to occur, for surely this was not just. This was not just.

He turned and saw Chief Wisdom standing near the cemetery's gate, waiting for him. Henry stood and dropped his head in his hand and then turned and walked a few hundred feet to his left. Then he took a short, paved path another couple hundred feet deeper into the cemetery and stopped after some time in front of his grandmother's headstone. He told her she would have loved Grace had she been alive to meet her. He admitted to her that he had demons he could not shake and that if he had been stronger and more resilient then his wife would be alive. He told his grandmother that, if she were still alive, perhaps he would be stronger. He told her quietly that he wished she were still here and that if she were then perhaps she could have helped and maybe Grace would still be alive. He said he knew that didn't make much sense, but somehow he believed the truth of it anyway.

He finally retreated toward the edge of the cemetery to find the chief still there, standing at the graveyard's gate like a lone lookout guarding against Henry's exit.

Henry stopped before Chief Wisdom and sighed and looked at his godfather.

The chief said he was sorry for Henry's loss and gripped Henry's shoulder and looked in the distance at his godson's wife's grave and beyond that toward the horizon which only a few miles away held the sea. The morning had not changed, still a celebratory sunshine in the face of such unhappiness. The air would warm as the morning turned to afternoon, and the Texas sun bathed the island in a thick, hazy heat.

Then the chief led Henry to his truck, and they drove toward Henry's neighborhood. In the truck Wisdom said again he was sorry, but they had to sort out a few things so the investigation could carry on. Henry said he understood and sadly peered out the passenger window. Before they arrived at Henry's home Wisdom stopped at Cal's and bought two large paper cups of coffee and brought them out to the truck, and then they were off again. At the house, Henry and his godfather sat at the small kitchen table with their hats off and their steaming cups of coffee before them, and there was a reticence that was deafening.

Wisdom said: "Let's start at the beginning, son." He had no small pad today but a larger notebook which he took from his briefcase, along with a pen.

"The beginning?"

The Heresy of Rain

"Yes, the very earliest point that you started playing poker for money."

Henry took a sip of his coffee, which was still too hot. "I learned to play poker from my grandmother. You remember her."

"Of course I do."

"After my dad died, Mom wasn't around so much. She left me with my grandmother for days at a time, starting when I was five or six."

"I remember."

"Three things she taught me were piano, poker, and shooting. Well, she didn't teach me piano so much as encourage my attempts at playing. She knew enough to tell me when I got something right or when I played a few bars that sounded like music."

"I can remember you playing bona fide music as early as when you were ten or eleven."

"Also, she taught me cards. Casino and gin and even old maid. When I was older, say eleven or so, she taught me poker. At first, five card draw. She and I would play five card draw until all hours of the night. Sometimes she would invite a few of her friends over to play. Jane Glover and Mary Lynn Francis would come over to the house. Who in the hell knows where Mom was. No one even asked. I'd be staying with Grandmother for a time, and Jane and Mary Lynn would show up. I'd play piano a while, and then we would eat supper and then settle into a poker game, each of us with a few hundred pennies to start. Me and three old widows playing poker till sunrise with ten dollars at stake. I loved those games."

"And shooting, you said?"

Henry offered a faint smile: "She took me to the gun range a few times. You should have seen her. She was something. We probably went to the gun range a dozen times. Maybe fifteen. She never took me hunting. Most of our spare time was spent playing cards."

"Did you win often?"

"At first they may have let me win from time to time. Then they didn't have to. I was pretty good by the time I was high school age."

"I'm sorry I wasn't around more."

"It's not your fault I didn't finish school."

"At least partly my fault, I imagine."

"I wasn't cut out for school. Cards and the blues, maybe, but not school. I've never been much of a reader or even a learner. It's not your fault."

"We all deserve a chance."

Both men sipped their coffees.

Henry continued: "I started playing at Sammie's every now and again when I was fifteen. Then after I quit school I played Thursday, Friday, and Saturday nights every week."

"That's about the time your grandma died." Wisdom wrote a few scribbles.

"Right, when I was almost sixteen."

"And your mother?"

"Mom had left for good by then. She and Howard left for Central Texas when I was still going to school."

"I remember. Are she and Howard Bernard still together?"

"I haven't got a clue, Grant. I don't much care."

"Did they ever get married?"

"A few years ago they did, maybe five or six years. I don't know."

"You kept on living at your grandma's place."

Henry nodded. "She owned it free and clear."

"Right."

"She left it to me, and all the furnishings. And what little she had in the bank. So I just stayed here, living by myself and playing weekends at Sammie's."

"And only sixteen years old. Jesus."

"Like I said, there wasn't anything you could have done. At any rate, I was fine with the arrangement."

"All the same, you should have been in school."

Henry shook his head and waved him off. "Anyway, I was making a little money and hardly had any expenses. I made enough to keep the lights on and have a little food on hand."

"What about taxes on the house?"

"It wasn't much. Mary Lynn took me to the courthouse each May and helped me get things squared away. Grandmother left me more than enough cash to take care of property taxes for a few years."

"Sounds like you had a support system."

"Sure."

Wisdom placed his pen on the table and rubbed his eyes. "Christ Almighty, I should have helped."

"Goddamn it, would you stop? You are my godfather, Grant, not my guardian angel. You've helped me plenty."

"Not enough. And you have to remember this is all about the time Lucille divorced me and took off—"

"Do you want to hear about the poker games, or are you going to sit there and feel sorry for yourself?"

Grant picked up his pen and gestured toward Henry.

"So I was working, but not very often. I slept during the day on weekends and even Monday, but I had a lot of time to kill during the week. So I would walk around the island, and usually I ended up at Sammie's. I would just sit at the bar, and Joe or Trav would get me a Coke. And I'd sit about, listening to the radio at the bar."

"It's bad enough they let you sit at the bar."

"They just gave me a Coke. They felt sorry for me."

"All right."

"I was seventeen when I noticed groups of men going in and out of the back."

"Back of Sammie's?"

"Yeah, sometimes one or two and sometimes several more than that. I asked Trav about it a couple of times, and he just shrugged me off. But when I asked Joe he told me it was the poker game."

"Just like that? He said it was the poker game?"

Henry nodded. "Sure. Just like that. Like it was no big deal to him. So I asked him who the men were, and he said they were Mr. Moretti's associates."

"Sammie Moretti."

"Right. Just a few days later I asked Joe if he thought they'd let me in on the poker game, and he just laughed. When I asked him what was so funny he said there's no way they'd let me back there on account of I had just turned seventeen and also on account of I'd need a thousand dollars just to get through the door."

Now Henry's godfather was seriously taking notes. This was no reminiscence about Henry's grandmother or walking to the courthouse with Mary Lynn Francis. As far as Grant Wisdom was concerned, Henry was a material witness to illegal gambling, possibly racketeering. And maybe murder. He nodded for Henry to continue.

"Several weeks later, I had the thousand. There was still a bit of Grandmother's money, plus I saved my wages and tips. Like I said, I didn't really have any expenses."

"Had you met Grace yet?"

Henry flinched, and then his eyes were glassy.

Wisdom said, "I'm sorry. I'm sorry, Henry. I know this is tough."

"Tough?"

"You know what I mean. But I have to know everything."

"Fine."

"Did you know Grace yet?"

Henry said quietly: "Not yet. Not quite yet."

"Okay."

Henry placed his hand on the table around the paper cup, which was still hot but no longer steaming but did not drink. He said again: "I hadn't yet met Grace."

"All right, son. You said you'd put together a thousand."

Henry cleared his throat, searching for the momentum that had gotten him this far in the story. "Right, I'd saved the thousand. Thinking that would get me in that back room."

"Why did you want to get in on the game?"

"What do you mean?"

"Seems as though you were making enough money to get by."

"I don't know. Maybe it was a chance to reconnect with Grandmother. I don't know."

"Maybe you were bored."

"Of course I was bored."

"Fine. So what happened next?"

"Once I had the thousand I showed up at the restaurant to hang around in the bar to chat with Joe and Trav and listen to the radio. Trav was overseeing a delivery and doing some inventory, so I called Joe over and said I had the thousand. Joe looked at me funny, and I said the thousand to get into the poker game."

"What was his reaction?"

"He looked at me like I was crazy, jaw dropped and everything. Then he shook his head and went back to what he was doing, wiping the bar and so forth. So I followed him down the bar and told him I was serious, and I had the money on me right then."

"Jesus."

"That's what he said. And he went back to ignoring me. So I kept pestering him. There was no one else at the bar. This was a Tuesday or

The Heresy of Rain

Wednesday at two o'clock in the afternoon or so. I followed him up the bar again. Finally, he stopped and told me to get out of there and put the money in the bank and stop thinking about the poker game."

"That was good advice."

Henry shrugged.

"Go on."

"So I offered him ten percent if he could get me in the game."

"Ten percent of your winnings?"

"Right. I told him to get me through that door, and I'd give him a share."

"What did he say then?"

"He asked me if I was any good, and I told him I was good enough."

"The entirety of your experience playing poker was with your grandmother and two old ladies from down the street?"

"More or less."

Grant shook his head and continued his notes.

Henry said: "So Joe thought about it for a minute and told me to hold on. He went into the back for a while, maybe five minutes, and came out shaking his head. He told me it was a bad idea but that if I wanted to play I should come back at nine that evening."

"Why do you think he went back there on your behalf?"

"I guess he had nothing to lose. Either I'd win some money and he'd get ten percent, or I'd lose my thousand and learn my lesson."

"I guess that's a fair assessment."

"So I went home for a few hours and returned that night."

"With the thousand."

"With the thousand."

"And they dealt you in?"

"Well, I went to the bar area again and asked Joe quietly to tell Mr. Moretti I was there. Joe told me Mr. Moretti doesn't have anything to do with who gets involved in the poker games."

Grant raised an eyebrow and pointed his pen at Henry. He said: "But Moretti gets a cut?"

"Right."

"How much?"

"I never asked, and no one ever told me. But I think twenty percent."

"What makes you think twenty percent?"

"Sometimes I saw dealers make notations or divide the take. Always looked like they were taking twenty off the top."

"Okay."

"So I played poker for several hours that night and walked away with my thousand plus five hundred."

"Draw?"

"Holdem."

"Had you ever played holdem before this?"

"No, but it's the same concept. Just have to understand betting strategy and get a feel for the other players' tendencies. I'm a fast learner when it comes to cards, like I said."

"And you gave Joe fifty?"

"Right."

"Tell me about the other players."

"That was four years ago. There were always different guys. Sometimes the same men will play for a few weeks then disappear then show up again. I don't know."

"Anyone from around town?"

"From Galveston? Of course. Businessmen and professors and politicians. Car dealers, pastors—"

"What?"

Henry looked at the table.

"Who else?"

Henry breathed heavily. "Over the years?" He shrugged. "Police officers. Sheriff's deputies. State troopers."

"Goddamn."

"There's a lot of money changing hands back there. A lot of the time it got too rich for me. There would be nights when you couldn't get through that door without five, ten grand."

"Who were the dealers?"

"Guys trusted by the boss, I guess. Or bosses, I don't know. Over the years there have been nine, ten dealers. They aren't running the show. The dealers answer to someone else who answers to someone else still."

This was the first time since Grace died that Henry was engrossed in something that demanded his attention and forced him to think of something other than Grace. Now and again though, while speaking with Wisdom, Henry would see past the chief and catch a panging glimpse of his grandmother's upright. Then he would imagine Grace emerging in the kitchen from the hallway. She appeared like a silhouette or a specter in the corner of his eye but was in an instant gone.

Grant Wisdom saw the gloom wash over Henry, and he said he was sorry to have to dredge up these memories at a time like this, and he wished he could go about his investigation some other way.

Henry nodded just slightly and ran his hand through his hair.

Wisdom asked: "Henry, what you've told me is very helpful. And I'm going to do everything in my power to protect you, legally and personally. I'm going to ask some specific questions about the gambling and other activities."

"Other activities?"

"For example, do the men in charge allow lines of credit?"

"Sometimes. When they allow guys to go into debt against the house it's just a couple hundred dollars."

"Sometimes?"

"It's not often."

"Fine. What happens to players who don't pay their debts?"

Henry dropped his hands from the tabletop to his lap and looked down. He took deep breaths and tried to will away the pain, but it would not pass. It would never pass.

Wisdom said softly: "I see."

Henry nodded again almost imperceptibly.

"Henry, how much?"

Henry shrugged. To speak would mean certain tears.

"How much, son?"

Henry held up his hand like a child and said five thousand through troubled breaths.

Wisdom shook his head and closed his eyes for a moment.

Then the chief asked if the five thousand included interest.

Henry rubbed his eyes. "I guess you could call it interest."

"What was the original amount they loaned you?"

"They let me get three thousand down one night. Several weeks ago."

"Did you have any way of getting the money?"

"Of course not. And every week they tacked on another three or four hundred. It got out of control. I tried to pay the fee, but they weren't interested."

"Who?"

"What do you mean, who?"

"I mean, who loaned the three grand, Henry? And who charged the interest? And who killed Grace? I think you know the answer to all of these questions."

"I doubt he's still around."

"Fair enough, but we need to start somewhere."

"It's a guy named Maddock. That's his name. Just Maddock."

"Maddock."

Henry nodded. "He answers to someone. I don't know who. Or maybe he doesn't, I don't know. He threatened me the day before Grace was killed. Or a warning anyway. He told me I had twenty-four hours. So I took what I'd saved, not quite six hundred dollars, and a put it in my pocket and left the house that morning, the morning Grace died. I walked around the island. Went to the bookshop. I ended up at the club, just looking for a soda. That's when I got your message."

"Was there any cash in the house?"

"No. I had it all with me. I knew Grace would be at her church lunch late in the morning, close to noon. I didn't know what I was doing. I had no design on the day. I was just walking."

"Goddamn, Henry. I'm sorry she got caught up in it."

"Me too. I don't know what to do. Grant, I'm lost."

"I know, son; I know."

"And now I'll be killed for talking to you."

"I'll protect you."

"Right."

"Henry, I can keep you safe from these men if I know who they are and where they operate. Are they racketeering?"

"You mean, laundering money?"

"Well, that's part of it. Are they charging businesses a regular fee, say monthly, in exchange for protection?"

"I haven't got any idea. I only involved myself with the poker game."

"What about weapons? Any of these characters carry weapons?"

Henry raised an eyebrow at the absurdity of the question.

"Of course they do, Chief. All of them. The guys in charge of the money, Maddock, probably the dealers. Hell, maybe Sammie too. Who knows."

"Tell me about Maddock."

He sighed. "He grew up on the island. I knew of him when I was a kid. Sometimes ran around with him. We had some of the same friends when we were young. He was two or three years ahead of me in school. He usually has a couple of other guys with him, like bodyguards."

"Does he live on the island now?"

"I don't know. I doubt it. But he stays close. His warning that night was strange. He mentioned Grace. Kept talking about my wife."

"I'm sorry, Henry. Goddamn."

"I know you are."

"What does Maddock look like?"

"He's a little taller than me. Maybe your height. Mexican or half Mexican or maybe black. I couldn't say. Never could tell."

"That's a lot of possibilities."

"I don't know. I guess it is a lot of possibilities. I've never asked the son of a bitch his family history."

"Calm down now, Henry. Stay with me here." Wisdom found his place in his notes. "So darker skin, a little taller than average."

"Right."

"And he's a bit older than you."

"I'd say twenty-three or twenty-four."

"That's pretty young to have as much responsibility and power as he's got."

"Yeah, I guess so. I suppose it doesn't take any certain age to turn into a murderer. To kill innocent women."

"All right, Henry. All right. This is something at least. Can you tell me about his voice?"

"His voice? Jesus, I don't know."

"By that I mean, does he have an accent or use any particular slang?"

"He sounds more or less like he's from around here. Texas, anyway."

"What kind of car does he drive?"

"He doesn't drive."

"Then what kind of car do his goons drive?"

"I've only seen him in a car once or twice. I just remember dark cars with dark windows. Maybe a Ford. I'm sorry."

"You're doing fine. Is 'Maddock' his first name? Last name?"

"We called him Billy when I was younger. William, maybe. Like I said, he's only ever been just Maddock since we got to be older."

"All right."

Henry leaned back in his chair. "Don't your deputies or the police detectives already know all this?"

"Some of it, sure. Corroborating witnesses only strengthen a case."

"All right."

"But we don't know enough."

Henry shrugged apologetically.

Wisdom said: "It's fine, we'll get him. It's tough to tie him to a particular scene though. He's a hard man to tail."

"I know he killed Grace."

"Henry, I don't believe anyone planned on killing Grace that day."

"You're probably right. But whatever the case, Maddock was close. No one does anything without his okay."

"Anything else you can remember?"

"Maybe, I don't know."

"You know where to find me if you think of anything. We'll keep an eye on your place and Sammie's."

"I can't imagine they'll keep the poker game going after all this."

"You're probably right. Maybe they'll move it somewhere else. We'll keep a lookout all the same."

"All right."

The two men stared at one another. One middle-aged man with his eyes on retirement. One young man looking at a long and lonely and terrible existence.

Then Wisdom said: "Henry, what do you remember about your dad?"

"My dad? Almost nothing. I have vague memories of his face, but I don't know if I actually remember his face or if I'm just going on what I've seen in photographs."

"I should have done a better job making sure you didn't forget him."

"He died when I was barely five years old. There aren't any memories. I was too young."

"You know he was the best officer on the island."

"I guess so. I know he was a popular guy with the rest of the officers."

"Not just the officers. With everybody. He twice, twice I tell you, talked suicidal people off the edge of the causeway. Just talked them off the edge. He had a way with people. They listened to him. People thought anything Ray King said was something worth listening to. And it was.

The Heresy of Rain

You know, he also resolved a hostage situation where this guy was holed up in his house with his pregnant girlfriend. The guy was a mess. Heroin, I think it was. Your dad got on the loudspeaker and talked to this guy for about half an hour. And then you see his pregnant girlfriend run out, crying and so forth. And then you see a gun slide out the front door. And then this guy just walks out with his hands up. Your dad was remarkable."

"I've heard about that hostage thing. Any idea what became of the girlfriend and her baby?"

"She moved to Louisiana with her mother. The guy served a few years on a gun charge and a drug charge. I don't know where he is now. But your dad, he was something else."

Henry just nodded and then looked down at the table.

Wisdom said: "That night he died, I should have been there."

"Chief, you can't keep doing this. It's not your fault I didn't finish high school. It's not your fault Grace died. It's not your fault my dad died. Give yourself a break."

"No, I mean I really should have been there. He was doing a simple seawall patrol."

"I know how he died."

"And this drunk son of a bitch comes—"

"I know."

"The son of a bitch comes flying down sixty-first and slams—"

"Chief."

"Slams into your father's car and sends your father over the edge of the goddamned seawall, and the drunk son of a bitch lives."

"What could you have done?"

"I was on patrol with him that night. I was late because Lucille and I had gotten into a fight. She was hollering and throwing stuff at me. Your dad started the patrol and was planning to pick me up just a few minutes after the accident. I was supposed to be with him."

"So my dad would be dead and my godfather would be dead too? What's the point in thinking about this? It's not your fault. And that's the last time I'm going to say it."

"He would be chief right now, you know."

"Maybe."

"There's no maybe about it. He was a great man."

"Chief, I'm tired. I'm sad as hell and I'm tired."

"I'm sorry. I'll leave you to yourself."

"Thank you for coming over."

Henry and the chief took a few steps across the small living room to the front door. They shook hands, and Grant Wisdom climbed into his pickup and drove into the early autumn afternoon.

Henry dialed the number and waited.

"Sammie's."

"Hey, Trav. It's Henry."

"It's good to hear you. People have been asking about you. Wait staff, customers, everyone. You doing all right?"

"I don't know. I guess. It's pretty tough."

"You know you can come in and hang out at the bar any time you want, just to have some company. You don't have to go back to playing in the dining room until you're ready."

"Thanks. I think I'll need some more time. Could you tell everyone I called and that I need another week or two and I'll come in or call again when I'm feeling a little better?"

"Yeah, no problem."

"All right. Thanks. Take care." Henry prepared to put the receiver back on the phone.

"Hey, Henry."

"Yeah?"

"I'm really sorry for you. Just wanted you to know."

"I know, Trav."

"All right."

Canto 1

HENRY WAS TEN YEARS OLD. It was a deep summer Galveston night, the kind of oppressive night that was unrelenting in its thickness. There was no relief. He sat in his bedroom by himself, reading the best he could a series of colorful books about important historical figures. There was a blue-tabbed volume about Abraham Lincoln and a yellow-tabbed volume about Ludwig Von Beethoven and a purple-tabbed volume about Marie Curie. Two dozen in all. He found most interesting the books about astronomy and music. Recently he had begun learning the piano at Grandmother Ballard's house, and his imagination delighted with the possibilities of music. He was sure most good music had been thought of before. But what if there was more? And if so: how much more? He imagined the thousands and millions of different combinations of notes that lay dormant for the unsuspecting pianist or harmonica or saxophone player to discover. He thought perhaps stars were like musical notes. Ethereal and whimsical entities all awash in mystery and magic.

His bedroom door was closed. He could hear in the living room or kitchen a fight between his mother and his mother's boyfriend, Howard. The fight had started as some kind of joke or comment in passing. Either his mother or Howard misunderstood the comment or misheard it and reacted defensively, and this led to a yelling match. This was not uncommon. Since Henry's father had died several years before, his mother brought men home and fought with them. Her relationship with Howard had been the most enduring.

Henry had grown accustomed to the fighting, but this night seemed different. He gingerly opened his bedroom door and tiptoed down the hall barefooted and peeked into the kitchen. His mother was hollering nonsensical expletives at Howard. He could see her now that he was in the hallway. Her arm was bleeding, and there was broken glass on the kitchen counter and floor. Howard stood several feet away in a defensive position with his hands up.

"Goddamnit, Howard," she roared. "I'll kill you if you come near me." She made sure he knew she was serious by grabbing a cleaver from the knifeblock near the refrigerator. Then she jabbed it a few times in the air for effect.

"Jesus, Tammy. For Christsakes, I was just talking to Linda. It weren't nothing else."

"Son of a bitch, Howard, I'll kill you." And so on and so forth.

This was the first time Henry could remember broken glass and real threats of violence. Typically Tammy and Howard passed out from excessive drinking before it came to blows.

So Henry retreated to his bedroom and put on his shoes, which he knew looked ridiculous with his red and black plaid pajamas. Then he paced quietly back to the end of the hall near the kitchen, where the skirmish intensified. It was as if the two of them weren't concerned so much with violence or sexual indiscretions or who said what so much as they were with who could yell the loudest. Henry knew he'd only have one chance to make a run for it, so he waited patiently through another bout of screaming.

"If you wake up Henry I swear to God I'll put this knife through your goddamn throat."

"He ain't asleep, Tammy. Jesus Christ, who could sleep through all of your goddamn hollering?"

"Son of a bitch, goddamnit."

Then Howard called Tammy a two-bit whore goddamnit.

His mother reared back with the knife, and that's when Henry made his move. He shot through the dining room and the tiled entry way and got to the door before his mother could do much about it. The door was unlocked, and he was gone. His mother got to the open door and screamed into the sweltering night for her son to get back in the house goddamnit or she would beat his ass.

He knew how to get to Temple Circle and had within a few minutes run the half mile from his mother's rundown bungalow to his grandmother's place. He hammered the door with his fist, and his grandmother answered his knocking with alarm but also with resignation toward the ongoing situation.

"Henry, what's the matter?" She led him into her den and sat him on a cushioned rocking chair and went into the kitchen to pour him a glass of water and get him a small piece of chocolate cake.

"It's Mom and Howard."

"Are they fighting again?"

"This time it's bad."

"Sweetheart, every time it's bad."

"Mom's bleeding." Henry accepted the glass of water from his grandmother and placed it on an end table and more eagerly accepted the piece of chocolate cake.

"How's that?"

"I'm not sure. There's broken glass on the floor. She's waving a knife at Howard."

She sighed and ran her hand through her hair and patted his knee and went back to the kitchen. Henry heard her take the phone off the hook and whirl the rotary several times. He could not see his grandmother from the den, but he imagined she was standing there shaking her head with one hand on her hip.

"Tammy. Listen…yes, he's here. I've got him right here. No, don't come get him."

There was a lull during which Henry imagined his mother was simultaneously screaming at Howard and his grandmother. He could then hear his grandmother muttering to herself.

"That's enough, Tammy. Leave him with me. He's not safe over there. I've got a mind to call the police and let them take you and Howard to city hall and put you in jail for a day or two."

Silence.

Then: "He told me there's broken glass and you're bleeding. Goddamnit, Tammy, he can hear everything you say and see everything you do. He's a little boy, not a pet, Jesus Christ."

Then she slammed the phone home and caused the bell to ding along with the clack of the receiver. Henry was finishing his cake.

She walked into the den slowly and said he could stay with her for a couple of days. She sat on a loveseat and put her elbow on the arm and leaned on her hand and smiled at him. The night seemed less oppressive and not so sweltering at his grandmother's house on Elm Court.

She said: "You know your mom loves you."

"I guess."

"She just misses your dad."

"He died a long time ago."

"Five years might seem forever to a boy, but to your mom, it's just a blink of the eye."

He sat wishing he'd thought to bring a book or two.

She said: "I'm not sure about that Howard, though. I'm a little worried."

"You should be. He gets drunk all the time and says mean things."

"To be fair, so does your mom."

"Yeah."

"Too bad she hasn't found someone sweet as you."

His cheeks turned red, and he reached for his glass of water just to have something to hold other than the small plate of chocolate crumbs.

"I'm serious," she said. "I know for a fact that you are a million times the man that Howard is."

"That's not saying much."

"When you're older, you'll know how to treat a girl, right?"

"Uh…"

"You'll treat your girl like she's a princess."

"I guess."

"You know what girls like in a young man?"

"What's that?"

"They love a musician. Want to learn a song?"

"Sure." He really didn't want to learn a song.

Then she led him over to the old piano for the first time and sat him down on the wobbly bench and showed him how to pick out "Twinkle, Twinkle, Little Star." He got it pretty quickly and continued to play it with his right hand while she sang the song. He'd never realized until then that the lullaby had more than one verse. He especially liked the third verse.

> *Then the traveler in the dark*
> *Thanks you for your tiny sparks;*
> *He could not see which way to go,*
> *If you did not twinkle so.*

Henry wasn't sure if this was the way to woo girls. He didn't think much about wooing girls at that age. But he was delighted by the music, the notes, the piano. He imagined while he was playing with his right hand the simple melody that he was soaring, a traveler indeed who relied on the stars' light to guide him.

Canto 2

HENRY AND GRACE WALKED ARM-IN-ARM along the street, which glistened after a short but fierce rainfall. The storm had passed while they were in a confectionary at Galveston's Strand. It was one of their earliest outings together, a few weeks after they had met at the church where Grace's parents were buried.

They arrived at the house where Grace lived with her sister and her sister's husband. The house was small but had a large porch or veranda. The porch lamp near the front door was lit. Henry walked Grace up the steps, and she tugged him over to the bench swing on the far side of the porch. It was tethered to the ceiling by two long chains. They sat together for a few minutes, swinging lazily back and forth. Henry had his right arm behind her, resting on the swing and just barely touching her shoulders. Henry attempted to initiate physical contact with uncertainty and hesitancy. Grace was fearless, though, and she reached up with her right hand and pulled Henry's arm down so that he was cradling her and brought his hand down and held it over her heart. She held his hand over her heart and leaned into him while clinging tightly. And so they sat, embraced and so swaying on the swing. He could feel her heart beat.

Then he turned slightly toward her and said her name softly and lightly clutched the back of her neck with his right hand, and with his left hand he reached up to her face and cupped her cheek and moved his hand to her ear and ran his finger along the nape of her neck and said her name softly again. She said his name softly and dropped her hands to her lap and let him pull her gently toward him. For a moment she had her head down, but then she leaned forward and parted her lips. He kissed her delicately. Her lips were soft and damp and warm. He pulled away after a short time, but she moved her hands to his sides, just under his arms, and pulled him back. They kissed again, softly and slowly. And then she smiled. He smiled too and asked her softly what was so funny.

"Nothing's funny," she said. "I'm only very happy."

He slid his hands to her back and pulled her close and embraced her tightly there on the swing. And he said: "I'm very happy too."

The Heresy of Rain

She laughed very quietly and said: "Would you believe me if I said that was my first kiss? Almost nineteen years old, and it's my first kiss."

"I would ask how did a girl this beautiful make it so long without being kissed?"

"Don't be silly."

"Would you believe me if I said it was my first kiss too?"

"No."

"Why?"

"You're a boy. And a musician."

"Well, I've never found a girl worth kissing till now."

"Is my sister watching us through the window?"

"No. The curtains are drawn."

"Then kiss me again."

Part II

"I did not know then that pride is a wonderful, terrible thing, a seed that bears two vines, life and death."

–James Hurst

The Heresy of Rain

THE NIGHT WAS COOL. Henry stepped outside and zipped tight his jacket and pulled his hat tight over his brow. His hands in his pockets, he started toward the street and once on the street walked quickly to the edge of his neighborhood and then beyond, into the unguessable Galveston blackness. Houses were mostly dark at this hour except for the occasional lighted window betraying an occupant's nighttime creeping within. Shops and other businesses were closed. Somewhere a dog barked and then was joined by other dogs in a chorus of yelps and howls that crescendoed until someone ordered one of the animals to quiet down. The moon waned above. In the distance waves crashed. Too, after several minutes of walking Henry could hear water lapping against the nearby pier of a small marina. He turned left on Broadway and then walked for a few minutes along the main drag until crossing and walking northwest on 3rd. The live oaks rustled in the night, and sometimes a bird called. Cats lurked and darted about like serpentine shadows of the evening.

Henry approached a bait shop and then stopped short, unsure of whether this was the right place. He had learned of the place listening to other men's conversations and half-revelations during poker games, especially when the other men had been drinking. The shop was closed. He stood for a time and then looked left and right and stepped closer to the shop. The writing on the windows offered live bait and lures and ice and fishing hooks and icechests and chum and fishing line and engine oil and buckets and cold drinks. Even standing outside the shop he could smell the place with its fishiness and other accoutrements.

The bait shop stood next to a service garage and between them was a paved walkway, cracked with weeds growing up through it. Henry walked slowly to the rear of the shop and saw that there was a dim gas lamp out back, and there were low, soft voices in the night. When he reached the back door of the bait shop he found two men who had been sitting in folding chairs but upon hearing his approach had risen defensively. Henry stopped and took his hands from his pockets as if to announce his benignity, and the men looked at one another and relaxed their shoulders.

One man wore a hat and smoked a cigarette. He asked what in the goddamn hell Henry wanted, especially at this time of night.

"I heard this is the place to buy a gun. Nothing fancy, just something basic."

"Then you heard wrong."

Henry pursed his lips and shook his head slightly. "I don't believe so. I have money, cash. Not much, but I suppose it's enough to buy a handgun."

"Who told you this was the place to buy a gun?"

"Just overheard it is all."

The men looked at each other again.

The man with the hat and cigarette said: "Are you a cop?"

"No, of course not. Christ. Do I look like a cop?"

"Turn out all your pockets and unbutton your jacket."

Henry did as ordered and then stuffed his pockets back into his trousers.

"Take off your hat."

"Goddamn, this is ridiculous." He removed his hat and then placed it back on his head.

"Why do you think you need a gun?"

"Same reason any other guy comes to you needing a gun."

"What reason is that?"

"Jesus Christ, I don't have time to dicker with you two clowns." Henry turned to leave. "Maybe someone else will sell me a gun without asking a hundred questions. I'll take my business somewhere else."

"Wait."

Henry stopped and turned back toward the two men and then stood there along the weedy pavement and put his hands in his pocket.

The one with the hat said: "Hold on, hold on. Just wait."

"All right. I'm not in any hurry if you'd like my business."

"What's your name?"

"Don't be ridiculous. Do you want my phone number and address too?"

The other man held up a finger and then put his finger to his lips. Henry stood still as this man ascended a creaking and flaking and chipped staircase that bore him to a small apartment above the bait shop. A light came on in the room above Henry and the man with the hat and cigarette.

The Heresy of Rain

The other man was gone for just a short while and then walked quietly but quickly down the stairs as the light above clicked off. Somewhere in the salty night a dog began to howl again, but the dog's owner admonished the dog before the chorus of yelping and moaning and yowling could begin anew. The man reached the bottom of the stairs and looked at his partner and nodded and whispered something in the behatted man's ear. This man nodded and shrugged and said quietly to Henry: "Thirty."

Henry took some bills from his pocket and placed three ten-dollar bills on the table between the men and him. Then Henry asked: "Bullets?"

The man without the hat leaned to his partner and held up five fingers.

"Another five dollars," said the man who spoke aloud.

Henry took out another ten and placed it on top of the first six and said he would like to double his order of ammunition. Both men shrugged and nodded.

The man then said very quietly: "Listen carefully. I'm going to give you these directions only once. No refunds. You understand?"

Henry understood.

"You know St. Michael's on Orchard just south of 50th?"

He nodded. "Sure." Henry had passed by the church a hundred times or more in his life but had never entered the building or even stepped onto its grounds.

"There's a big marble and limestone mausoleum near the east edge of the graveyard. It belongs to the Santacruz family."

"I know of it."

"There's a pedestal on each side of the entrance. You'll find your purchase in the leftside pedestal after nine tomorrow night. Don't ever come here again."

"All right."

Henry nodded his thanks to the two men and then looked up toward the apartment over the bait shop and then turned to leave, the cash still untouched on the table. As he turned onto the sidewalk to head back home he heard a distant clap of thunder. Then the neighborhood dogs began again, but no one bothered to quiet them.

THE FOLLOWING MORNING DAWNED with the promise of renewal for everyone in the world save Henry King. The clock's seven o'clock chime was harsh and discordant. Henry jerked awake and found himself on the living room sofa, as had happened most mornings since Grace died, and felt a wrench of sadness ripple through him. He rubbed his eyes and sat for a while on the sofa, trying to piece together the previous night. He remembered the directions about St. Michael's and stood slowly. His jacket was hanging on the back of a kitchen chair. He walked to the chair and took from the jacket pocket a sheaf of bills. It was all the money he had. After his purchase from the previous night he had five hundred twenty-nine dollars. He made a cup of instant coffee, which was bitter and too hot. Gritty.

A cold front had sneaked through the area overnight, so the air was gentle and refreshing and the sky cerulean forever and ever in each direction. Henry walked to the mailbox out front. He found inside the mailbox a couple of advertisements for local stores and a sympathy letter from Sammie's. The staff offered its condolences, and restaurant management offered him all the time he needed to recover. He was missed, the note said. It also reminded him that the restaurant's employees and patrons were his family and would support him in any way possible. He stuffed the note and the other items back into the mailbox and set off.

Just less than an hour later Henry was the first customer at Gulfside Automobiles, a used car lot with a modest selection of vehicles. The dealership sat on three commercial lots at a busy intersection. Henry supposed there were a hundred vehicles. The place was bedecked in flags and banners and signs and painted windows in all kinds of gaudy colors. A small, windowed office sat in the center of the lot, and a few salesmen were now snaking about, sweating already in their suits, and cigarettes hanging from their lips. Traffic was heavy but not unusually so, and Henry crossed the street and walked onto the dealership's grounds and muttered to himself a reminder to be polite.

The Heresy of Rain

One of the leering and tousled salesmen spotted him immediately and darted in his direction, stamping out his cigarette as he approached. He wore a brown suit a size too small, and his wiry combed-over hair was wet with perspiration. He was fat and unsightly, his squat round body over-working itself. His hair flapped about, and his tie flew over his shoulder in the wind.

"Good mornin," the salesman said as he hustled over.

Henry said hello.

The salesman offered his name and shook Henry's hand. Henry did not offer his name.

"Anything special you lookin for?"

"Something cheap that runs fine."

"You got a family?"

"No."

"Plan doing some travelin in your new car?"

"Hadn't thought about it."

"Live on the island?"

"More or less."

"What's your budget?

"Like I said, cheap."

"You lookin to finance?"

"Maybe."

The salesman put his finger to his chin in a ridiculous attempt to convince Henry that he was some silly genie from a lamp, conjuring the perfect automobile for him. Henry rolled his eyes and shook his head. The salesman didn't notice.

Then the suited and sweating man offered a fifty-one Chevy deluxe coupe with only one previous owner and just forty thousand miles. The man said it was a steal at nine hundred ninety-five dollars.

"I said, cheap."

"Well, I could probably knock it down to nine fifty."

Henry shook his head and began to pace the lot. The salesman trailed as best he could. Another customer or two had arrived, and the other wolves circled these potential commissions. Henry stopped and peered ahead.

"How about that truck?"

The salesman pretended not to see the truck. "What truck?"

Henry folded his arms and gave the salesman a look. "The only god-damn truck on the lot."

"Oh, the black one?"

"I'm losing my patience with you."

"Sure, all right. That's fine, that's fine. Let's have a look at the truck."

It was a forty-six Ford pickup, black with some dings and dents about the body. A close inspection revealed a relatively clean interior but nothing pretty. The driverside mirror bore a crack, and the tailgate was missing.

The salesman said: "Two ninety-five for this one. Been on the lot a couple weeks. We bought it at an impound auction."

"For someone who didn't seem to realize this truck was on the lot you seem to know more than a little about it."

The man shrugged.

Henry asked if the truck ran.

"She runs." He used the sleeve of his suit to wipe at his brow. "Runs just fine."

"How new are the tires?"

"You shouldn't have any problem gettin another five or ten thousand miles out of them." The man glanced about the lot and saw people asking the other salesmen about cars whose prices would yield more promising paydays.

"I can pay two fifty cash if it runs and if you'll fill it up at that service station across the street."

The salesman dropped his head and looked at the ground, defeated and embarrassed as he marched slowly to the office.

Three minutes later he emerged and told Henry he had a deal. A half hour after that Henry drove his pickup off the lot. Having had little practice as an automobile driver Henry drove the truck about the island for some time, becoming accustomed to the vehicle's responsiveness, transmission, and handling. Then he refilled the half-empty gas tank at a service station. He pulled into the parking lot of a church near his neighborhood and walked home from the church in the warming sunshine.

At nine o'clock that evening he was standing in his home, at the wide threshold where the kitchen and living room met. He looked around and tried to focus on everything, so he could remember it. He walked over to the piano and touched the topboard and then played very softly a few bars without sitting and then picked up a small, framed photograph from the coffee table and removed the photograph from the frame and glass and slid it into this shirt pocket. He ran his hand over the sofa's arm with his lip trembling, and he dropped his head in one hand before going over to the kitchen table and taking up his hat. He remembered something and walked over to one of the kitchen drawers and removed a slip of light blue paper from beneath the drawer's sundry contents; he put this blue slip of paper in his billfold and slipped the billfold back into his trouser pocket. He had cut off all the lights save the kitchen light. He took up his small duffle bag which held two changes of clothes and his shave kit and another pair of shoes. He pocketed his keys and fingered his jacket pocket to confirm the presence of what cash he had left and slid through the back door and shut it quietly behind him.

Just minutes later Henry was parked along the street near St. Michael's. The cemetery was dark and appeared empty of visitors. He cut the engine and climbed out of the truck and closed the door quietly before convincing himself he was alone, and he stepped through the wrought iron gate and onto the churchyard grounds. There were a few gas lamps about, but they offered little light. With his hands in his pockets he paced slowly by the headstones and monuments and crucifixes. He could read some of the headstones if he strained his eyes. He stopped to admire one of the monuments, which belonged to someone named Cartwright. John Cartwright had been born in 1799, according to his headstone, and he lived a peaceful life if the stone was to be believed until he died in 1901. Henry was overwhelmed by John Cartwright's life, and he stood on Mr. Cartwright's hallowed ground as he pondered a life that saw three centuries, countless wars and battles, slavery, abolition, the advent of modern banking, the establishment of an electric grid, and an uncountable number of other milestones, both societal and personal. What it must be like to cheat the universe and live longer than one man deserves to live. John Cartwright must have been a lucky son of a bitch.

Henry remembered his purpose and moved on, making his way to the eastern edge of the cemetery. For every John Cartwright, who lived a hundred and two years, there were twenty dead children. Deceased babies, cut down by destiny or fate or the universe before being allowed to make a go of it. Some monuments bore flowers or potted plants or even plush animals and toys for the children. There were teddy bears and pale-faced dolls with curly hair and wooden puzzles and tractors and books. A child's grave is surely the saddest sight. It is one thing if an adult dies, even a young adult, for an adult has had an opportunity to make his mark on the world, a chance to be seen and heard and most of all to contribute something great and material. A child has had no such opportunity. It is not only a matter of what if. It is a matter of why so. It is difficult to determine a purpose in such a thing. Some graves—mostly those belonging to adults—were unadorned, and Henry figured those monuments belonged to people whose benefactors had at some point joined them in this final resting place or some other burying grounds.

After some time he reached the large stone mausoleum, marked Santacruz. A hundred tons of marble and limestone with landscaping and pillars and torches. He stood in the night admiring the building for some time. Centuries and generations of a family housed in a stonework shrine that in time, if not now, will be little more than a charnel house. When he was sure there was no one near he went to the pedestal to the left of the mausoleum entrance and found there was a small bowl or receptacle on top of the short pillar, probably a container for flowers. The bowl was empty save a cloth bag. Henry took the small bag and its contents and shoved it into his jacket pocket. He noticed a gate near this monument, which led to a small grassy area near the church's entrance, and he left through this gate with the intention of walking around the cemetery and back to his truck, which was parked a few hundred yards away.

"Good evening."

Henry flinched and turned around to see someone approaching him in the dark.

"I didn't mean to scare you."

"It's all right. I just didn't realize anyone else was out here."

The figure came closer, and Henry realized it was the priest, dressed almost entirely in black with the white collar beneath his chin.

"I'm Father James Valdez."

Henry nodded a hello but didn't offer anything else by way of a greeting. He ran the last five minutes back again in his mind in an effort to convince himself Father Valdez couldn't have seen him take the gun from the mausoleum's pedestal. He was not confident of this.

The priest said: "Is everything all right?"

"Fine. I was admiring the headstones."

"As a mourner or a historian? I don't believe I've seen you here."

"Neither, I suppose. Just happened to be driving by and realized I've never been in this cemetery before."

Father Valdez smiled. "It is a wondrous, hallowed place. It's amazing some of these graves have survived. The 1900 storm shifted so many corpses this way and that."

"I noticed some of the tombstones seemed shorter than they ought to be."

"The entire island was raised an average of four feet after the storm. Some places, more or less. That the island survived such carnage is a sign of Galvestonians' resilience, don't you think?"

"I think you're probably right."

"I was just preparing to do my nightly walk of the sanctuary. Won't you join me inside?"

"I should go."

"Oh, I insist." Father Valdez raised an eyebrow and held out his hand in a gesture of authoritative gentility.

"Well, all right." Henry didn't like the idea of accompanying the priest into the church while carrying an illegal firearm, but he also didn't want to further arouse the priest's suspicion. And the man seemed harmless enough.

Henry followed Father Valdez into the nave. St. Michael's was not a very large church, but it was old and grand all the same. It boasted regal wooden beams and icons of stained glass and rich red carpeting. Just behind the choir area was an apse with a large, sculpted passion of Christ, replete with a crown of thorns and forlorn eyes cast downward. The nave was quiet. There were candles lit about the transepts and small chapels beyond the apse. All was veiled in an inaudible and unknowable ether. Clothed in this ghostly and fragile transparence.

Father Valdez said: "Please sit with me."

The priest motioned for Henry to slide into a pew near the back of the nave, near the center aisle. Then the priest sat next to Henry, close to the aisle. Father Valdez crossed himself and bowed his head silently for just a moment. They could have been two worshipers early for mass or two wedding guests before the ceremony.

"I come here every night," said the priest, "to this exact spot in the nave. Each and every night without fail. There are three very important things I achieve by visiting the back of this church each evening. One is obvious, and the other two are less obvious, but I think no less important. And you might be surprised that I say that when I tell you what those reasons are."

"All right."

"I failed to get your name earlier."

"Henry."

Father Valdez reached over and patted Henry's knee the way a grandfather might. "It's good to know you, Henry." The man's voice resonated in such a way that suggested he had learned how to tailor his voice to the building. He had mastered the acoustics.

Henry tipped his hat for the sake of politeness and then realized he ought not wear a hat inside the church. He removed the hat and placed it on the pew to his right.

"Sorry I didn't take off the hat sooner. I don't go to church much and forgot the rules."

Father Valdez waved him off. "Churches have too many rules. Is it polite to remove your hat? Sure. Does God care whether you are wearing a hat? I doubt it. Anyone who thinks our salvation is somehow bound to hat wearing is misguided at the very least."

Henry smiled softly, relaxing a bit.

"All right then, Henry," said the priest, "I was telling you there are three reasons I come every evening at this very time and sit here in the sanctuary. The first is the obvious reason: I get a good look at Jesus." The priest gestured toward the passion sculpture at the head of the building. "I am reminded of his suffering. His suffering. I think too many clergymen spend too much time looking the other direction, wouldn't you agree? They stand up front and pontificate and carry on about staying out of hell or tithing or confessing but sometimes forget about the suffering. When I remind myself that Jesus suffered, it helps me to remember that my worshipers are suffering. Henry, they are suffering. And what is my job if not to aid the suffering?"

"That's reasonable."

Father Valdez smiled. "I'm glad you agree. There is so much suffering in this world."

Henry only nodded.

The Heresy of Rain

"So much suffering," the priest continued, "and there are two important things about suffering we should always remember. Are you ready?" He said this like a teacher might prepare students to note a couple of important facts in a lecture.

"Sure."

"Okay, those two important things about suffering that you should always remember are this. One, we cannot measure another person's suffering. Do you see what I am saying?"

"I'm not sure I follow."

"In other words, we shouldn't presume to understand someone else's sadness or grief or pain or heartbreak. Even if you have experienced something similar, your own grief cannot be a measuring stick to gauge the other person's grief. We are all different."

"I see now."

"Right. We are all different. Do not presume to know what someone else is feeling. I remind myself of this a hundred times per day. I cannot possibly understand what someone else is feeling. If he is talking to me on the street, in a confessional, in pre-wedding counseling, at a funeral, whatever the case. I cannot measure another person's pain. It's unwise and impossible. I can listen and offer support and can even offer a path to salvation, but I cannot presume to know his sadness. That is vital. We must remember this. The second important thing about suffering is this: ready?"

"Yes."

"It is this: suffering is redemptive." The priest was becoming more animated but not quite turning all the way to face Henry.

"All right."

"I'm glad you understand, because this is important. Our suffering allows us to become clean."

"Clean."

"Yes, it is through suffering that we are purified."

"I've suffered plenty, and I don't feel purified."

Father Valdez folded his hands in his lap. He said: "Perhaps you need perspective. Time. Often we are not acutely aware of our growth, of our purification. It takes time for us to realize how our pain and misery have redeemed us."

"That seems too simple."

"What do you mean, simple?"

"I mean the world is more complicated than that."

"Perhaps. Perhaps."

"We don't sit around and wait after we've experienced something bad. We don't hold still until God sends us a sign that we've survived some kind of test."

"True, our world is not the world of the Old Testament."

Henry shrugged.

"That is why, young man, we have a redeemer. We take all our troubles and pain and suffering and transgressions, and we unburden ourselves by heaping our collective yoke onto Jesus' back."

"I guess."

"Fair enough. Just try to remember those two things about suffering. First, that we cannot measure another person's pain. Second, that we are redeemed through our suffering. All right?"

"Fine."

"All right. You'll remember there are two other reasons why I sit in this spot every night at this time. The second reason is time."

"Time?"

"Yes, time. That is, it is a reminder to me that I should slow down. People, they move too quickly. It wasn't always this way, but it is now. Everyone is zipping by."

Henry shifted his weight in the pew.

The priest continued. "When I was a child I loved the sky, everything about the night sky. The stars, the moon, all of the wonderful worlds up there. I would climb trees at night with the hope that I'd have a closer, clearer view of the sky's offerings. To this day I am captivated by the celestial world. The thing that most mesmerized me when I was young, though, was Orion's belt."

"Orion's belt?"

"Yes, the three stars that make up the belt of the mythical hunter, Orion."

"All right."

"People have for thousands of years used that line of three stars as a religious or navigational or architectural guide. It has never changed in the history of humanity. Always it is there. And I've forever been enchanted that millions of people have so esteemed those three stars throughout history. Can you imagine? Some of the world's most important ancient or even prehistoric creations are aligned with those three stars of the hunter's belt. So every night as I was growing up I reminded myself to go outside and find Orion's belt. Not only was it a way for me to connect with people across millennia—for they too stared at these three stars—but it also reminded me to slow down. Sometimes I truly had to hunt the skies to find Orion's belt. It might take many minutes, minutes during which I stopped to establish perspective, perhaps literally and figuratively. Life is more fulfilling at a measured pace."

"Maybe."

"There's no maybe about it. Everyone should take some time each day to pause and take a deep breath. Slow down. I don't make it outside every night to find Orion's belt anymore, but I do sit here every evening for a few minutes. This perspective reminds me of suffering, and it reminds me to slow down."

"What's the third thing?"

Father Valdez smiled. "The third thing," he said, "is it allows me to hear."

"To hear what?"

"To hear whether someone is walking near the Santacruz mausoleum and rummaging about the monument."

Henry lowered his head a bit and shifted his gaze from the priest.

"It's all right, young man. It's all right. Sometimes I can convince the visitor to come in and talk to me. Usually he just runs away."

"I'm sorry. I don't know what to say."

"Ah, don't say anything, Henry. In many respects I'm just a silly old man. I appreciate that you've given me your attention for these many minutes. You are kind to humor the ravings of a lunatic." The priest turned to face Henry and raised an eyebrow and smiled.

"I don't think you're a lunatic."

"Well, thank you for saying that. I often wonder if my parishioners truly believe what I'm saying, or if they simply feel sorry for me."

"Does it matter?"

"I guess I've never thought about whether it matters."

"Your life's work is about getting souls into heaven. To do that, you need people in the seats, people listening to your message."

"Yes."

"So it shouldn't matter whether they are coming for the salvation or coming because they like you or coming for the coffee and cookies you put out after mass."

Father Valdez turned his palms upward in concession. "You make a good point, Henry. What matters is people are coming."

"I would think so."

"I thank you again for sitting with me. I can tell by looking at you that you are a serious and soulful person."

"I'm a blues musician."

"Ha! Well, that's it, then. Maybe I should go into the palm reading business. At any rate, I can see also that you are burdened. Something is bothering you. I hope you enter into a time of intense reflective introspection."

"I'm usually a quiet person."

"Introspection is not only about being quiet. To be introspective one must truly face himself. He must ask himself difficult questions and search for difficult answers. He must be honest with himself, and he must admit to himself that he is vulnerable and imperfect."

"Isn't that what prayer is for?"

"Some people, they won't talk to God. This is the next best thing. If I can't get a person to face God I think maybe I can get him to face himself. Self-discovery and honesty, those are important as well as piety. Maybe in some cases more important. I don't know."

"All right."

The priest looked as though he was going to stand but instead turned to his pupil: "Henry, you have an opportunity to unburden yourself right now if you wish."

"I don't think that's possible, Father."

"Of course it's possible."

Henry shook his head. "Anyway, I wouldn't know how."

"It's easy, really. You just say it."

"Say what?"

"Whatever it is that's troubling you."

Henry turned to the priest and looked the older man in the eyes and told the older man that his wife had been murdered recently.

The priest relaxed and let his head drop a bit, and he breathed a heavy sigh of genuine sadness.

"I'm so sorry."

Henry dropped his head in one hand and had his elbow on a knee and willed himself against sobbing in the presence of God's messenger.

Father Valdez asked very quietly if it was the murder of the young blind woman he had read about in the paper.

Henry nodded and squeezed his eyes shut and covered his eyes with his hand and trembled with such incredible pain and sadness and loss.

"I see. I can't imagine your misery, Henry. I cannot imagine."

Henry sat with his shoulders slumped and his eyes closed tightly, for what could he say?

"Tell me her name."

"Grace."

"That's a beautiful name, Henry. Was she very beautiful?"

"Yes, she was."

"Of course, of course."

"It was my fault."

"You cannot blame yourself for the senselessness of others."

"I should have known. I should never have let her out of my sight."

"You were her husband, Henry, not her bodyguard. Not her father. You weren't Grace's keeper."

Henry shook his head.

"Henry, listen to me. Please. Look up. Look at me, son."

Henry wiped his eyes and looked at the priest.

"Henry, listen. You cannot change anything. Do you understand that? Your job is to live your life in such a way that honors Grace's memory. You have an opportunity to lift your wife's memory and legacy and render her someone to behold."

Henry nodded, ready to loose himself from the sanctuary.

"All right. Please remember I am here. I am always here. I see confusion and anger in your eyes. I see misery and pain but also fury. Please return to this church if you need to talk or pray or sit in a quiet place. Please, Henry."

Henry only nodded again.

The priest rose from the pew and backed away into the aisle and allowed Henry to scoot over and rise from the pew and walk a few steps to the door at the rear of the nave. Before he left he turned again to say goodnight to Father Valdez, but the priest had already turned toward the front of the nave and was walking slowly toward the transept with his head bowed in prayer or sadness. Henry pushed the door open and was soon outside again. He paused for a moment and looked at the sky. It was a clear night, and there were many stars. He peered into the darkness for a bit, trying to find Orion's belt. There were many small groups of stars that could have been the hunter's sash. He could not tell one from the other. Perhaps he would try again at some other time. He put his hands in his jacket pocket and reassured himself that his weapon was still there and walked toward his truck.

Minutes later he pulled into a cinema parking lot and took an empty space and idled for a moment before cutting the engine and rolling the driverside window down a few inches. There were young people entering and exiting the building, and they were full of joy and youth and fun. They were just younger than Henry, who had never seen a movie in the theater. As a boy there was no opportunity or money for movies, and as a young man he was busy. Grace hadn't been interested in films. She preferred radio shows, which were designed within an audiological framework. Anyway, for Grace the movies had been their seaside chats about the cool wind and the sky and the moon and the universe that birthed it all. Henry watched the moviegoers for some time and then checked his watch: ten thirty. He figured he had time for a short nap and shut his eyes.

Less than an hour later Henry was leaving a service station, having filled up again and having purchased a Texas road map and two Cokes and a bag of shelled peanuts. Everything but one of the sodas went into his glovebox. He drove slowly about the northwest edge of the island for some time. Just before midnight he pulled over to the side of the road and cut his lights while idling. He rolled down the driverside window about halfway. Less than a block ahead of him was the bait shop where he'd purchased his gun. After his short nap and cold beverage he was alert. He tried not to think of Grace as he watched the bait shop. Instead he pondered the priest's lesson about suffering and redemption. He wondered if a person could exist outside redemption's reach, his soul so black it was beyond reclamation. He wondered if God existed even, or if the world was a chaotic place of zinging and zipping forces that clashed and conflicted and only served to augment the chaos. Perhaps suffering meant nothing. Perhaps the trick is to figure out how to avoid suffering because there is no redemption. Henry figured this notion was too dark and that he ought to keep his eyes on the bait shop.

The Heresy of Rain

After some time—Henry's watch read twelve nineteen—a sedan backed out of the shop's long driveway and headed south toward Broadway. Henry pulled from the roadside and followed the sedan, careful to keep his distance and leave his headlights off. The sedan turned onto Broadway and went north toward the Strand. Henry flipped his headlights on before following onto Broadway but kept his distance. There were a few other travelers on the road. Partyers creeping back to their hotels, residents on their way to work or leaving work, sinners easing into or out of an evening of debauchery.

Henry trailed the sedan in his black truck for a few miles as the car's driver traveled along the island's main street and then turned right on 50th, toward a seedier part of town with a vibrant if troubled nightlife. He trailed the car a few minutes more and then stopped when the driver pulled the sedan into a small parking lot adjacent to a tavern. The tavern's lot was lit by a single gas lamp, and the establishment itself was a dim place, with a wooden sign that bore its name and a long porch for revelers who wished to drink and fight outside. Henry took the Coke from his glovebox and then put it back without drinking but took the gun instead and looked at it in the darkness. The weapon was a .38 Special, its chrome scuffed and tarnished, and its heavy black handle rubbed and worn. In the cloth bag were the twelve rounds. He slid six of the bullets into the chamber and stuffed six of the remaining twelve in his jacket pocket. He looked up in time to see one of the sedan's riders walk to the tavern's entrance and shake the hand of a man who stood on the shadowy porch. He could not say for certain the identity of any of the men.

The moon was in and out of shadows as Henry quietly exited his truck and stood by for a moment. He switched the truck key from his left pocket to his right, and he stuffed the gun in the back of his trousers the way men did in adventure novels and on television. He pulled his hat low and began the slow gravelly walk toward the tavern, all obscured in dimness and vagueness and sin. He did not know what he was doing. Powered on by grief and rage, he walked slowly forward. When he was less than one hundred feet from the tavern entrance the door opened, and Maddock stepped into the cool and breezy night air. Henry stopped and stood near a parked car, one of a dozen or so. He looked on as Maddock walked a distance from the front door and spoke with one of the men from the sedan and one other man. Henry was not close enough to hear what they were talking about but was close enough to see the bright orange dot alight each time one of the men took a drag on his cigarette. The other two men laughed loudly, and one man took a pull of the bottle he held. Another man exited the sedan; this was the driver. The men who sold him the gun at the bait shop were not present; these were different men. Other customers or acquaintances or hired men he did not know. This last man, the driver, entered the tavern and left the other three to their joking.

Henry took the gun from his trousers and knelt. His aim had been good when he was a boy, taking shots at paper targets at the gun range, but that was a decade in the past, and these were not paper targets. They were men who breathed and talked and prayed. Who was Henry to decide whether they had a right to live, a right to die? He crouched among the parked cars and plodded slowly forward. Soon he was in the open, concealed by only the night and his dark clothes. The men did not see him. He pulled back his gun's hammer. The men did not hear the click.

Henry said loudly: "Maddock."

Maddock turned and peered into the darkness as Henry fired. The blast was deafening and atomic. Maddock was hit, and he screamed into the night, yowling like a shot cur as he held his left shoulder with his right hand and fell and scrambled back to the tavern's steps. Screaming and cursing, he crawled into the tavern as Henry fired four more shots and strode toward the building. Both of the other men were hit, but only one fell. The other made it inside, and the tavern door slammed shut again and again. Henry scrambled to the fallen man and looked at him in the eyes and saw the look of desperation, of near-death, an ugly and unwelcome stare from a wounded footsoldier. The man's breathing was labored and wheezy. The fallen man had in the commotion dropped his cigarette and beer bottle and a matchbook. Henry knelt. He refused to look the man in the eyes because then the man would become human again. He would be real. Henry took up the matchbook and pocketed it and sprinted back to his truck. A man exited the tavern and began firing at Henry as he returned to the truck, and one of the bullets struck the gravel near his foot, and another round caromed off the top of his windshield, leaving a small webbed crack.

Then Henry heard sirens; someone had alerted the police. The man firing at Henry heard the siren as well and cursed loudly and returned to the inside of the tavern. Henry stood next to his truck with little notion of what to do next. He fished two more bullets out from his pocket and slid them into the Colt's chamber. Then he ran quickly back to the sedan and fired a round into the rear driverside tire and scrambled back to his truck. The siren grew louder. Before Henry could climb back onto the driver's seat the patrol car was nearing the tavern and within seconds had stopped a hundred feet from the tavern and from Henry's truck. The patrol car and truck and tavern were in a kind of triangle, and the patrol car blocked Henry from Broadway. No one had exited the tavern in almost a minute. The patrol car's sirens were silent, but the lights flashed a phantasmagoric pulse. Other than those flashing lights there was nothing in the air. The night was still and heavy. Henry kept the truckdoor open but knelt a little so that he could see the patrol car but still be protected by the door.

Someone exited the cruiser. Henry could not identify the officer until he spoke loudly in the night: "Put the gun down and walk toward me with your hands where I can see them." It was Grant Wisdom.

Henry said nothing. He could not tell if the chief had his service revolver drawn.

Wisdom continued: "Let's take it easy, son. There doesn't need to be any more violence tonight. Just drop your weapon and walk slowly toward me with your hands where I can see them. There are some people here who I understand are hurt badly. We need to see about those folks. Officers and sheriff's deputies will be here in just a minute."

Henry said brazenly: "I don't think anyone else is on the way."

"Don't be ridiculous, Henry. Just walk away from your vehicle."

Henry reasoned the chief would never harm him. Calling his godfather's bluff, he hopped up to the seat and threw the truck in gear and sprayed gravel behind him as he bore directly for the patrol car. As he suspected, the chief did nothing as Henry veered sharply around the patrol car and over the curb with a jolt and headed for Broadway. Once he hit the main road he had to make a decision. He thought for a few seconds about returning to St. Michael's and holing up there so that law enforcement couldn't get to him. He knew, though, that if he did that he'd never make it off the island. So he took a right and drove for the mainland. With his chest heaving and his head full of possibilities he crossed the bay on the causeway and kept going from there.

He drove all night, traveling at a comfortable pace to avoid attention. He knew the area in Galveston County well, but once he was on the roads deeper onto the mainland he was in unfamiliar territory. He had enough gasoline to take him through Brazoria County, then Harris County and all the way to Walker County. Once he was a couple hundred miles from the coast he pulled into a service station to fill up and get another soda and a sweet roll. Then he drove another hundred miles on the highway, where there were no billboard advertisements and where other travelers were few and then found a roadside rest stop in Madison County where he pulled over and rolled the windows down a few inches and slept.

The Heresy of Rain

HE WOKE LATE IN THE MORNING. It was a small rest area off the main highway. A few brown leaves had fallen from the oaks onto his truck's hood. The ground was covered with weeds and gravel and leaves and in the near distance brown and yellow pine needles. There were a few picnic tables and a restroom and a pay phone. The parking lot was large enough for only a dozen vehicles. His was the only one there. He stepped out of his truck to stretch, careful to stay out of the view of passersby. After using the restroom and looking at his map he sat in the truck for several minutes and did nothing. The air was cooler here than Galveston, and the trees around him browner. It was early October, and the sky was overcast. The day would turn warm again in the early afternoon.

He reached into his pocket and pulled out the small scrap of paper he'd taken from the kitchen drawer at the house in Galveston. On the paper there was printed in his grandmother's neat handwriting a simple address. 27 Ranch Street Sweetwater Texas. He stared at the address for a long time. Then he sighed heavily and rolled up the window a bit and shook his head and threw his truck into gear and headed northwest toward Sweetwater.

THE ROADS FROM MADISON COUNTY TO SWEETWATER were lonely. Towns were few and offered little for the weary traveler. The land was sometimes flat and endless and at other times hilly and endless. Trees stretched as far as he could see in any direction. Flocks of dark birds appeared neverending as they crossed the blue sky like some airborne train. There seemed to be enough space in Texas alone to house all the people in the world. Having lived his entire life on an island along the coast, Henry knew little of the rest of the state. He found its vastness incredible and sometimes intimidating but also comforting. It seemed like an easy enough place to get lost in for a while. Before entering the town of Sweetwater he stopped at a café that doubled as a filling station and got a cup of coffee and some gas and a Dallas paper. Back in the truck he drank the coffee and scanned every headline of the newspaper until he saw a small article in the "State" section. The article mentioned a shooting in Galveston. One man injured critically and two others injured but not as seriously at a small tavern on the north side of the island. According to the article there were no suspects nor any witnesses who were willing to describe the shooter or his vehicle. Anyway, there was little to go on because of the darkness and the late hour of the crime. Anyone with information should contact the Galveston County Sheriff or the Galveston Police Department. Satisfied that he had at least a few days he tossed the paper to the passenger seat and drove on to Sweetwater.

Once in the town Henry stopped at the small post office and asked if the woman behind the counter could point him in the direction of Ranch Street, and the post office clerk told him to drive another two or three minutes until County Road 259 and take a left. Less than five minutes later he was at 27 Ranch Street. He left the truck on the gravel driveway and approached the small house with deference for the situation's precariousness. It was a house made of wood with a covered raised porch, and it was a house in need of paint and new windows. In truth it seemed a house in need of a new soul altogether. It rested sagging and depressed on a small parcel of thirsty land. There was dust all about. In the past day and a half he had driven through nothing but expansive forests, and this house seemed to be built on the only parcel of land devoid of vegetation within a thousand miles. The dust blew up in the wind and hung over the land and blinded all seers from the truth of the horizon. The ground below was gray and the sky gray with no line of demarcation, no sense of up or down save the beholder's own understanding of direction. The house sat quietly, surrounded by the gray dust that sometimes swirled red, and there was something that must have amounted to a lawn with occasional patches of faded green weeds. Henry pulled his hat low to his eyes for fear of the wind and climbed the splintered steps to the front porch. He took the folded paper out of his pocket and checked the number against the number nailed to the boards next to the door and then shoved the paper back into his pocket. He fingered the chipped and flaking numbers on the house and then knocked softly and reluctantly.

Almost a minute went by, and he had raised his fist again to knock more loudly when the door slowly opened and revealed the occupant he'd expected to find. Two old and tired eyes peered from within as if they were confused and searching. The eyes blinked and strained for a time.

"Henry?"

He nodded once. "It's me."

The moment was slow to unfold. Even after Henry's mother recognized the son she had a decade before abandoned she made no move to hasten any sort of reconciliation. She opened the door just a bit wider and continued to stare at him like he was a dream or a ghost.

"I don't know what to say."

"You don't have to say anything," he said, "but I thought I owed it to you to stop by for a bit."

"Owed it to me? What's happening?"

"If you'll give me just a few minutes of your time."

She nodded slowly and opened the door to allow him to enter. Henry tried to recognize some of the furnishings but could not. The place was spartan and dim; she must have accumulated these few possessions and furnishings after leaving Galveston. There appeared to be a solitary working lamp along with the dusty radio and a few wooden chairs. Too, there was a colorless rug and a stumpy four-legged table in the center of the room. There were no photographs or any other reminder of the past.

She motioned for him to sit in a tattered chair but offered him nothing more.

He sat and swallowed hard. Within him was a foreign feeling, something like imbalance or unfamiliarity. This was his mother before him, seated small and frail and too old. Too old for mothering and too old for compassion and too old for listening. She was only in her mid-forties but with few teeth and stringy faded hair and leathery wind-beaten skin she could have passed for twenty years older and maybe did.

He asked: "Is Howard still around?"

"What do you mean is Howard still around?"

"It was my understanding you two got married soon after you left Galveston."

"That's true, we did." She fidgeted with her fingers and constantly moved her thin emotionless mouth, and her eyes darted about.

"Is he still alive? Are you still married? Is he here?"

She fingered the hem of her worn dress and looked about the room, anywhere but at her son. She was skittish and never stopped moving her fingers. Like a child or an addict.

"Well, we're still married."

"All right, you know what? I shouldn't have asked. I surprised you showing up like this unannounced."

"It's fine. No, it's fine, Henry. Howard got put in prison a few years back."

"For fighting? Stealing?"

"For everything, I guess. He was skimming from the cashbox where he worked. The hardware store in town. When his boss confronted him he got in a fight. He got ten years for it, theft and assault. He'll be out in fifty-seven."

It did not occur to her that Henry's guess regarding his stepfather's transgressions was rooted in anything other than luck.

"I'm sorry to hear that, I suppose. To be honest I never knew him well, but I'd be lying if I said I'm surprised."

She shrugged. "I visit when I can."

Then there was a dust-filled silence that lasted both seconds and more than forever.

He said: "You're probably wondering how I knew to find you here."

"I suppose your grandmother gave you the address before she passed."

He nodded. "Then you knew she was dead."

"They got word to me."

"Who got word to you?"

"Her neighbors. Friends, you know, those women she played cards with."

"But you weren't at her funeral."

"Things were complicated back then. Things are still complicated."

"It wasn't that long ago."

"I'm sorry. I'm sorry."

He shook his head and looked toward a dusty window as if to say he did not believe in her sorrow and he did not even believe in her maternity. He did not believe that anywhere in his mother there was any goodness. He believed in her self-interest and in her greed and in her laziness. He believed in her shame and in her demons. But not in her sorrow. Certainly not her sorrow.

"Anyhow," he said, "I thought I ought to stop by. Stop by before I head out again."

"You came all this way just to head out again?"

"I've got to be on my way shortly."

"Well."

Henry could see the confusion in her eyes, and he could hear the uneasiness in her voice, which was quavering and tinny.

"Look," he said, "what I really came to say is I'm in some trouble."

"Henry you know I don't have any money."

"I'm not asking for money. Goddamn. You haven't changed at all."

"All right."

"I just need to square things with you because you're my only living relative, and I imagine the police or maybe the Rangers will track you down."

"Henry. What have you done? Last I knew you were playing the piano."

"I got married." He paused and sighed. For a moment she looked hopeful.

He continued: "But my wife was killed, and I went after the guys who did it."

She put her hand to her mouth, and for the briefest instance there may have been compassion or even maternity in those sad and colorless eyes.

She said: "I'm sorry to hear that. I am."

He ignored her. "I shot a few of these guys in Galveston. At least one is hurt badly. Maybe all three, I don't know. Then I took off and came here. I supposed I could get here pretty easy without being followed."

"What will you do now?"

"I'll head out. I have a truck and a little cash. I've got one more guy to find."

"Who? Who else?"

"The guy who ordered Grace dead."

"Grace?"

"My wife."

His mother slumped in her chair a little and then looked toward the window but said nothing. There was nothing to say. What can be said at a moment like this, when a parent realizes she has failed? Failed her son and failed herself and failed the world. These are the moments that define our lives, benchmarks upon which we measure our value. It is a terrible and sad thing to realize upon such a moment that one's life has not amounted to anything more prized or commendable than the swirling dust neither she nor anyone else could escape. That she bore into this world a gifted child does not matter. It does not matter.

Henry said: "So that's it. I figured you should hear directly from me what has happened. I'm not proud of shooting those guys, but I'd do it again if I had the chance. Maybe you know what it's like to love someone so much it hurts, but I suppose you don't. And she died because of something I did, and the pain is too much."

"Why do you need to do that? Maybe you could just go somewhere else, settle down. I wouldn't say you came here. I doubt anyone could find me."

"Chief Wisdom will find you."

"Grant Wisdom?"

Henry nodded.

"He's still police chief?"

"It'll take him a few days to find you, but he will."

"And then what?"

"He'll ask if I came here."

"What should I tell him?"

"It doesn't matter what you tell him. When I leave here you won't know where I'm headed."

"Do you have to do it? Is revenge that important?"

"If I don't take care of it, then nobody will. Any man in my position would feel the same way."

"I'm so sorry."

Henry readied to stand.

"I never meant for any of this to happen," she said quietly.

"Of course you didn't. But you left all the same."

"You were too young to remember your father. When he died I didn't know what to do."

"Sure you did. You started drinking and quit taking care of me."

"Don't say that."

"What? Don't say that? How else would you describe it?"

"I was young."

"You were older then than I am now."

"I was heartbroken. Your father, Henry. He meant so much to me."

"But I didn't?"

"Henry."

"It worked out for the best. Grandmother did fine, more than fine. She gave me opportunities that I never would have had with you."

"I've never heard you play the piano."

Henry shrugged and then stood, ready to quit this uncomfortable conversation and this dusty home so filled with staleness and coldness and misguided sentimentalities.

"It doesn't matter anyway."

"I'm sorry."

"You keep apologizing, but I don't think you know what you're apologizing for. And I don't think you mean it."

"Of course I mean it."

"Guilt and sorrow are not the same."

She appeared ready to apologize again but said nothing.

"Are you still hooked?"

"What do you mean?" she asked.

"You know what I mean. You and Howard. Or I guess just you now. Beer, whiskey, pills, whatever else you could find. When I was young, anything you could find to escape your reality if even for a minute."

"That's not true."

"Don't be ridiculous. Of course it's true. You didn't try to hide it from me when I was a boy, but now you'll lie?"

"Henry."

He said: "Anyway, I just thought you should hear it from me that I got in some trouble and the authorities will follow me. I'll be on my way."

He left the room, stepping outside and into the dust and wind, which was a refreshing reprieve against the house's damp and suffocating interior. He looked toward the house as he climbed into his truck, and he saw through the dust-streaked window a ghastly and unfamiliar face staring at him, like some vulgar and sunken and skeletal being, one he abhorred, for this form was an aberration of the world. This was not a mother. This was not a mother. This was a woman beholden to sin. Sin and indulgence and self-gratification. A woman of abandonment who now found herself alone and withering in her own dregs. He thought again to himself that sorrow and guilt are not the same.

Canto 3

Henry and his grandmother walked from the elementary school to her house. He was eleven. Fourth grade. His beaten brown backpack was slung over his shoulder. His grandmother carried his lunchbox. She rarely picked him up from school.

He asked: "Where's my mom?"

There was no answer. His grandmother touched the back of his hair as they walked and combed it gently with her fingers.

"Grandmother?"

"I heard you, dear."

"How come she didn't pick me up today?"

She sighed and even after having several hours to prepare an adequate answer to the question she knew was forthcoming she could say nothing. After a few more seconds of silence, she told him the truth. They turned onto her street.

"Henry, your mother hasn't been herself lately."

"I know. Since she met Howard."

"Maybe so. You're probably right."

He shrugged. They were a few houses short of her small but cheerful home.

"She and Howard have left, Henry. They've moved away for a while."

"For how long?"

"I'm not sure, son. I'm not sure."

"Am I going to stay with you?"

They arrived at her house and stood now at the end of her single-car driveway. She turned to face him and put a hand on her shoulder.

"Yes, you'll stay with me. Is that all right with you?"

"Sure. Will you keep teaching me piano?"

She smiled and tousled his hair. "You're already about a thousand times better than I am. I've got nothing left to teach you."

He smiled shyly, and they walked into the house together.

Canto 4

HENRY AND GRACE WERE BARELY NINETEEN YEARS OLD, and Henry had saved enough money to buy a simple gold band that was plain but shiny and expensive. It was a soupy August night on the beach, and they had walked along the shore. Her hand was small and soft and cool in his. Somehow she was guiding him along the shore, ever aware of the water's edge. He stopped and held tightly her hand and took her other hand and held her at arm's length facing him. Her brow furrowed, and she cocked her head a bit with curiosity. He then brought her close to his face and did not kneel but rather embraced her.

He told her he loved her so fiercely there were no words. And he told her she was uncommonly beautiful and had a gentle and beautiful soul. He said he didn't know if he would grow old because sometimes people die young, but however old he got to be he wanted it to be with her. He took the gold band from his pocket and slid it on her finger and said please say you'll marry me. Please say yes.

Her lip trembled, and she nodded yes and began to cry gently. He slid his thumbs beneath her eyes to wipe the tears, and she said yes and I love you.

And then she held him tightly there on the beach, and she said: "I will protect you. I won't let you die."

Then there was a soft rain that masked their tears.

Part III

"There is within me (and with sadness I have watched it in others) a knot of cruelty borne by the stream of love, much as our blood sometimes bears the seed of our destruction."

–James Hurst

The Heresy of Rain

THE LARGE RED AND YELLOW AND WHITE SIGN read WELCOME TO AN-
DREWS: STAY A WHILE. Henry supposed this was as good a place as any.
The next sign along the road informed him he was in Andrews city limits
and that the population of the seat of Andrews County was 8,098. Tired
and hungry, Henry looked for a place to hole up for a bit. This was far
West Texas, near the New Mexico border. Desert land. It was flat and
dusty but sometimes brown and weedy, and always it seemed a steady
wind. A mile inside city limits he saw Andrews Motel, a long one-floor
building with several doors that led directly from the rooms to the parking
lot. The theme seemed to be light blue. The doors were blue, the window
shutters were blue, the awning near the front desk was blue, and the roof
was also blue. He went inside with his duffle bag and inquired about a
room. The marquee outside advertised single occupancy rooms as low as
six dollars per night.

The clerk was a pleasant young woman a little older than Henry. She
had short dark hair and too much lipstick but was nonetheless cute. She
smiled nicely and informed Henry that all the rooms were booked for the
next few nights on account of a fair a few counties away.

"Goddamn."

The young woman continued to smile nicely.

"Sorry, it's not your fault. I've just been driving for a couple of days
and need a spot to rest before I move along."

"I understand, sir. Would you like to register for a room startin next
week?"

Henry shook his head. "Is there any other motel around here?"

She shrugged cutely and smiled with apology. "Just us."

"Well."

There was a pause for a few moments, during which Henry tried to
decide what to do next, and the clerk smiled unblinkingly at Henry. Then
there was an epiphany.

"Oh! The Whitmans are lookin to rent out their little apartment. I'm friends with their grandniece, Connie, and she said yesterday they had the room over their garage fixed up for a renter. If you're lookin to stay in Andrews a while. Or maybe they'd let you stay for just a few days."

"Where are the Whitmans?"

The clerk wrote the directions to the Whitmans' house, just a few miles away, on a sheet of Andrews Motel paper. Henry folded the paper and put it in his shirt pocket.

"Thanks very much…"

"Darla." She flashed her cute, dimply smile.

"Thanks, Darla."

Ten minutes later Henry was knocking on the Whitmans' front door. Mr. and Mrs. Whitman were older folks who were kind and methodical. They seemed to Henry to embody the very essence of "grandparents." Mr. Whitman braved the stairs to show Henry the room above their garage. It was a simple affair with a twin bed and a sofa and a dresser. There was a small bathroom and a sink and a very small refrigerator that fit under what Henry supposed was the kitchen counter. There was no closet, but Henry didn't need one.

"What do you think?"

"Looks pretty good," Henry said. "How much are you asking?"

"Fifteen a week, due each Monday evening."

Henry nodded while doing some tabulations in his head.

"All right," he said. "I think I can do that."

"Do you have a job?"

"Not yet. But I can give you the first two weeks' rent right now."

"What's your name again?"

"Henry."

"It's good to have you, Henry. Supper each evening is included. Clara—that's my wife—usually has it on the table around six."

"That sounds good."

"You're on your own for other meals."

"All right." Henry took the thirty dollars out of his pocket and handed it over to Mr. Whitman.

"Well, that's about it," said Mr. Whitman. "You're just in time for supper tonight. I reckon you should wash up and head down in a few minutes."

"I'll be right down."

Mr. Whitman had his hand on the doorknob but turned. "Oh, and one more thing. We don't mind if you have friends over, but no loud noise or music. And do your best to keep lady visitors a secret from Clara. She's very old-fashioned."

Henry smiled and nodded.

Mr. Whitman said he'd see Henry in a few minutes and shut the door behind him. Henry fell to the sofa and put his head in his hand and wondered almost aloud how long he would be able to do this. Before going down to the Whitmans' dining room for supper he emptied his pockets and placed the contents on top of the dresser. The scrap of paper with his mother's address and a few loose coins and the matchbook he took from the wounded man outside the tavern on the island. He turned over the matchbook in his fingers a few times. The cover read CATTLEMAN GRILL, ALPINE TEXAS. He would take out his map later and figure things out. He took his gun and what few bullets remained from his duffle and wrapped it all back in the cloth sack and shoved it under the sofa cushions and pressed down on the sofa and then sat for a moment to make sure it couldn't be detected in the unlikely event he'd have a guest. He looked out the room's lone window. It was almost dark. He imagined Grant Wisdom driving all of those lonely roads and then finally strolling into Andrews with his sirens blazing and his gun drawn. He shook his head and put the matchbook on the dresser. Then he looked in the small mirror and rinsed his face and went down to supper with Mr. and Mrs. Whitman.

TWO MORNINGS LATER Henry was wandering about Andrews, trying to figure out what he would do next and how long he would stay. He located a service station and a hunting and outdoors shop and the post office. He saw a small café or diner and passed it by and then turned around. The diner's marquee read ANDREWS DINER OPEN 24 HOURS.

Henry pulled the truck into the restaurant's small parking lot. Still cautious, he sat in the truck and observed the area for a while. There were a few other vehicles parked in the lot. The diner was in need of some cosmetic updating, but it didn't look shabby or rundown. He hopped down from the seat and walked toward the entrance and noticed in a window near the door a sign handwritten with black marker taped to the window: DISHWASHER WANTED. He stopped for just a second and then went inside to the sound of the bell jangling above his head.

The diner was not large, but there was room for several booths and a row of stools at the counter. The place was done up in red vinyl and chrome. Henry took one of the stools and thanked the waitress behind the counter when she handed him a menu and said she'd get him some coffee as soon as this fresh pot was ready. He decided on the three eggs and ham special and handed the menu back to the waitress who smiled and gave him his fresh coffee in exchange. The place smelled old-fashioned and bready and familiar.

The few customers in the restaurant appeared to be regulars. Two older women—both with beehives for hair, one with pink hair and the other blue—were gossiping over steaming coffee in one of the booths. A truck driver who seemed friendly with the nice waitress sat a few seats from Henry at the counter. He wore a green baseball cap with plastic webbing and a heavy jacket over his denim shirt. A couple of college-age boys, about Henry's age, were having breakfast in the corner. A stack of textbooks sat on the table. Henry thought about college for a moment and what it must be like and whether he would like it, but he soon dismissed such a ridiculous line of thinking on account of he had never cared for school.

His meal arrived, and he ate it hungrily. The waitress, whose nametag said "Suzanne," filled his coffee twice more and seemed to be genuinely appreciative when Henry complimented the coffee and the food. Suzanne was a friendly older woman with red and gray hair that was done up in a bun. She wore lipstick and too much makeup about her eyes. Henry almost asked her if she knew Darla from the motel.

When she brought Henry his check Henry got her attention before she went back over to the truck driver.

"What do you need, hon?"

"Nothing really. I was just wondering if the sign out front in the window is still good."

"What sign is that?"

"The handwritten note about you all needing a dishwasher."

"Well, I don't know. Let me go ask."

She pushed through the white swinging door and was gone for thirty seconds, and when she returned from the back of the diner she said: "Jack said the sign is still good. Our last two daytime dishwashers didn't work out so good. One got himself fired for being late too many times, and the other got himself arrested for driving drunk."

"Well, I'd be interested. What does it pay?"

"Hold on, hon."

Suzanne went back to the rear of the restaurant and was gone for another thirty seconds. During this time the truck driver look annoyed, and Henry shrugged and smiled apologetically. She came back and said: "It's seventy-five an hour. Goes up to eighty-five if you do a good job and don't get fired after a month. Or arrested for being a drunk."

"How do I apply?"

"We're not so formal about applications. I guess I can get Jack up here to see about you."

"I'd appreciate it."

Before she made her third trip to whatever was behind the swinging door Suzanne put one hand on her hip and the other on the counter and said she'd never seen Henry before.

"I'm new to the area."

"Hm. Where do you live?"

"I took the apartment over the Whitmans' garage, over there on County Road Nine-sixteen. I just arrived a few days ago."

"All right. I remember hearing they all was going to rent that out."

"Yes ma'am."

"What's your name darlin?"

"Henry."

"All right, Henry. Give me just a second. I'll run and get Jack for you."

She winked and held up a finger in the direction of the truck driver and disappeared again. When she returned a minute later she brought with her a middle-aged man who wore a short-sleeved dress shirt and a tie with little hamburgers and pink milkshakes all about it.

"Suzanne tells me you're interested in bein a dishwasher."

"Yes sir."

"It pays seventy-five an hour with a dime raise after thirty days if you're still around."

Suzanne said loudly from the other end of the counter: "Jack, I already told him that."

Jack ignored Suzanne.

"Hours are six-thirty in the mornin till three-thirty in the afternoon."

"All right."

"You get free fountain drinks and coffee and twenty percent off menu items. But don't overdue the drinks. It don't grow on trees."

Suzanne said: "Jack, coffee does grow on trees."

Jack closed his eyes and shook his head and then sighed heavily. Suzanne winked at Henry. Henry smiled nicely.

Then Henry said: "That sounds good."

"Workdays are Monday through Friday with some Saturdays. I'll try to give you plenty of notice when I'll need you on a Saturday." Jack said his days of the week so that the "day" syllable sounded like "dee." So it was Mondee, Tuesdee, and so forth.

"I'm pretty much available whenever you need me."

"Payday is every other Friday, and I pay in cash."

"All right."

"Suzanne tells me you're new around here."

"Staying at the Whitmans' apartment."

"That's what she said. And your name is Henry?"

"Yes sir."

"Where you from, Henry?"

"Down south."

Jack chortled as if Henry had told a joke.

"Son, we are down south."

"Sorry. I mean down by the coast."

"You been to school?"

"I graduated high school," he lied.

"No college?"

"No sir."

"What brings you up this way?"

"Change in scenery, I guess."

"You seem like a nice enough fella."

Suzanne hollered from the back of the diner where she was checking her lipstick: "Goddamnit, Jack. Just give him the job. He ain't a criminal. He's just a boy. Call the Whitmans if you want to check up on him."

"Jesus, Suzanne! What did I say about your language? Christ almighty."

Jack looked at Henry for a bit. He said: "I reckon I will give the Whitmans a call. How long you been at them all's place?"

"Just a couple of days."

"What are they chargin you?"

"Fifteen a week."

"Seems more than reasonable."

"They are nice folks."

Jack eyed Henry for another few seconds and then nodded his head. "All right," he said, "we could use you tomorrow."

"I'll be here."

"It ain't just dishwashin. There's also some moppin and loadin inventory from the truck and so forth."

"I'll do anything you all need."

"All right." Jack stuck out his hand. "See you at six-thirty."

Henry smiled and shook Jack's hand and laid a couple of dollars on the counter for his check and Suzanne's tip.

"Thank you, sir."

Jack started for the back again, and Henry was almost through the door when Jack turned and said: "Say, son."

Henry turned with the glass door half open and the bell in mid jangle. "Yes sir?"

"I didn't catch your last name. I'll need it for payroll records."

Without pausing Henry said "Ballard."

"Ballard. You related to the Waco Ballards?"

"I wouldn't know, sir. There are Ballards all over Texas as I understand it."

"There sure are. Anyhow, we'll see you tomorrow. Provided the Whitmans don't have anything incriminating to say."

Suzanne looked up from the college students' table where she was filling their coffee mugs. "Hon, he's just teasin is all."

"It's fine, ma'am. I'll see you all tomorrow."

The Heresy of Rain

IT WAS JUST AFTER HENRY SETTLED IN ANDREWS that his nightmares began. They were all variations of a single terrible dream. In the dream he was walking along a dusty and windy land that was neither hot nor cold. Just wind. And he always struggled with his footing, tripping or stumbling over his feet even when there was nothing to obstruct him. The angry overcast sky, roiling and red. After several moments of walking and stumbling over this dusty land Henry approached a small wooden house. It was a rundown house, faded and gray with no windows he could see. Eventually he made his way to the house, stumbling up the chipped and faded steps to the front door, which was closed. Dizzy and confused, he pounded on the door with his fist. The wind and dust flew about. After a short time the door opened just a crack, and two beady eyes gazed out. He understood in the dream that these were his mother's eyes, but when the door opened it was revealed to Henry that they were Grace's eyes. She was dead, but her eyes were open and staring horribly, not at Henry but beyond Henry into some dark and deep yonder behind him. And in the dream Henry fell back out of the house and down the steps and back onto the dusty and confusing land, struggling to get his footing.

HENRY SPENT HIS DAYS in the back of the diner, washing dishes and loading inventory and generally keeping the kitchen tidy with chores that though not part of his job description kept him from boredom. There were a few different cooks who worked days at the diner, but all they did was make messes. It was Henry's job to clean up the messes. Henry's work was honest work, and he worked hard. He arrived at six-thirty every morning and stayed late when asked. It was a routine, one that suited Henry just fine. He didn't have to do any thinking. Dishwashing was rote. Rhythmic. It was repetitive and measurable. Not unlike playing the piano. At the end of the shift there was resolution, a sense of completion. He paid his rent and took many of his meals at the diner and often had supper with the Whitmans. He got along with his co-workers. Suzanne continued to baby him. She seemed to be a sort of maternal figure for the entire staff. And because he was working out of the public eye and living off the beaten path Henry didn't feel the need to turn and look over his shoulder very often. Henry's work was constant. He didn't have much downtime at the diner. Occasionally he would think of Grace, especially if he had had a dream the night before. Or perhaps a smell or sound would make him think of her, and he would be beset by a raw pang. It seemed no one caught him wiping away the periodic tears.

It was early November when Charlotte began working at the diner. The lunch rush had just subsided, and Jack entered the small kitchen area with the new employee.

"Henry," Jack said while Henry's back was turned to the swinging door.

Henry turned around while saying, "Yes sir?"

Jack was standing with a young lady Henry had not seen before.

"This here's Charlotte. She's goin to start waitin tables for us, eleven till seven. Charlotte, this here's Henry. He's been here about month, washes dishes and what not."

Henry nodded his head toward Charlotte, smiled, and said a polite hello. He figured her to be about his age, maybe a little younger. She was pretty, with sandy hair and a few freckles on each cheek. She tucked her hair behind her ear and shyly said hello back to Henry.

Jack said: "Charlotte's the daughter of an old friend of mine. She's a good kid. Knows her way around town and ought to do a hell of a job for us. Anyhow, just wanted to show her around the place. She'll start in a couple days."

Henry said, "Good to meet you," and then he nodded again and turned back to the dishes as Jack and Charlotte went back to the front of the diner.

IT WAS A FEW WEEKS LATER, almost Thanksgiving, and Henry was working some extra hours. At three o'clock he heard Charlotte talking on the phone, and though he didn't catch the context of the conversation he could tell she was agitated. She came out of Jack's office where the phone was and folded her arms and shook her head. Pouting.

Henry asked if everything was all right.

"I guess. That was my dad. He can't give me a ride home after all, at least not at seven when I'm off here."

"How late will it be before he can make it over here?"

"He said ten."

"That's pretty late."

"That's way too late to be hanging out here."

"Why don't you let me take you home?"

"Henry, I can't ask you to stay till seven."

"I'll be here until six anyway. Jack asked me to work a few extra hours."

"Are you sure? I live twenty minutes away. I hate to take up so much of your time."

"If there's one thing I have it's time. I don't have anything else to do." She smiled. "Are you sure?"

"I'm positive, Charlotte. I'm happy to help."

"All right. If you're sure."

He nodded and then walked over to the corner and grabbed a mop, and she said thank you and ran her hands along the pleats of her blue diner-issue dress and went back to work.

Henry drank coffee and read the newspaper until seven when Charlotte was ready to leave. She gave Henry directions to her parents' house, and they left. After a minute of silence Charlotte asked Henry where he's from.

"Way down by the coast."

"Corpus Christi?"

"Not far from there," he lied. The towns were more than two hundred miles apart, but she didn't need to know the specifics of his past.

"Do you have family up here?"

"No. I don't have much family anywhere."

"I'm sorry to hear that."

He shrugged. "It's all right."

Then there was a pause. Nothing said for a minute or more than a minute. An uncomfortable lull during which Henry tried to think of something benign but interesting to talk about, for he knew what was coming next.

"You know," she said, turning to look at him from the passenger seat, "they say you're a drifter who just showed up one day looking for work."

He raised an eyebrow. "By *they*, do you mean Suzanne?"

She laughed and put her back to the seat again. "Yeah, I guess so."

"Well, I guess I am a drifter. I like it here in Andrews, though."

"Really? I can't wait to leave. I've been here all my life. That's why I'm working at the diner. To save money for a car and then I'm gone."

"Where will you go?"

"I don't know. I guess I haven't thought much about that part of my plan. I've always liked the idea of leaving Andrews, but I really don't know where I'd go. California maybe. Or New York. Or New Orleans. New Orleans seems interesting."

"Maybe."

"I don't know. Just anywhere but here I guess."

Henry craned his head to see a road sign and turned left.

Charlotte asked if he had any hobbies.

"I play the piano some. I haven't had a chance to play much lately. The Whitmans have a piano in their house, but I haven't asked them if I could play it. Seems like a strange thing for me to ask."

"What kind of music do you play?"

"The blues, mostly."

"I don't know anyone else who plays the piano. I'd like to hear you play sometime."

He smiled. "We'll see. Maybe I'll work up the nerve to ask Mrs. Whitman if I can have a look at their piano. Who knows. I played at a club for a while before I came out this way."

"A club? I bet you've had lots of girlfriends then."

Henry said nothing. He just pursed his lips and stared at the road.

She said: "I'm sorry. I shouldn't have said that. It's none of my business." She turned to the passenger window and folded her hands in her lap.

"That's all right. Don't worry about it."

"Have you had a chance to make many friends around here?"

"Just one. Or at least I hope I can call you a friend."

She looked over at him, and he could see her beaming even in the darkness.

"Of course you can."

A few minutes later he dropped her off at her parents' home, a typical ranch style one-story with white or yellow shutters; he couldn't tell in the darkness of the early evening.

"Thanks, Henry. I really appreciate your help. And sorry if I talked too much."

"Talked too much? I'm happy to have had the company, Charlotte. I'll see you tomorrow."

She waved goodbye and smiled very sweetly and headed inside.

The Heresy of Rain

THE FOLLOWING DAY Henry was seated at supper with Mr. and Mrs. Whitman. Toward the end of the meal, while Mr. Whitman was gathering plates and dishes and taking them to the kitchen to be washed, Henry asked Mrs. Whitman about the piano.

He said: "I see you all have a piano sitting over in the den. Does it get much playing?"

Mrs. Whitman smiled. "No, dear, not anymore. Our Jane played when she was young. She loved to play that piano, didn't she, Edgar?"

Mr. Whitman said from the kitchen: "You bet. She was the best around."

"Then Jane grew up and went away to school," Mrs. Whitman said, "and now she has her own family up in Michigan. I have it tuned every two years, but Edgar and I don't play. Every now and again Joyce and her family will visit from up north, and she'll play a few songs."

"That's too bad, it just sitting there and all."

Mrs. Whitman perked up. "Henry, do you play?"

"I play a little." He smiled shyly. "But I'm a bit out of practice."

"Do play, dear! Please. I'd love to hear that old thing again."

"Well. Are you sure?"

"Of course. What sorts of things do you play? Classical music? Show tunes?"

"Mostly the blues."

"Edgar, come on in here. Henry's fixing to play some of the music the blacks like."

"I'm just in the kitchen, Clara. I can hear him fine in here. And I don't think we're supposed to call it black music anymore."

Mrs. Whitman gave Henry a quizzical look, and Henry just shrugged.

"Well, go on," she said, shooing him over to the other room.

Henry pulled the bench out from under the piano and then sat down and lifted the fallboard and scooted himself up to the instrument. He took a deep breath and grasped the edges of the bench and took another deep breath and then relaxed his shoulders and closed his eyes. And he imagined Grace, not Mrs. Whitman, sitting in that room waiting for a performance. He started low, with a slow-paced introduction or vamp that he repeated a few times to get used to this piano's timbre and to get a feel for the music again. He had not played in two months, the longest he had gone without playing the piano for many years. Soon he found his rhythm, his direction. And he imagined not Mrs. Whitman but Grace listening. He lost himself in the music, improvising soulful melody after melody. He played high and low and switched keys from C to F and back to C again. This was home. Two months of demons and anxiety and anger and guilt flew from his body as he entered into a catharsis the likes of which the Whitmans had never observed. He had been playing for almost half an hour—to him it seemed mere minutes—when he opened his eyes and resolved the tune and turned around. The Whitmans were sitting together on the sofa, staring at Henry as if he were some angel or ghost. Their mouths were agape and their eyebrows furrowed in awe and surprise. Henry shrugged and dropped his head apologetically. He was embarrassed for having played so long without stopping.

"I'm sorry," he said, "I should have stopped long ago. I lost track of time. That happens sometimes when I play."

Mr. Whitman was the first to speak. "Son, I've never heard anything like that before. Not on the radio and not on a record."

Mrs. Whitman asked, "Where did you learn to play like that?"

"I guess I just sort of figured it out when I was younger. My grandmother played a little bit and showed me how to get around the keyboard and taught me some things before I got the hang of it on my own."

Mr. Whitman said, "Whatever the case, that was amazing, son." Mrs. Whitman nodded her head in agreement. "Have you considered a career in music?"

"I've played a little in restaurants and churches before. Maybe I will again someday."

The Whitmans then encouraged Henry to play a few more tunes before he went up to his small apartment and to bed for the night.

The Heresy of Rain

BEFORE LONG MOST OF ANDREWS KNEW there was a genuine musician renting the room above the Whitmans' garage. Henry played at a couple of churches and refused payment. His renditions of "Amazing Grace" and "Down to the River to Pray" and "A Closer Walk with Thee" were moving and resonant. He was uncomfortable with the attention and tried to deflect it. And he knew this was not the way to blend into a town and keep clear of law enforcement. So in the end he politely turned down a few gigs. By Christmastime, he was thinking seriously about leaving. Every evening before he went to bed he picked up the matchbook and stared at the name of the restaurant it advertised.

In the middle of December he had gotten off work for the day. It was Friday afternoon. He removed his apron and hung it on the peg near the kitchen door and waved to Jack and told Suzanne he'd see her tomorrow.

"Henry, wait." It was Charlotte. There existed between them an awkward friendship. Henry had had few female friends in his life. He turned and smiled, uncertain and timid.

"Why is it that I am the only person in this town who has not heard you play the piano?" She had her hands on her hips.

Henry shrugged and looked toward the ground. "I don't know."

"I keep hearing about the blues-playing dishwasher from down at the diner."

"Well, I'm sorry it's worked out this way. I never meant to exclude you."

"I think you owe me a concert."

"Owe you a concert?

"Yep."

"I'm not sure what you mean."

"My dad is the vice president of the board at our church."

"All right."

"It's the Methodist church at Smithfield and Route Six."

"I know where that is."

"Anyhow, everyone knows me over there. The cleaning staff is there late on Sundays, and they all will let me in. You and I can go there, and we'll have the whole place to ourselves except the cleaning ladies. They won't bother us."

"I don't know, Charlotte. I wouldn't want to get us in trouble." This sounded to Henry weird and sneaky.

"They know me." She crossed her arms and dared Henry to refuse. "Besides, we have a very handsome piano that needs playing."

"If you think it's okay."

She winked at him and told him to pick her up at five on Sunday.

He spent the next two days in a fog of confusion and anxiety. The Whitmans both sensed something was on his mind and asked him at supper Saturday if anything was wrong. He assured him he was all right, but they weren't convinced. Mr. Whitman followed Henry out to the garage after the meal as Henry was about to climb the stairs to his room.

"Henry, you sure there isn't anything wrong?"

"I'm sure. It's just an adjustment for me, being in a new place and all."

"Especially around the holidays, I would imagine."

"I guess so."

"You thinking about home, wherever that is?"

"Sometimes. There are a lot of things on my mind, I guess." Henry sat on the first step, and Mr. Whitman pulled over a wooden chair and sat with him.

"Are you thinking about someone from back home?"

Henry was silent for a moment. "Yes. Almost all the time."

"Is she pretty?"

"Very pretty. Beautiful."

"I bet she likes your piano playing."

"She did. Very much. I wrote some songs for her. I miss her. I really miss her." And suddenly Henry was overcome by emotion. His eyes clouded, and his face turned red. His lips trembling, he apologized to Mr. Whitman. "I'm sorry. I just…" He trailed off, unsure of what to say.

"I see. Are you sure you're all right?"

Henry used his shirtsleeve to wipe his eyes and stood up. "I'll be all right, Mr. Whitman. I apologize. I'm acting like a kid."

"You've got nothing to apologize for." Mr. Whitman stood as well. "Clara and I like having you around. I hate to see you upset. You let us know if there's anything we can do for you."

"I appreciate it, sir."

Henry turned toward the steps, but Mr. Whitman stopped him. He was walking toward the end of the long driveway. He called Henry to join him. Henry walked out to the end of the driveway where Mr. Whitman now stood.

Mr. Whitman said: "Look at it." He waved with his hand to gesture toward the sky.

Henry looked up. The night sky was bright and milky. Swaths of pale and translucent matter stretched about and whirled above. Stars were clustered, and they glowed and sparkled brilliantly against the night.

Mr. Whitman said: "Sometimes when I'm feeling out of sorts I'll come out here and just look at the night sky. It's almost as if its vastness reminds me of my place."

"Recently someone told me about Orion's belt. I've tried a few times, but I can't find it. I don't know it from any other group of three stars."

"This is a good time to find it. It's most visible in the southwest sky during the winter. Look at the Millers' house down the street, with the weather vane."

"All right."

"That's out toward the southwest. Now look straight up. You'll see three bright stars sort of on an incline, from left to right."

"Well."

"Do you see it?"

"Yeah, I actually think I do."

Mr. Whitman said: "Anyway, sometimes I find comfort in the night sky." Mr. Whitman put a hand on Henry's shoulder and then turned to go inside.

Henry said: "Thanks for everything, sir."

"Nobody calls me sir anymore. Especially not family."

"All right." Henry then walked up to his room where he fell asleep that night holding the matchbook.

THE FOLLOWING EVENING Henry pulled up to Charlotte's place a few minutes before five. He was unsure of the protocol regarding this sort of outing, but Charlotte made things easy for him by bolting through the front door and letting herself into the truck without Henry having to move a muscle. She was wearing a wool jacket and a long skirt, and her hair was down.

He didn't realize he'd been staring at her for several seconds after she got in the truck.

She tilted her head and smiled. "What?"

"I'm sorry. I guess I've never seen you with your hair like that."

"You mean, not in a bun for work?"

"Yeah, I guess that's it."

She laughed. "Let's go, silly. We've got to get there before the cleaning ladies are done."

On the way to the church Henry asked how long Charlotte's family had lived in that house. She told him all her life.

"My parents bought it in thirty-three, the year before I was born. In the middle of the Depression. Daddy says they got such a good deal he could sell the house now for nearly eight times what he paid for it."

Henry nodded and did the math on Charlotte's age.

Just minutes later they were pulling into the Methodist church parking lot.

Henry again expressed his misgivings. "Charlotte, I don't know about this. I feel really odd breaking into a church and playing the piano without permission."

She had one hand on the door already. "We aren't breaking into anything. I can already see Dolores cleaning the windows. Come on."

She was right. The maintenance staff knew her and let her into the building, even gave her a hug.

"See?"

"All right, all right."

The Heresy of Rain

Henry thought the church building was large for a town this size. There were four sections of pews with five aisles, including the ones on the sides. Everything seemed to be done up in an opulent green. Behind the altar there were two enclaves: one for the organ and one for the piano. The piano was a stunning black JC Fischer grand.

"My God," he said, "you were right. This is a beautiful instrument." The topboard was already propped open, and the piano had been dusted and polished. It was sleek and lovely, and Henry sat on the green cushioned bench and rested his left hand on the sideboard and covered his mouth in amazement with his right hand and then turned to see Charlotte, who was already seated on the first-row pew, her hands in her lap. She smiled broadly. Just before Henry began to play something Dolores the cleaning lady stuck her head in the sanctuary and told Charlotte they were leaving and the door was locked and that she would see her next week. Then they were alone. The lights were not all switched on. Inside the building there was a palpable energy, not unlike his experience at St. Michael's on Galveston.

"Are you just going to sit there, or are you going to play for me?"

Henry shook his head and turned and said: "Sorry. Any idea what you want me to play?"

"Whatever you know I'll like."

"All right."

And so he played. He played hymns that were the anthems of salvation and the dirges of despair, and he played spirituals that spoke of manacles and hopelessness and victory, and he played syncopated rags that shuffled and skitted and jaunted about, and he played Dixieland marches and patriotic ballads, and he played Gershwin and Ellington and Joplin and all the rest. After half an hour he stopped and turned to Charlotte who seemed spellbound by it all.

"Keep going," she implored. "I can't remember the last time I felt so relaxed. I've never known anyone so talented as you. At anything."

"I doubt that."

"Please play a few more songs. Please please please!"

For the next fifteen minutes Henry played a few of the tunes he had written for Grace. Lullabies. Sweet nighttime songs that hung in the air. Ethereal melodies that he'd not shared with anyone but Grace. He closed his eyes against the memories, tried to focus on the notes. He took deep breaths as he played. This was the blues, yes. But different. Special slow jazz that stood for something else, something that mattered. Like a prayer or a poem or an orthodox incantation. When he finished he kept his eyes closed and his head down and did not move his hands from the keys and did not think of Charlotte or anything but Grace and her wonderful smell and her lips and also of her sister Diana's sad smile at the funeral and then finally of the men at the cemetery shoveling dirt over her coffin and closing her off from the world forever. Closing her off from him.

He stayed like this for a whole minute or more. Then with another deep breath he opened his eyes and turned partway on the green velvet bench and looked at Charlotte. She still sat there on the first pew. One arm was across her midsection and the other elbow propped on the arm and her hand over her mouth. Even from fifteen feet away he could see that her eyes were glassy.

He shrugged slightly and then looked down, not sure what else to do. He was in a locked church, playing the blues in the memory of his murdered wife while a lovely young lady cried at the beauty of the notes. He did not know what to do next.

She took a tissue from her purse and dabbed just under her eyes and then smiled.

"I would clap," she said, almost laughing at the absurdity of it all, "but I'm not sure that's quite the right response. You deserve much more than applause."

"I don't know. Thanks."

She stood and walked toward the piano enclave and stopped with her hands folded and resting on the nearby railing.

"I've never heard anything like that."

He smiled and laughed lightly. "I've gotten a lot of that lately."

"I'm serious. I mean, I've heard the blues, of course. But that was something else. What you play is special."

"I don't know about that."

"And the songs you played last. I didn't recognize them."

Henry looked away and swallowed hard. "Those were just a few tunes I wrote some time ago."

She stared hard at him. He would not look at her. He played with the raised seam at the edge of the green velvet bench. He took deep breaths. He sensed in her something warm and familiar but also complicated.

"When you drove me home last month. Remember?"

"Sure."

"I said something about girlfriends back home."

He shrugged.

She said: "You seemed, not upset, but sentimental maybe? Emotional."

"I guess."

"Those songs. The ones you just played for me. They once were for someone else."

"Did you like them?"

"Of course."

"Then that's all that matters. You wanted a concert, so I played for you just about everything I know."

"Well. Thank you, Henry."

"You're welcome."

Then she tilted her head a bit and said: "There's something about you."

"What do you mean?"

"I don't know. A drifting diner dishwasher"—she smiled—"who plays the piano like that? I don't know, Henry. I think you must have some secrets."

"We all have secrets. I'll bet you've got some of your own."

"Sure, I suppose. Of course we do. But we don't all play the piano the way you do." She held out her hand, face up. He reached out and took her hand and helped her up. Her hand was soft and warm but unfamiliar. "Thanks again for the show," she said. She led him with her hand down the steps from the enclave to the center aisle and then patted his back the way a mother might and then squeezed his shoulder and then clasped her hands behind her back, and they walked out of the church into the chilly West Texas December evening.

"It was my pleasure," he said. Then they climbed into the truck and drove away, two friends engaged in an unknowable relationship, with secrets plentiful.

HENRY PULLED UP to one of the two service stations in Andrews. It was Pete's Automotive. Outside there were tires stacked about and gas cans and oil cans scattered among the tires. Henry pushed through the glass door. The man behind the counter was Pete.

Pete said: "How can I help you?"

"I noticed a knocking sound earlier today when I was driving to work. Some folks recommended I bring my truck to you."

"All right. That black truck?" Pete gestured to the parking lot.

"Yes sir."

"Forty-seven?"

"Forty-six."

"You have time to wait a bit while we take a look at it?"

"Sure."

Henry sat on one of the vinyl chairs in the small waiting area. The chairs' cushions were green, and they were ripped with the stuffing showing. On the small table were some hunting and fishing magazines from two years ago and an ashtray. Pete drove the truck up and down the street a couple of times and then pulled the truck up to the garage and entered the small office again.

Pete said: "Sounds like spark plugs and tubes and maybe valves need replacing. It's a pretty easy fix. We've got the parts. It'll be ten dollars, and we can do it while you wait."

"All right. Sounds good."

Pete nodded and tapped the counter a couple of times in what appeared to be some sort of tic and then went out to the garage and talked to the mechanic, a young man who appeared to be about Henry's age. Then the younger man nodded and pulled the truck all the way into the garage while Pete re-entered the office.

He said to Henry: "Okay. Arthur will get it taken care of. Should be a half hour or so."

Henry nodded and said thanks.

The Heresy of Rain

Forty minutes later the tune-up was complete, and Henry paid the ten dollars and went out to retrieve his truck from Arthur.

The truck was back in the parking lot, and Henry nodded his thanks toward Arthur—who was still in the garage—and began to climb back into the truck. Arthur held up a finger as if to tell Henry to wait, and he walked quickly out of the garage to the truck.

Arthur said: "You Henry? The new guy that works at the diner?"

"Yeah."

"Been going around with Charlotte?"

Henry had placed one foot on the sidestep but now took his foot off and closed the door and took a step toward Arthur.

Henry said: "I don't see how that's any of your business."

Arthur put his hands up in defense. "Well, you've been going around in public with her, so it's not a secret."

"Then what's your point in asking about it? Charlotte and I are friends. We work at the same place."

"Just friends, huh?"

"I'm just about to lose my patience with you. If you've got something to say, then say it instead of being a goddamn mealy-mouth."

"Calm down, man."

"Don't tell me to calm down. Man."

"I'm just saying, be careful. I'm telling you for your own good. People start talking and so forth. You know how that is."

"No. I really don't know how that is."

"Look, I don't know what Charlotte has told you, but, well shit." The young man paused, uncomfortable. "She's spoken for is what I'm saying."

"Spoken for? Like she's got a boyfriend?"

"Something like that."

"Christ, you are a quibbling son of a bitch."

"Shit, just be careful." Arthur turned around and started heading back into the garage.

Henry said: "Hey." Arthur turned around. Henry continued: "She and I aren't going around. We're friends. Just friends. She and I have a firm understanding about that. And like I said, it's none of your goddamn business anyway."

Arthur nodded. "All right. That's good. See you around."

MRS. WHITMAN PLACED TWO MUGS OF COFFEE on the dining table and sat opposite Henry. Then she returned to the kitchen and brought back to the table a tray of cookies she had baked earlier that morning. The house smelled of the holidays, of a crackling fireplace and coffee and baking and warmth. Mrs. Whitman wore a light sweater of greens and reds with gold and silver circles all about it. She smiled at Henry and told him his coffee would get cool if he let it sit there.

"Thanks for inviting me down here today, Mrs. Whitman," Henry said, and then he took a sip of the coffee, which was very hot and spiced with chicory and cinnamon.

"I'm happy to visit with you, Henry. And would you please call me Clara?"

"I'll try, but I can't promise anything."

"Well, whatever makes you most comfortable. At any rate, Edgar will be in town for hours today."

"What is he doing?"

"Shopping for my Christmas gift. This happens every year. It's something of a tradition, I guess. He disappears on a Saturday a couple of weeks before Christmas and then returns late in the evening, complaining about the huge crowds of people at the shops. But I think he secretly enjoys it."

"Crowds of people? I can't imagine more than a dozen people being in the same place at the same time around here."

"He's fussy."

"He's not so bad."

"You're right. He isn't so bad at all."

"How long have you two been married?"

"Next June will be our fiftieth anniversary."

"Congratulations."

"We haven't made it there yet."

"You seem very happy together." Henry reached for a cookie. It was in the shape of a Christmas tree and iced green.

"Most of the time, yes. In fact, almost all of the time."

"What's the secret?"

"It's pretty simple. When he zigs, I zag."

"That's it?"

"More or less. People need their space. Just because two people have been married for a lifetime doesn't mean they need to be together twenty-four hours a day. So we give each other enough space to live, to breathe. To think."

Henry smiled and nodded. A sad smile born of nostalgia and memories and sorrow.

Mrs. Whitman poured cream into her cup and stirred the coffee deliberately, and then she took a sip and then crossed her arms with both elbows on the table and looked pensive and curious.

She said: "So you and the Mayfield girl."

"The Mayfield girl?" Henry was uncertain. "You mean Charlotte?"

Mrs. Whitman smiled and nodded and even winked as if entering into some clandestine dialogue that would reveal to her important information to which only the privileged were privy.

Henry said: "I didn't even know her last name until now."

"Well?"

"Well what?"

"Well, are you two an item?"

"An item? No, we're only friends."

"You two have been seeing a lot of each other."

"We work together, Mrs. Whitman. Really, that's all. We're good friends."

"She's very pretty, you know."

"Of course I know. I see her all the time." Henry took another one of the tree cookies and broke off a piece and crammed it in his mouth as if perhaps keeping a full mouth would absolve him from further engaging in the line of discussion.

"Well, I'm only saying."

"What are you only saying?"

"That you two make a very handsome couple."

"Mrs. Whitman, we aren't a couple. I think you're not listening to me."

"All right, all right." She chuckled and waved him off with both hands as if to say she did not believe him or at least that he did not know what was good for him. It's the way older people dismiss the notions of younger people in such a way that is patronizing but playful.

Henry said: "She's been wonderful, Charlotte has. Along with you and Mr. Whitman, of course. You've all been welcoming and friendly. It wouldn't have been so easy otherwise."

Mrs. Whitman stared into Henry's eyes for a few moments. Then she said: "You are a nice young man. You work hard, and you are a talented musician. Charlotte Mayfield is a very pretty young lady who, from what I understand, has eyes for you. It seems odd that you wouldn't want to date her."

"It isn't so much that I don't want to date her." Henry propped an elbow on the table and looked down and ran his hands through his hair and looked back up at Mrs. Whitman.

"Then what is it?"

They stared at one another across the table, two half-filled coffee mugs and a plate of cookies and a holiday centerpiece of pinecones and feathers and candles between them.

Finally, Henry said: "I recently lost someone important to me. It wouldn't be fair to Charlotte or to this person's memory if Charlotte and I became a couple."

Mrs. Whitman leaned back and crossed her legs and folded her arms on her chest.

She said: "Oh. All right. I understand, then. I'm sorry to hear that."

"It's all right."

Then Henry paused. It was one of those moments in a person's life that can shape what's going to happen from then on. Sometimes we divulge, and sometimes we don't. Often it is better that we don't divulge. To be the caretaker of information, even if the information is some seemingly insignificant fact, is a responsibility whose importance we must honor. Once we offer the information, once we give wings to the words, it is gone. It is no longer ours. Now it is flitting about, and we haven't the power to get it back again. This was such a moment for Henry. And the information was not insignificant.

"It was my wife," he said.

Mrs. Whitman covered her mouth and closed her eyes for a moment as if trying to unhear the words, or maybe as if in prayer. She said: "Oh, dear. Henry, I'm sorry to have brought it up."

"It's not your fault."

"How long ago?"

"A few months."

Now Mrs. Whitman's hand was over her heart, and her eyes were drawn.

She said: "And you just left town?"

"A day or two after her funeral. Sometimes it's best to head out for a while, I think."

"Will you return home?"

"If you mean the coast, then no, probably not. I consider home to be the room above your garage, to be honest."

She nodded solemnly. "Well, you just stay as long as you'd like."

"I appreciate it."

"Do you mind if I ask your wife's name?"

"Not at all. It was Grace." Upon saying her name Henry's eyes welled up. It was unexpected and sudden. He took a cloth napkin from the table and covered his eyes for a moment and then wiped away the tears and took a deep breath and cleared his throat and took another deep breath.

"I'm sorry. I thought I could say her name by now."

"Bless your heart."

Henry took a long drink from his coffee and then cleared his throat and then moved to rise and refill his mug, but Mrs. Whitman waved him back to his chair and took both mugs into the kitchen and refilled them herself.

He said: "I'd appreciate it if that stayed between you and me. About my wife and all."

"Oh, of course, sweetheart. I wouldn't think of telling anyone."

"Even Mr. Whitman."

"My lips are sealed." She gestured across her mouth as if it were a zipper.

Henry took another sip of coffee. He said: "Sometimes I imagine her before me, just floating about, watching me. Often when my eyes are closed I have this sensation that she's with me and that if I open my eyes quickly enough I'll see her. But I never do. She disappears too quickly."

"No doubt she's your angel."

"Maybe, but I don't think of her as an angel. I think of her as a spirit."

"Like a ghost?"

"More like that, I guess. But I don't imagine she's haunting me. Or haunting anyone. Not like that. Just that she's with me."

"I'm sure she is."

"I imagine that she's beside me, watching my decisions and choices. I still feel accountable to her. I don't think I'll ever be able to get rid of that feeling."

"Why would you want to? She's part of who you are. You see?" Henry nodded.

Then she said: "Henry, let me tell you something. I've mentioned our daughter, Jane, right?"

"You said she plays the piano."

"Right. She's our only living child. A couple of years before Jane was born, I had a baby girl. This was about a year after Edgar and I were married. A little baby girl. We named her Hannah. God's grace. She was the most beautiful newborn you've ever seen. Almost immediately the doctor and the nurses were concerned. She was listless, didn't cry much. A specialist came in and did an exam. He concluded very quickly that Hannah's lungs and kidneys were not fully developed. She wasn't breathing well. I asked the doctor, the specialist, about treatment, about a cure. I asked him what do we do now? There's got to be something we can do. Something that can be done. He only shook his head and said there's no treatment. He said the only thing to do is hold her for a few hours until she dies. Hold her until she goes." Mrs. Whitman paused and smiled bravely, fighting decades-old tears. "So they gave her some pain medication so she would be comfortable, and they wrapped her tight and warm and handed her to me. I held her for more than four hours. I wouldn't let anyone else touch her. Not even Edgar. I held that baby girl until she died in my arms. And then I was devastated."

"Jesus, Mrs. Whitman. I'm sorry to have made you think of that."

"Henry, that's my point. I always think about her. I think about Hannah when I'm grocery shopping, when I'm cooking, when I'm driving through town, when I'm talking to my friends, when I'm playing bridge, sitting in church, always. Always I think about her. Almost fifty years later, Henry, I haven't forgotten what she looked like. I don't want to forget."

Henry nodded.

She said: "And you won't forget about Grace. You loved her. You still love her. And you'll think about her all the time."

"I don't think I'll be able to love anyone again."

"I didn't think I'd be able to love a child as much as I loved Hannah. For more than a year I refused to discuss more children. I thought having another child would somehow dishonor Hannah's memory. That's a ridiculous notion; I know that now."

"But I understand the feeling."

"Of course." There was then a long pause, but a comfortable pause. "But in time you'll begin to feel differently. We don't forget those we've loved. And we don't besmirch their memories by moving on. It just takes time."

"All right."

"Perhaps this sounds silly to you, but I can imagine your Grace holding my little Hannah in heaven. I can imagine them free of pain and free of worries. And I can imagine them loving one another very much."

"That's a nice thought."

"It is a nice thought. Sometimes all we have are nice thoughts. Distant memories and nice thoughts amid all the pain and suffering we endure."

Then they were silent again for a moment. A reticent and throbbing lull that bore in that moment the weight of eternity. As if these two had engaged themselves in some powerful and weighty or perhaps sacred discourse.

Then Henry looked up and said: "Can I ask you something?"

"Of course."

"It might be an odd question. But it's something that's been on my mind."

"Go on."

Henry said: "Do you—do you think our suffering is redemptive?"

Mrs. Whitman offered a solemn and knowing smile.

Then she said: "I have to believe it is, because if it's not then what is the point? Our misery and heartbreak and pain. Our sadness. It must in the end mean something. It must."

"I hope so."

"We are all tested. We are all bound up in human tragedy. Every person you pass on the street has a story, every one of them. Right? It's the one thing we have in common, the one thing that links every person in the world. We have suffered. Some of us more or less than others, but we all know the truth of misery. The burden of despair."

"Did you ever dream of your daughter?"

"Of course. I still do. I dream of her as a baby. I dream that I'm pregnant with her. I dream of her as a child, an adult. Sometimes I have these terrible dreams that someone is slipping away from me, as if over a cliff or into the ocean, and I know somehow in my dream that it's Hannah. Do you dream of Grace?"

"Yeah, I do. I have this recurring dream where Grace and my mother are somehow mixed up together like they are the same person. I'm walking up to my mom's house, and my mom opens the door but somehow I'm tricked, and it turns out to be Grace, and she's staring horribly not at me but through me or around me."

"Is your mother still alive?"

"Yeah. She left me when I was a kid. Left me with my grandmother. I've only seen her once since I was eleven."

"Maybe with this recurring dream your mind is trying to reconcile the woman for whom you harbor the most love with the woman for whom you harbor the most resentment."

"You're probably right."

"I would imagine," Mrs. Whitman said, "that the two most important females in most men's lives are their wives and their mothers. In a way, you've lost both of yours. It's no surprise your mind weighs on both."

"That makes sense." Henry took the mugs up and put his hand out when Mrs. Whitman protested and went to refill the mugs. He came back and said it was his turn to fill the mugs.

She said: "Probably I should have put the coffee in the silver carafe and brought it to the table."

"This'll be my last cup," Henry said. Then he said: "You're right about Charlotte. She is pretty and young and very nice. Perhaps if our lives had taken us on different paths and we met in another time and place, maybe then we could be more than friends."

"Oh, you never know, Henry. You could feel differently a week, a month, a year from now. Maybe one day you'll wake up and you'll be ready to love again. And maybe then you can see Charlotte differently, more than just a friend."

"That's a nice thought too. But I don't think so."

"Give it time," she said.

Then the front door opened, and Mr. Whitman bustled his way in and began complaining about the crowds at the shops in town.

The Heresy of Rain

HENRY AND CHARLOTTE SAT ON THE OLD FOOTBRIDGE that spanned Mill Creek just outside Andrews city limits. It was Christmas Eve. The desert air was chilly and dry and electric. The creek was low and the bridge ramshackle. They sat like children with their legs hung over the edge of the bridge, dangling leisurely in the cold night. The two were mostly silent, listening to the sounds of the night. Coyotes and rabbits and sometimes a deer rustling in the weeds.

"Thanks for coming out here with me," she said. "I know it's silly."

"It isn't silly."

"Well. Thanks also for saying that."

"You care too much about what other people are thinking about you."

"I know."

"Well, stop."

She turned away and laughed lightly. "If only it were so easy to dismiss the judgment of others."

"Are you often judged?"

"No, I'm just talking nonsense."

Then he said: "Anyhow, I can imagine you've had enough mingling and chatting and celebrating for one evening."

"I always forget how much family I have. Then I'm reminded every Christmas of all the aunts and uncles and cousins and second cousins and step-cousins and all of that. And they are maddening. Rude, demanding, judgmental. The holidays do that; they remind us how much we hate each other."

"I've never thought of that. Maybe you're right. But won't your parents be upset when they realize you've left?"

"They won't realize I've left until I get back."

They were silent for a moment. Then she said: "I've always come to this spot when I feel overwhelmed. Ever since I was a little girl. There's nothing scenic or beautiful about this place. I mean, it's a rotting bridge over muddy water. But somehow, I find it comforting."

"It's important to have a safe place."

"Yeah. It is. Did you have a safe place?"

"I guess it was my grandmother's house. Then when my mom took off I lived with my grandmother, so I always felt safe until she died."

"What was your grandmother like?"

"She would have done anything for me. She taught me things you can't learn in school. But she didn't take herself too seriously. That's what I remember most. She never let life get the better of her. She laughed. She always laughed, smiled no matter what."

"Do you have any brothers or sisters?"

He shook his head and looked away from her.

"I'm sorry," she said. "I didn't mean to pry."

"It's all right."

"I'm sorry all the same."

"Look at all those stars."

"I get lost trying to figure them out. I wonder how many there are."

He said: "Millions, I guess. Or more."

"Do you think we'll ever have it all sorted out?"

"Have what sorted out?"

"The sky. The stars and the moon and whatever else is up there."

"It seems as though lately I've been looking at the stars a lot. I sometimes wonder that myself, whether we'll ever have it sorted out. It just seems like too much. Too much space, too many stars, so much distance between us and them. I'm not even sure it would be worth it. Maybe we're better off not knowing. What's the harm in us looking at the night sky and wondering about things? Why do we think we have to know everything?"

"I don't know. Maybe you're right. Maybe we ought not try to know everything. Sometimes there are dust storms out here, and for hours or days you can't see anything. Not anything right in front of you and surely not the stars. That's the most disappointing thing about those storms. They deprive me of the stars."

"I guess it doesn't rain much out here in the desert."

"Almost never. Maybe that's the one redeeming thing about Andrews. I've never liked the rain. It's dreary and leaves everything muddy and soggy."

"Someone told me once that the rain is a promise being paid off by the sky. The rain is renewal. And refreshes and nourishes. It's like everything has gotten a bath, she said."

"Who said that?"

Henry closed his eyes and took a breath and willed the moment to pass.

She said again: "Who, Henry?"

"Someone," he said, but his words got caught in his throat. He felt like he was drowning. "Someone who was very important to me. Someone who loved me."

"Are you a difficult person to love?"

"That's the second time someone's asked me that question."

"Well?"

"I don't know. But I know she was not a difficult person to love."

"What happened?"

"She passed away."

"I'm sorry."

"It's not your fault."

"I seem to have a way of asking the wrong questions."

"There's nothing wrong with a friend asking another friend a question."

"Am I still your only friend in Andrews?"

He smiled. "Yeah, I think so. And I guess the Whitmans. And Suzanne, maybe?"

"I wish I could know what you're thinking."

"Wouldn't that be something."

"No, I'm serious. There's something, I just don't know what. I wish I could figure out what's going on in your mind so that I could help you unburden it. You are a lockbox of secrets and angst and darkness. What if I could help you square the past and reconcile your demons?"

"Do you think it's actually possible to square the past and reconcile demons?"

"I'm not sure. But it's worth a try."

"I guess I agree with you on that account. It's worth a try."

They were silent for more than a minute. The dry, cold wind chilled the air.

She said: "Where will you go next?"

"I don't know."

"When will you leave?"

"I don't know that either. I can't stay here forever."

"Neither can I."

"I guess we have that in common as well."

"As well as what?"

"Us working at a diner. And us trying to reconcile our pasts."

After a moment she said, quietly, almost to herself: "I always thought I'd marry a musician."

"Is that right?"

"Yeah. Some musician on the road in Andrews; I'd catch his eye, and he'd take me with him to his next stop and then all the way to California. And he would marry me out in California, and I would take pictures of our wonderful life and send the pictures back to Texas with letters describing our big, glittery home. I would give birth to wonderful little children who played the guitar or harmonica, and they would sing for everyone, and we'd be happy."

"Sounds like a nice life."

"Maybe. Now I'm not so sure. I think it's probably more important to marry someone I love rather than someone who's famous and wealthy."

"If you're lucky you'll fall in love with someone who's famous and wealthy."

"You've been married, haven't you?"

For a long time he did not answer, as if his taciturn pause might help Charlotte forget she had asked the question.

Then he said: "Yeah. I have."

"Thank you for being honest."

"I trust you. I'm not sure why, but I do."

"It's hard to trust people."

He nodded silently there on the bridge.

"Will you take me with you?" She had turned to face Henry, confronting him with the full force of not only the question but also her fraught pleading. She looked him square in his moonlit face, and her eyes and mouth were serious and unrelenting.

He gave her a sympathetic smile. Then he said, honestly: "Sweetheart, you sure are some kind of pretty."

She sighed and furrowed her brow and then pursed her lips. "You're avoiding the question."

"If you and I met under a thousand other circumstances I'd have already left with you. We would be on our way to Kansas City or New

The Heresy of Rain

Orleans or Chicago where I could play the piano and you could do whatever you wanted. You could go to college, study whatever you want, be a writer, anything in the world. But in our current circumstance, I'm sorry. Charlotte, I'm sorry."

In the darkness he could see her tears. "But why?"

"Because I haven't yet reconciled my past. Also, because my past is still too fresh."

She looked out at the small creek and shook her head. "I can hardly stand it."

"I know."

"I've never known a guy before who I could talk to so easily."

"Nah, you just haven't met many guys."

"No, really. Other boys have always been too aggressive or too proud or too shy or too inconsiderate. You are just right."

"I think maybe I'm lucky is all. I've just guessed the right things to say when I'm around you."

"Oh, please."

It's true about men and women. No man is comfortable around women. And beautiful women terrify men. The notion that any man is at ease with women is a notion propagated by fools and men who have never been around women.

She forced a relaxed smile and wiped her eyes with her jacket sleeve. "You're being silly."

"No, I'm just being honest."

"Don't be ridiculous."

Henry was serious. He realized, as many men have realized over the course of human history, that the idea that men regarded women as second rate is a ruse.

She laughed and shook her head. She said: "I have a gift for you."

"That's exactly what I'm talking about. I don't have anything for you. You didn't say anything about presents."

"It's a surprise, silly. For Christmas." She reached into her small purse that sat next to her on the footbridge and took out a very small package and held it out for Henry to take from her hand.

He took the package and carefully removed the white twine and brown paper. Beneath the paper was a black velvet clamshell box. Henry looked at Charlotte questioningly.

She said: "Go on, open it."

He lifted the lid. Inside the box was a small sterling silver treble clef. It looked splendid against the black box in the light of the moon. He took it in his hand.

"It's a lapel pin," she said. "I know you don't wear jackets very often, but I wanted to get you something to remember me by. A ring seemed over the top. And you don't wear a watch. Turn it over."

He looked at the back of the pin and in the moonlight could just make out the tiny inscription: "To Henry, From Charlotte."

He said: "Now I have a reason to wear a jacket."

She laughed. "Now we're best friends."

"You've only just known me for a few months."

"And I already think you're pretty wonderful. Your wife was lucky indeed."

He put the pin gently back into the clamshell box and closed it and gave Charlotte a hug. Then Henry asked Charlotte if she had a boyfriend.

"Of course not. You'd know if I did. You and I spend a lot of time together."

"Nobody at all?"

"Nobody at all."

"Arthur at the service station says differently."

"Arthur Truman?"

"I don't know. Just Arthur. Light brown crew cut, real red in the face."

She rolled her eyes and shook her head with exasperation. "Yeah, that's Arthur. We were friends when we were kids."

"Why did he tell me to stay away from you? Hell, I even told him you and I were just friends."

She turned and looked at Henry and then smiled broadly. Then she laughed and said: "Because I've got lots of jealous boyfriends. You'd better watch out." Then she laughed again into the night. Henry thanked her again for the lapel pin, and she rested her head on his shoulder.

The Heresy of Rain

IT WAS THE MIDDLE OF THE NIGHT, some days later. Henry slept on his bed above the Whitman garage. There were three soft knocks. Then three more, a little louder than before. Henry woke, confused at first. Then he realized someone was at the door, and he got out of bed and pulled on a t-shirt and some blue jeans. He rushed to the door and opened it. Charlotte stood outside on the landing.

"Charlotte? What are you doing?"

"I came to visit you. Can I come in?"

Henry stepped aside so Charlotte could enter. She wore her work uniform and a long coat over it, unbuttoned but pulled tight. Henry went out to the landing and peered around the outside of the building and the driveway.

"How did you get here?" he asked. "Did you walk?"

"Yeah."

"It's almost five miles from your house to the Whitmans' house."

"I didn't come here from my house." She sat on the bed. In the dark she was grainy and unclear. She slipped out of her coat and let it fall to the bed. There she sat, on Henry's bed in the dark in the middle of the night, wearing her waitress dress with her hair in a sloppy bun.

"Have you been drinking?"

"Of course not, Henry. I've been sitting down on the Mill Creek bridge."

"For six hours?"

"More or less."

Henry walked to the nightstand and switched on the light. In the shadows she looked sad and tired and beautiful. She was the sum of all human emotion. And she was worn out.

Henry then walked to the foot of the bed and knelt and looked her in the eyes.

"Why did you come here?"

"To seduce you."

Henry closed his eyes and shook his head.

She said: "Do I have a chance?"

"Charlotte, I—"

"I know. I know. We've had this discussion. But I thought if I showed up in the middle of the night some romantic impulse would take over, and you'd not be able to resist me."

"You sure you haven't been drinking?"

"Goddamnit, Henry."

"Sorry."

She stood and did her best to smooth her dress. She stepped over to the dresser. Then she took up the small, framed photograph of Grace, and she brought it close to her face and stared at the picture for several moments. She turned and held up the photograph to show Henry, as if she had just discovered something new and wanted to share it with him.

"This is her, right? Your wife?"

He nodded and said: "Grace. My wife. She was my wife."

She ran her finger over the photo and then told Henry she was beautiful.

"I know."

"I shouldn't have come here, Henry. I'm sorry."

"It's all right. Now you can keep me company while I drive over to your house."

She smiled. "You're pretty funny."

He took up her coat and held it open for her, and she slid her arms in and pulled it tight again. Then she stood on her toes and gave Henry a kiss on the cheek and said again she was sorry. He told her to stop apologizing and put on his shoes and jacket and drove her home.

The Heresy of Rain

MID-JANUARY. The air was cold and biting, and the wind was a constant grating and punishing force. Henry stayed indoors as much as possible, and he and Charlotte met semi-regularly at the diner Saturday nights for coffee and conversation. Their topics ranged from politics to science to history. Henry found Charlotte's ideas to be intellectual, worldly, and intimidating, but that was nothing new. He'd felt like the academic inferior against all the important females in his life.

On this Saturday evening it was almost seven o'clock. The diner was busy but not impossibly so. Henry and Charlotte sat in a small booth, Henry with his back to the diner's entrance. It was during an easy discussion between two friends that this unfortunate scene unfolded.

Henry was taking a sip of his coffee.

Charlotte saw something alarming through the diner windows, and her eyes widened and would have screamed if eyes could scream, and she covered her mouth with her hands. Her sudden movements caused her coffee to slosh about, but she did not care.

She said, "Oh my God oh my God oh my God."

Henry heard the door open hard against the wire newspaper stand, and he heard the bell above the door jangle wildly and clang about. And some unknown voice said: "Is this him?"

He couldn't even get his head swiveled to see his assailant before the person grabbed him under his arms and dragged him violently from the booth to the floor, his legs first crashing the underside of the table and then splaying about the table, making a mess of the coffee and saucers and sugar cubes.

"I come back from Korea, and I'm greeted by this?" Henry heard the other man speak as if from a distance. As if he were not actually there. The voice was edgy. It was a bark, strained and gruff.

Henry's head slammed every solid surface from the booth to the floor, then his attacker belted him in the stomach. Henry tried to cover his face, but it didn't do any good. The man landed punch after punch to his cheeks and eyes and lips. At first there was intense pain and panic, and then after a while only numbness and acceptance. Henry had the vague notion that employees and customers alike were intervening on his behalf.

He heard Charlotte screaming: "Davey, no! Davey! No, stop!"

Davey did not stop. He pummeled Henry until Henry could no longer move, all the while hollering about returning from Korea and expecting to find his girl waiting for him and instead finding his girl going steady with some candyass piano player. That Charlotte pleaded with Davey and assured Davey that she and Henry weren't dating did no good.

The last thing Henry heard was something about him being a goddamn musician son of a bitch. Then there was darkness.

The Heresy of Rain

THE NEXT FEW DAYS WERE HAZY. Henry glided in and out of consciousness, his whole face aching, and his chest feeling broken and fractured and splintered. Jagged. Sometimes he was in a room with lights, and sometimes it was dark. Sometimes there were people around him, and sometimes he was alone. Occasionally the people talked, but mostly he could not understand them, nor did he care. He sensed a menagerie of whispers and sighs and sometimes panic and urgency. He felt a series of prods and pokes and other intrusions. His wounds were wrapped and unwrapped and rewrapped and covered and uncovered. Sometimes the people would urge him to sip some water and take a pill of some kind or another. Sometimes someone would tell him this'll just sting a little. But he never felt anything but a constant and intense ache in his head.

Often when he slept his dream returned, and he saw his mother's eyes in that dim room, and the eyes became Grace's eyes. Every time he dreamt this horrible sequence he relived it, relived something terrible that had not actually happened.

Then finally he opened his eyes and sensed everything and put it all together. He remembered the evening with Charlotte when they were talking over coffee at the diner. And he remembered being attacked. Bit by bit, he even remembered what the attacker said to him and to Charlotte. Punch by punch. And he remembered Charlotte's protestations. He thought he remembered some other folks trying to pull the man off him, but he couldn't be sure about that. His head ached so very much.

He tried to turn his head to see a clock or perhaps a window or some other item that might help him determine what day it was or what time of day it was. But everything was too painful, and he went back to sleep.

"Henry, how are you feeling? Can you hear me, Henry?"

He opened his eyes again, this time able to focus a little better.

"Can you hear me?"

"I can hear you."

"Great, great. That's wonderful, Henry. You're doing a lot better now. It was a little dicey a few days ago, but you sure are a fighter."

He didn't feel like a fighter.

"Think you can open your eyes again for a bit?"

"That light is really goddamn bright."

"Okay, okay. I'll see what I can do."

The man grabbed ahold of the bedside lamp and swiveled it so that the bulb was focused the other direction.

"Thanks."

"Great, great. I'm going to shine a little light in your eyes. Try to follow the light."

He did so, and Henry followed it.

"Wonderful. Henry, my name is Dr. Baker. Do you know where you are?" Dr. Baker was a kind-looking middle-aged man with wire-rim glasses and a white coat.

"No. Some hospital?"

"Yes. You're at the Andrews County Medical Center."

"What day is it?"

"It's Thursday."

"Jesus Christ almighty."

"Yes sir, you've been through quite an ordeal. Do you remember anything?"

"I remember getting the shit kicked out of me by some cheap shot artist."

"Well, that's pretty much the long and short of it, Henry." The doctor paused. "Henry, we've been trying to determine over the last few days whether you've got any family."

"I don't."

"All right, that answers that. Do you feel strong enough to talk to me for a few minutes?"

"Sure."

"Okay, all right. Henry, you've got a severe concussion. You're going to have a headache and some blurred vision for a few more days at least."

"All right. Thanks."

"Oh, that's not all. Also, we've repaired your nose."

"What was wrong with it?"

"It was broken pretty good. And your jaw is fractured, but that will heal on its own as long as you rest plenty."

"Why does it hurt to breathe?"

The Heresy of Rain

"That's the broken ribs. Three of them. We'll keep you here for a few more days, and then we'll wrap you up real tight and send you home to rest there. But Henry, my main concern is your head injury. It's difficult to gauge the severity of brain trauma. The only way we'll know how far along you've come is from your perspective. When you feel nauseated or if you are seeing double, that sort of thing, you've got to let us know. Also, if you begin to remember things a little better, tell us that as well."

"All right."

"Good, good. We aren't going to allow you to have visitors until tomorrow. There are a couple of folks who've been anxious to see you. We'll see how you feel tomorrow morning."

"All right."

Then he was asleep again.

This time there was no dream.

THE FOLLOWING MORNING he ate some toast and chicken broth and didn't vomit, so the doctor thought he was all right to see a visitor as long as his head wasn't aching too badly.

"Henry?"

He looked over toward the door and saw Charlotte entering tentatively. He nodded and said Charlotte's name.

"How are you feeling?"

"About like you'd imagine, I guess."

He looked her as square as his double vision would allow and saw her lip trembling and tears welling up in her eyes.

She said: "Oh my God, I'm so sorry." She put one hand to her mouth and with the other hand touched Henry's arm.

"Have they put your boyfriend in jail?"

"Henry, he's not my boyfriend exactly."

"He's not not your boyfriend exactly either as far as I can tell."

"His name is Davey."

"I know. I heard you screaming his name while he was breaking my nose."

"Just listen, please. His name is Davey. We dated in high school and a little after high school. He gave me a promise ring before he went off to Korea with the Army."

"It appears you aren't a very good promiser."

"Henry, that was more than two years ago."

"All right."

"He wrote me less and less frequently, and I wrote him less frequently until we weren't writing each other at all. That was about a year ago."

"It's a good thing I didn't try to marry you like the musician in your fantasies. Imagine the beating he would have given me then."

"It's not funny."

"You're sure as hell right it's not funny."

"I'm sorry, Henry. If I'd have known he was coming back that night I wouldn't have been sitting with you in a public place. I never wanted you to get hurt."

"So is he in jail?"

"He was arrested later that night when the sheriff caught up with him. He's out on bail. They've already charged him with assault. Some people around here are whispering about the possibility of attempted murder."

"That seems reasonable."

"He's under house arrest, though. I refuse to go see him."

"Atta girl."

"Henry!"

"Charlotte, I don't know what you want from me. You hedged your relationship with a trained killer against me, and I became your friend. And now I've got broken ribs and a broken face and a goddamned brain injury. Jesus Christ. I asked you if you had any boyfriends, and you said no."

"I told you he's not my boyfriend."

He reached for a cup of ice water with a straw and couldn't quite get it, so Charlotte helped him sip it. He hated her and loved her at the same time. He reckoned to himself that friendship is complicated.

Then he said: "I'm sorry. It's not your fault."

"Yes, it is."

"All right, then yes, it is."

Then she tried to smile but instead started sobbing and couldn't stop crying for anything. She said she'd been afraid he was going to die and that she didn't know what she was going to do or how to contact his family. And she said she couldn't stop thinking about how he told her she was pretty and how they were best friends and that was okay with her. In the middle of all this a nurse heard the commotion and brought in a box of tissues, nearly the whole of which Charlotte used during her meltdown.

"Charlotte, calm down."

Between sobs she asked if he forgave her, and he said yes, he forgave her. He reached up as best as he could, and she leaned over and hugged him.

"Not too hard," he said. "Your army man has broken half my chest."

He was only trying to be funny, but she started her crying again. He told her he was getting tired, and would she sit with him a while until he fell asleep again?

And of course, she said yes, she would.

The Heresy of Rain

THE FOLLOWING DAY WAS SATURDAY, a week after the incident. He had another visitor, someone he was glad to see.

"Good morning, Henry." It was Mr. Whitman, who entered the room with cautious authority and walked over to the chair near Henry's bed and sat down and smiled at his tenant who was all beat to hell.

He told Henry: "You look all beat to hell."

"That's about how I feel."

"Any better, though?"

"Yeah, actually. I feel better every day. I think they'll let me out of here Monday."

"Clara has been getting our den ready for you. You can stay there for a week or two until the doctor thinks you're ready to get about on your own."

"That's awfully nice of you all."

"Son, you've been through a hell of an ordeal."

"If you go up to my room above the garage, you'll find some money—"

"Don't be ridiculous. I'll not discuss rent with a man who's clinging to his life."

"I'm not clinging to my life any longer."

"All right. You know, that lady friend of yours has been a mess."

"Charlotte. She feels bad about it is all."

Mr. Whitman nodded and smiled and patted Henry's arm. And then his demeanor changed. He slid his palms along his slacks and stayed with his hands on his knees and his head down for a moment, and then he sighed audibly and reached into his shirt pocket and took out a slip of paper and held it out for Henry to take.

Henry reached through the pain and took the paper from his landlord and realized right away it was a newspaper clipping. He unfolded it gently.

Mr. Whitman said: "It's from Wednesday's paper. Three days ago."

Henry finished unfolding the clipping and started reading the short paragraph as best he could, all things considered, though he knew what it would say. The blurb was an update on the story from last fall about the Galveston shooting. There were still no named suspects, but local officials sought a person of interest who might be driving a dark-colored pickup and who may have fled to another part of the state. The three shooting victims had survived, but the suspect could be indicted for three counts of attempted murder if found. The reward for information leading to that person's capture and arrest was raised from one thousand dollars to two thousand dollars.

"Is this from the Odessa paper?"

"Yes. They run notable state stories every now and then."

"All right."

"This is your opportunity to explain yourself, son."

"All right. Who all knows?"

"Right now, it seems I'm the only one to read the Odessa paper and put two and two together. It won't be long before someone else connects the dots."

"All right."

"Tell me everything."

So Henry told him everything. He told Mr. Whitman about meeting Grace when he was eighteen and how she was beautiful and generous and sweet and blind. About how he played the piano for her at night so she could sleep, and about how he described to her the night sky. He began crying as he told Mr. Whitman about his job as the pianist at Sammie's and about how he began playing poker with bad people and these people allowed him to run up a debt he could not repay. He told Mr. Whitman the men murdered his wife while they were looting his home. And he told him how he bought a gun and the pickup and tried to kill the man who killed Grace or at least the man who was in charge of the guys who did it but instead wounded him and almost killed two other men. He told Mr. Whitman he ended up in Andrews by chance.

Mr. Whitman was silent for a few moments.

Then he said: "I'm not going to ask you where that gun is because I suspect it's on my property, and I'd rather not know."

"All right."

"Are you telling the truth about the truck?"

"What do you mean?"

"You didn't steal it?"

"No, I bought it. Title's in the glove box."

Mr. Whitman sighed. "Son, I don't know what to say. I honestly think ten out of ten men who were in your position would have handled things the same way."

"I appreciate you saying that."

"But ninety-nine out of a hundred men wouldn't have been in that situation to start with."

"That's fair."

"I like you, Henry. You're a good kid who pays his rent on time, and Clara thinks the world of you."

"Does she know?"

"Hell no."

"All right."

"So I'm going to help you get out of here in a couple of days. And then you'll recuperate downstairs at the house. Then in a week or whenever you're healthy you're going to get the hell out of here. Don't try to tangle with Davey and leave Miss Charlotte alone. All right?"

"Yes sir."

"And just get the hell out. Don't tell me where you're headed."

"Fine."

"And when someone else figures it all out, or when the authorities finally take hold of your scent and arrive in Andrews? I'll tell them the truth: that you were a good citizen, that you got the shit kicked out of you by your lady friend's old boyfriend, and that you took off without saying where you were headed."

Henry nodded.

Mr. Whitman stood and said: "Clara is cooking up a storm for you. Get on out of here so there'll be someone to eat it all."

Then he walked over to the door and nodded to Henry and shut the door as he left.

ON MONDAY MORNING Henry was released from the hospital. Mr. Whitman was waiting out in his car. The nurses and other hospital personnel were tending to Henry's bandages and gauze and fussing with his medications and so forth. By and by, it seemed a few of them were sweet on Henry. He didn't care. He just wanted to leave. He sat there in a wheelchair, annoyed and petulant and tired.

Dr. Baker was the last one in his room. He looked over the discharge papers and signed a few forms and wrote a few prescriptions. Then he shoved all the important paperwork into a large envelope and dropped it on Henry's lap.

Dr. Baker said: "Well, son, I guess that's about it. Your discharge instructions are in there with your prescriptions. Hazel will wheel you out to Mr. Whitman's car. He patted Henry's shoulder and strode toward the door.

"Dr. Baker."

The doctor stopped at the door and had one hand on the doorjamb. "Yes?"

"I can't pay for any of this."

"What do you mean?"

"The surgeries, the hospital stay, all the treatments and medicine. I can't come close to being able to afford it."

"Son, you didn't know?"

"Know what?"

"The folks at the diner held a collection for you, got all the employees and even a bunch of regulars to chip in. Also the folks at the Methodist church. They paid for more than half of your bills. Mr. Whitman took care of the rest."

"Goddamn."

"You got lots of people who care about you." Then he left.

Hazel got Henry out the door and on to Mr. Whitman's waiting car.

The Heresy of Rain

HENRY SPENT SIX DAYS in the Whitmans' den. They had done up the room so that Henry had just about everything he needed. The old sofa was perfectly comfortable as a bed, and Mrs. Whitman moved the radio close to the sofa. She jaunted about, humming to herself and looking after Henry. Henry wondered how long it had been since Mrs. Whitman felt a sense of purpose such as this. She seemed a natural caretaker. Mr. Whitman spent most of his time pacing. It seemed every five minutes he walked over to the window that overlooked the street and driveway and parted the blinds and gazed in all directions as if he were expecting a visitor. Several times, Henry caught Mr. Whitman staring at him, as if trying to bore down to Henry's soul.

Charlotte visited Henry on his fifth day of convalescence.

Mrs. Whitman told Henry Charlotte from the diner was there—as if there were any other Charlottes—and would he mind visiting for a while? Henry said of course he could visit with her.

Charlotte entered tentatively.

"You look better," she said cheerfully.

"Thanks. I feel better. Still all bruised to hell, but I think I'll make it."

She sat on an ottoman near Henry. She smelled like vanilla. She wore almost no makeup, but she was stunning with her bright eyes and freckles and wonderful voice. Henry for a moment considered giving up on his quest and taking Charlotte to some faraway place like Canada or Brazil or Ireland but dismissed the notion as impractical and unfair to Charlotte. Perhaps, too, Henry felt it was unfair to Grace or Grace's memory. It happens sometimes that guilt and sadness and pain are all combined, and the resulting sensation is something like confusion.

"We miss you at the diner."

"Tell Jack and Suzanne and all the others I'll be back as soon as I can," he lied.

"Jack complains every day that the boy he's got on dishwashing duty isn't half the worker you are."

"Dishwashing isn't difficult work."

"Not everyone's as hard a worker as you."

"I sure appreciate you all's help paying my hospital bills."

"We were happy to help. You've made quite an impression on people around here."

"I don't know what I've done to deserve people's goodwill."

"You are patient and kind. People like you." Her voice began to break.

"If you say so."

Charlotte turned her head and looked toward the main part of the house to make sure the Whitmans were not close by, and she lowered her voice nearly to a whisper.

"Henry, I have to say something."

"All right."

She turned again and then faced Henry square. Her face was solemn and anxious, as if she believed what she was preparing to say carried the weight of all the world and all of the world to come. She closed her eyes for just an instant and pursed her lips and then sighed.

"I love you."

"Charlotte. No, you don't."

"Don't say that. I do. I know I do."

Henry cast his gaze downward and sighed and shook his head. In truth, he believed her.

"Just listen," she said. "I know you don't feel the same about me. I know your wife died and it broke your heart. I know you have a hundred secrets you'll never share. I know you're running from someone."

He looked at her now.

She said: "I know all that. And I know you'll leave soon, somehow I know it, and you won't take me. I've already made peace with that, though I wish you'd reconsider. I knew I wouldn't be able to live with myself if I didn't tell you how I feel. You have a gentle soul and a good heart." His lip quavered, and her eyes misted.

"You're right about most of that. Maybe if you knew all my secrets you would change your mind about me."

"I'd only love you more."

"I don't think so."

"I would. I know I would."

The Heresy of Rain

Henry only looked away.

Then she said: "We don't get to choose whom we love."

He didn't say anything at first. He only sighed and nodded a solemn agreement. What a truth that was: we don't get to choose whom we love. Then he said: "You're right. I'm going to leave soon. And I'm going to miss you terribly. I meant what I said about you and me meeting under different circumstances. We could have been something, right?"

Her eyes were glassy as she nodded and tucked a strand of sandy hair behind her ear.

"But listen to me," he said, "listen. Don't marry that Davey."

"I won't. I promise. He is probably going to prison for a while anyway."

"I know you say you won't. But if you're still around in a few years he'll sweet talk you like a son of a bitch. Goddamnit, don't marry him."

"Why don't you marry me, so I can avoid the issue altogether?"

"Charlotte, I've been straight with you from the beginning."

"I know."

They stared at one another for a moment.

Then she said: "You're right."

"About what?" he asked.

She smiled sadly and said: "We could have been something."

She leaned over and kissed him on the forehead.

Then she was gone.

HENRY THOUGHT OF HIS UPCOMING DEPARTURE and little else. A night-time getaway seemed to make the most sense, but he needed the house to be free for a while. The Whitmans were home most of the time, and Mr. Whitman was like some skittish animal, alert and attentive as if some bird of prey would at any moment descend upon him and carry him away to a place unseen. In the end Henry reckoned the most sensible thing was to wait until Sunday morning while the Whitmans were at church. While the whole of Andrews was at church.

A little before nine o'clock Sunday morning the Whitmans were headed out the door. Mr. Whitman turned to Henry. He was wearing his usual Sunday ensemble of chinos and a dress shirt and a tweed shooting jacket with elbow pads. He wore no tie. He waved briefly to Henry, who was still resting in the den.

Then he said to Henry: "We'll be going out to lunch after the service this morning. Be home around one. Maybe one-thirty."

"All right."

Mr. Whitman held the door open for a second longer, peering into the den at his mysterious fugitive houseguest as if he still didn't know what to make of it all.

"You take care," Mr. Whitman said.

"Thank you. For helping with the bills at the hospital. For everything."

"You're surely welcome."

"I'll never be able to repay you."

"That's the thing about a gift, Henry. It isn't meant to be repaid."

Then Mr. Whitman nodded and left, closing the front door behind him.

It took Henry two hours to get his act together. Mrs. Whitman had urged him to go up and down a few stairs every day to get his strength back. Even so, Henry's ascent to his old room above the garage took a whole minute. Everything was as he'd left it. He crammed his belongings into his duffle. The gun was where he had hidden it in the sofa, which he'd been expecting. He put the gun and the couple of bullets he had left into his bag and then shaved and put the shave kit into his bag as well. He spent a whole minute looking at his face in the mirror and decided he didn't look half bad, all things considered. He took what was on the dresser—a few coins and the matchbook—and slipped it all into his trouser pocket and grabbed his duffle and headed back down.

Henry hobbled into the Whitmans' kitchen and poked around in the cabinets and the pantry and then finally found what he was looking for. Mrs. Whitman had cultivated a small library of the local church member directories. He found the collection of spiral-bound books in a drawer. After several minutes of flipping through the pictures of the smiling families and their addresses and phone numbers he found the address he wanted. He copied it on a sheet of paper from Mrs. Whitman's grocery list pad and put the books back into the drawer and hurried about to leave.

He tried to clean up the den a bit before leaving but found the job impossible. So he turned his attention before he left for good to the task of writing the Whitmans a note. In the end he couldn't think of anything that would sufficiently convey his appreciation, so he thanked them again for their kindness, particularly with the medical bills and his recovery. Then Henry sat for a minute on the sofa and sized himself up. His head hurt like hell but less so every day. He had almost three hundred dollars. He counted it again and shoved the cash in his pocket. Then he walked out to his truck and set his duffle bag in the passenger seat and placed the gun carefully in the glovebox and took the map out of the glovebox. He took the map around to the driver's seat and got a general feeling for the direction he needed to go. Then he reached over to the duffle bag and pulled the photo of Grace from an inner pocket and wedged it up in the temperature gauge, so he could see it at all times. He took the matchbook out of his shirt pocket and turned it over a few times and then placed it in the ashtray. And then he pulled backward out of the Whitmans' driveway and winced as he got to the end of the driveway and bounced a bit and was reminded painfully of his fractured ribs. And then he headed out.

Before he left Andrews he had one stop to make. By now he was familiar enough with the town that he had little trouble finding the address on the small sheet of paper he had less than an hour before copied from the church directory in the Whitmans' kitchen. The house was larger than the Whitmans' house and larger than Charlotte's family's house, but not terribly so. It was a two-story redbricked structure with white trim and a tidy lawn. Henry double-checked the address on the sheet of paper against the number on the house's mailbox and idled there at the curb for a moment and then cut the engine and climbed down onto the pavement and walked slowly to the door, with its deep oak finish and frosted glass. He readied his fist to knock but then changed his mind and pushed the doorbell. Several seconds passed, and then he could see the form of someone approaching the door from the inside, and then that person opened the door and upon realizing who was standing on her front porch Davey's mother frowned.

She said: "I don't think you should be here."

Henry shrugged and nodded. "You're probably right, but I think I ought to have the chance to explain myself. And I thought maybe Davey would like to explain himself to me. We owe each other that at least."

Davey's mother looked doubtful. She stood with one hand on the door's handle and the other braced against the doorframe and closed her eyes for a bit and then sighed.

She said: "Hold on just a minute." She held up a finger and closed the door but did not lock it and then disappeared as a form into the house's interior the same way she had materialized moments ago. Henry stepped back from the door and waited.

She returned and opened the door wider and stepped aside while peering to the street to make sure no one saw. Her effort was in vain: everyone else was at church. She motioned for Henry to enter and then said almost in a whisper: "Just a few minutes. He's not supposed to be within a hundred feet of you. The judge said so."

"I won't tell anyone if you don't."

She led Henry into a kind of study or library. There were two leather chairs and floor-to-ceiling shelves with hundreds of books or perhaps thousands. There was a desk with a few writing implements and a brass banker's light. Along one wall was a small fireplace, where a fire now burned. The room was warm and homey. Davey sat in one of the leather chairs. He wore a menacing scowl that Henry suspected must have required some effort to maintain.

His mother gestured toward the empty chair and reminded Henry that he should only stay for a short time. Henry nodded and took the seat.

After several seconds of silence, Davey said: "I don't have anything to say to you."

"Don't be ridiculous. Of course you do."

Davey closed his eyes and shook his head slowly like a pouting child.

"Fine," Henry said, "then I'll talk."

Davey folded his arms now and refused to look at Henry directly.

Henry said: "I showed up in Andrews a few months ago with no plans to stay, no plans to do much of anything really. But the Whitmans had a place available for cheap, and I jumped at the opportunity and saw a sign at the diner advertising a dishwashing position. So I took that job and washed dishes. After a few weeks Charlotte started waiting tables at the diner, and we became friends."

At this, Davey scowled a more sullen scowl and stuck his chin out and made a show of folding his arms again. Henry rolled his eyes and shook his head.

"Anyway," Henry said, "Charlotte and I became friends. We had coffee together on Saturday nights and talked about the kinds of things friends talk about. And sometimes I gave her a ride home after work. And she took me to the footbridge over Mill Creek where it's quiet. I played the piano for her. And that's it."

Davey said: "I don't believe you."

"Of course you don't. If you believed me you wouldn't have assaulted me from behind like a cheap shot son of a bitch."

"I could kill you right now."

"Christ, why are you so angry?"

"Why am I angry?"

"Yeah."

Davey unfolded his arms and leaned forward and put his elbows on his knees. He said very quietly: "I fought at Inchon. I fought at Bloody Ridge. I fought at Triangle Hill. And I fought at Kumsong. At every turn I lost friends. My brothers in arms were picked off by snipers while standing just inches from me. I carried wounded American soldiers across battlefields and put them down on cots in the medical tents only to have the medical tents explode or burn down minutes later. I was shot twice. Once on my arm and once on my hip." He pointed to both places on his body as if Henry didn't know where Davey's arm and hip were.

Henry only stared emotionless at Davey and continued to stare as Davey spoke.

Davey continued: "There were times when I almost gave up. We were surrounded, or I had run out of food or water, or I got lost. But I didn't give up. I kept going. I fought a little harder to make it out alive. You know why?"

Henry just stared.

"Because," Davey continued, "I knew Charlotte was waiting for me. I never gave up because my girl was back at home, praying for my return."

"What does all this have to do with me?"

"When I got home from Korea I heard Charlotte was running around with some musician from out of town. Some goddamn piano player."

"Running around?"

"Arthur Truman told me he even warned you."

"Are you not listening to me? Charlotte and I are just friends."

"You didn't look like just friends to me."

Henry shook his head and rolled his eyes. "I've told you—"

"You don't know what it's like to—"

Henry stood now, and as he stood he did his best to ignore the pain that shot through his hips and chest and sides. He said loudly: "You don't know a goddamn thing about me. You don't know my pain, my suffering, my history. Don't you tell me what I have or have not experienced. Don't you tell me anything."

Davey leaned back in his chair, surprised by Henry's sudden emotion. Davey's mother appeared at the room's door, bearing a look of concern.

Henry continued: "I came here thinking maybe I'd gotten the wrong impression of you while you were trying to kill me a couple of weeks ago. I see now you're every bit the piece of shit meathead I thought you were. I don't give a goddamn about the battles you've fought or your heroics while on duty or what it was like to leave your girl back at home. None of that shit matters to me. You're either too stupid or too insecure to realize I don't love Charlotte. I'm a couple of minutes away from leaving this town, and you'll never see me again. But you should know that Charlotte thinks you're every bit the piece of shit I think you are. Also, what if we were running around together, as you put it? What if she had decided she didn't want to be your girlfriend anymore? What does that say about you?"

The Heresy of Rain

Davey's face twisted into some hideous expression of rage, and he leapt from the chair to within inches of Henry. And he seethed, his breathing loud and animalistic. He was like some raging bull or some other wild beast finally taunted too many times.

Henry smiled. He said: "Go ahead and hit me. Try to kill me. You're the big, strong soldier, and I'm the candyass musician."

Davey's mother hurried to Davey's side and held his arm and pleaded with him not to hit Henry and then ordered Henry to leave. Davey's face was red, and his chest heaved with anger. His mother tried to soothe him by stroking his arm and whispering.

Henry said: "Charlotte and I are friends; that's all. I may never see her again. But I know for sure she'll never love you. And that gives me great comfort."

Henry stared at Davey and his mother for a few seconds more while the fire popped behind him and then left the room and walked to the front door and showed himself out. He heard the lock behind him. Once outside he walked out to the street where his truck was parked and climbed up into the driver's seat and winced and sucked in air because of the pain. He looked up at the house once more and saw Davey in one of the windows. He stood there, seething still. Henry only returned the stare, and Davey disappeared into the bowels of the house. And then Henry took a deep breath and unzipped his duffle bag and took out the cloth sack with the gun and bullets and put the sack into the glovebox and started the engine and drove to the end of the street and then out of Andrews.

Canto 5

THEY WERE SEATED AT THE DINNER TABLE. Henry stared at his plate of baked chicken and mashed potatoes and occasionally chased a green bean or carrot around his plate with a fork. He'd said almost nothing since arriving home from school more than two hours before. She looked upon him without judgment and finally asked what was on his mind.

"I don't know," he said with an adolescent shrug. "Nothing."

"All right," said his grandmother. "If you say so."

He took a passive bite of potatoes and made another stab at a green bean. She took a deep breath and placed her napkin on the table and leaned forward and rested her chin on her fist with her elbow on the table.

"It doesn't seem like nothing."

He shrugged again.

She said: "A couple of days ago I read in the school newsletter that the eighth grade dance is coming up."

He committed nothing on the matter.

"You feeling sad and being quiet doesn't have anything to do with the dance?"

Shrug.

"All right. I'll leave you alone."

She took up her plate and iced tea glass and stood and turned toward the kitchen.

He said: "I asked a girl." It was a soft and hesitant revelation.

She stopped and looked over her shoulder toward her grandson and nodded pensively. Then she took her plate and glass into the kitchen and placed the plate in the sink and refilled her tea glass and went back to the table where Henry sat unmoved.

"You did?" she asked.

"Yeah."

"Do you mind if I ask who?"

He shrugged. "Peggy. Peggy Alexander."

His grandmother again nodded thoughtfully. "Addie Alexander's girl?"

"Yeah."

"I'm guessing she has other plans."

He nodded.

"I'm sorry to hear that, Henry. I really am."

"She told me she's not going with any one boy. She said instead she was going with a group of her girlfriends."

"Well, that's not so bad. Maybe she'll have a change of heart once she sees you there neat and clean and dapper." She tried to urge him on with a smile and wink.

"Later I found out Charlie Lewis asked her a few minutes after I asked her, and she told him yes."

"Ah."

He sighed and put his fork on his plate and slouched in his chair, staring at his grandmother with a look of exhaustion and defeat.

"I'm so embarrassed."

"Her taste in men is horrible. She'll regret not going with you after the fourth or fifth time Charlie Lewis talks with his mouth full. Or after he burps or tells one of the stupid jokes he's learned from that vulgar father of his."

Henry softened but didn't quite smile. "I guess."

She reached across the table and patted his hand.

She said: "Girls can be exasperating, can't they?"

"I guess."

She smiled. "A few years from now you'll meet the perfect girl. She'll be wonderful. Beautiful and gentle and honest and loyal and sweet. And you'll forget all about Peggy Alexander and Charlie Lewis. She'll be perfect. I promise. She's out there."

"I guess."

"Every Peggy you've ever met will become a distant memory, some faraway dream. You'll know she's the one. There will be something special about her. Her smile, her hair, her intelligence, her style, her moxie. Maybe all of those things. And you'll think 'hmm, that grandmother of mine was right.' And you'll be so proud to introduce her to me."

He shrugged, dubious.

"She's out there, Henry. She's out there."

Canto 6

"DO YOU EVER WISH you could see?"

"Of course."

"I'm sorry. That was a stupid question."

She said: "It's not a stupid question. I think for a lot of blind people, people who have been blind since birth, sight would be a painful and disappointing sensation. Can you imagine how confusing it would be? If darkness or nothingness is all you know, it's normal in some sense."

"But you've seen before."

"Long ago. I remember very little. There are some things I'd love to see again. My sister's face. The stars. The ocean. I wonder what it must be like to read a book."

"Do you every wonder what I look like?"

"I know what you look like."

"How do you mean?"

"I can touch your face and trace your features, and I can feel your hair and your arms and your shoulders."

"But what if your understanding of my appearance, your image of me, what if it's wrong?"

She smiled and chuckled lightly. "How can it be wrong? I can't possibly describe to you how I imagine you must look. Maybe it's way off. Maybe my memory of colors and shapes is so distant that what I'm thinking of is actually a frog. Or a guitar. Or a lamp or a tree. What difference does it make?"

He touched the side of her face and tucked a strand of brown hair behind her ear.

Then he said: "I hope you don't think I look like a frog."

She laughed. "But what if my memory of a frog is actually an umbrella? See? It doesn't matter. I'm perfectly happy. And you shouldn't worry about me. Also, I've asked my sister. She says you're plenty good-looking."

He laughed lightly, embarrassed.

The Heresy of Rain

"Anyway," she said, "if I were sighted I may not have met you."

"That's a troubling thought."

"Yes," she said. "Yes, it is."

An Interlude
1939

THE BOY WAS ELEVEN YEARS OLD, *gangly and awkward. His hair was short but unruly, difficult to tame. His feet were overlarge. But his teeth: they were the very root of his pre-adolescent insecurity. Snaggled and crosswise. Missing here and there. Altogether misaligned, a sad and unavoidable stratagem of an unforgiving aversive. A humiliation. He seldom smiled or laughed, and he only spoke when addressed. Sometimes he pretended not to hear when someone asked him a question or made a passing comment. He feigned illness to avoid the photographer on picture day at school. Or he just skipped school entirely on those days. After some time, skipping school became a habit. It became normal.*

On this day the boy had skipped school once more. He spent the day on a secluded section of the beach. It was late winter. No revelers. Nor any fishermen. A slate sky above and forever out to sea. He stole an apple from an outdoor market at noon and retreated to his spot near the wharf. There were no boats on this day—just the dark gray rocks and a few gulls, who glided and swooped about like bats and sometimes darted flimsily in the wind.

When the afternoon waned he began his trudge toward his house, a three-mile walk. After twenty minutes he approached his neighborhood. The wind had turned cold. He buttoned his thin jacket to his neck and shoved his hands in his trouser pockets. As he neared his street he saw a familiar group of boys who were returning home after school. It was six or seven boys, all just a bit younger than he. They walked ahead of him and didn't see him approaching. He quickened his step. He was still more than a dozen paces behind the boys when they stopped; they began laughing. At first in mild amusement but then louder and more boisterous. He took refuge behind a large live oak and listened as they joked.

"Hey look, everyone: I'm Billy!"

It was Charlie Lewis. He had folded a few scraps of paper and shoved them between his teeth and lips so that he appeared clownish and silly, his pretend teeth missized and terrible. They continued their laughter. The boy didn't know Charlie well.

The Heresy of Rain

Another young boy of the group, Henry King, laughed along with the others. He laughed more than the others. And more loudly. Then Henry walked over to Charlie and tousled Charlie's hair.

Then Henry said: "Now you look just like him. Ugly hair and all."

They laughed some more, and then Charlie took the paper out of his mouth and threw it to the ground and smoothed his hair and said: "I heard he skipped again today. Is he stupid or something?"

The boy turned and ran, and he did not stop running until he reached his house.

His mother said "William!" as he entered. She grabbed him by the arm and turned him to face her and said: "How many times am I going to get a phone call during the school day and hear 'I'm sorry to say, Mrs. Maddock, but William isn't at school again today'?"

He was silent.

"What am I going to do with you, William?"

He did not reply. What was there to say?

So he wrenched free and hurried to his room and slammed the door and cried.

Part IV

"A white veil came over the eyes and the long white beak unhinged. Its legs were crossed and its clawlike feet were delicately curved at rest. Even death did not mar its grace, for it lay on the earth like a broken vase of red flowers, and we stood around it, awed by its exotic beauty."

–James Hurst

The Heresy of Rain

THE DRIVE FROM ANDREWS COUNTY to Brewster County would be half a day at most, so Henry took his time. There was no need to attract the attention of law enforcement officials by speeding or driving otherwise recklessly. The road was endless and barren. Route 67 took him southward. Less than an hour outside of Andrews he stopped at a service station and filled up and changed a five-dollar bill for dimes and walked out to the pay phone in the parking lot. He dialed the number and then after hearing from the operator how much the call would cost fed a handful of dimes into the slot.

"Galveston Police. How may I direct your call?"

"Could you tell me if Chief Wisdom is in the office today?"

"He's not in today. Would you like to leave a message or speak with an officer?"

"No, that's all right. When is he expected back?"

"He's out of town on a case right now. He'll come back next week to check in at the office and then head back out West if necessary."

"All right."

She repeated: "Would you like to leave him a message?"

"No, but thank you."

Henry placed the receiver back on the hook and got on his way.

To pass the time that day and keep himself alert he counted dead deer on the side of the road. He lost count or lost interest in the seventies. Seventy deer splayed about on the highway's shoulder, having been the victims of human encroachment. He wondered if any of the drivers involved in those accidents had been hurt or killed. He wondered what it would be like to be killed violently and then left out in the open to rot like some ancient, crucified criminal or like a brown and stale and withering tree in the middle of a grand and green forest.

By early afternoon he was hungry, so he stopped at a café near Fort Stockton. He took a deep breath before he left the car and willed himself to walk from his truck to the cafe's entrance without betraying his soreness to the other patrons, who were very few in number. Henry took a seat at the counter near an old man who drank black coffee and was otherwise still. He figured the man's age at over eighty. Maybe ninety. Henry ordered coffee and eggs and toast.

The proprietor of the café—which Henry noticed was very similar to the Andrews Diner where he was still daytime dishwasher until tomorrow when he would not be at work or perhaps Tuesday if Jack cut him some slack which he knew Jack would—poured Henry a cup of steaming coffee. Henry thanked the man.

The proprietor was a tall, cleanshaven man in his late forties or perhaps early fifties.

He said: "Haven't seen you here before."

Henry told the proprietor he was passing through.

"This sure is good coffee," Henry said.

"I'm happy to hear that on account of we make our living selling this stuff."

"Well, it's sure good. I'll have to remember you all if I pass through again."

"Where you headed?"

"Brewster County."

"You're only an hour away from the county line. You got family there? It's mainly private ranches and the state park."

"Sure. A few relatives."

"What's the family name? Maybe I know you all."

Henry sipped his coffee and cleared his throat. "Family name's Ballard."

"I don't reckon I know any Ballards in Brewster County. I knew some Ballards in Waco, though. You related to the Waco Ballards?"

"No, I'm not familiar with the Waco Ballards, though this isn't the first time someone's asked."

"Well, all right then."

Finally, the proprietor left him in peace for a few moments. And a short time later he had his eggs and toast, and the proprietor kept his coffee cup full. The old man next to Henry just drank his coffee in silence. Then the man turned to Henry and slowly nodded a hello. Henry touched the brim of his hat and said howdy because that's what people said in this part of the state, and then he removed his hat and placed it on the counter to his left on account of having good table manners. He felt nervous and agitated suddenly, as if a whole task force of constables and deputies would charge the café and arrest him or engage him in some kind of Wild West shootout.

The old man took a sip of his coffee. Then he said to Henry: "I hope you got a few licks in on the other guy."

Henry asked: "I'm sorry?"

The man nodded toward Henry and said: "You look like you've been in a fight, son."

Henry relaxed and pushed his plate away and said: "Well. To be honest, no. He was a cheap shot, sucker-punching son of a bitch. I didn't get any licks in. I was laid up for a couple of weeks."

"Sorry to hear that."

Henry shrugged. "I've got a few busted ribs too. I'm doing much better than I was a week ago."

"Was it over a girl?"

"Yeah, but it was a misunderstanding. I was just friends with her."

"Was?"

"Well. I guess I still am. Hell, I don't know."

The old man motioned for the proprietor to refill his cup and Henry's as well. Then the old man said: "I'll tell you what, son. There are lots of reasons to fight another man: money, honor, reputation, baseball, cattle, family, horses, property, any number of things. I've found that the only *good* reason to fight another man is if it's about a woman, and the woman is worth the effort. And they almost always are."

"I guess I can't disagree."

The old man stared at Henry, similar to the way Mr. Whitman looked at him over this past week. Like the man was piercing Henry's façade and drilling to his vulnerable core.

Then the old man said: "I hope you find peace."

"Peace with what?"

"Peace with whatever is burdening you."

"Burdening?"

"Yes. I can see in your eyes something. Something like sadness."

"What makes you think I'm burdened with sadness?"

"Sadness, heartbreak. Maybe guilt."

"I've just had a rough go of it lately."

The old man stared into Henry's eyes.

Henry said: "I've only just recently gotten out of the hospital and up and driving and so forth. I'll be fine."

"No, it isn't physical. Or at least it isn't only physical. There's more. Your eyes divulge your burden, young man."

Henry said nothing.

The old man continued: "Maybe there's more than one cause. Or maybe there's more than one feeling, these things burdening you. Maybe it's all bound up together. I'm old and tired, but I can see these things."

"What things?"

"Everything. Everything. And often what we see in other people the people themselves fail to realize. They don't have the proper perspective."

"You think I lack perspective?"

"Of course. We all do. But that isn't the point. The point is that you are bothered by something in your life. Something in your past or maybe your future."

"We're all burdened by something in our past," Henry said. "In that way I'm no different than anyone else."

"Look at that man." The old man gestured to the proprietor. "Or these ladies over here," he said while pointing to a pair of women sipping coffee in a booth. "Sure, they are burdened, but their eyes don't speak the same kind of sadness and worry your eyes do. Of some peril. Some great pain."

"What difference does it make if my sadness or worry or burden or peril exists right now or recently as opposed to these other people whose experiences are memories? In time I'll have gained the perspective you speak of, and I'll be like everyone else in here."

"That may be true, and that's a fair point about perspective. But some of us face more peril than others, and it's a fact of the human condition that we fail to account for our own place in the world. And sometimes there is more urgency with some of us than others."

Henry looked up for the proprietor. But the proprietor was counting eggs or loaves of bread and had his back turned.

"Does my case suggest to you a greater sense of urgency than others?"

"Perhaps. Only you know the answer to that question."

"Why does it matter?"

"Why does what matter?"

"All of it. Why does my burden matter, and why does its urgency matter?"

"Are you concerned about your soul?"

"My soul." Henry furrowed his brow and took a sip of his coffee.

"Yes. Yes. Your soul. One day," the old man said, sweeping his hand across an imaginary panorama, "there will be a reckoning."

"Like in the bible?"

"I don't think so. A reckoning. A great accounting. An accounting of our lives. Our lives—when we have died—will be adjudicated. We will be measured against our deeds, good and bad."

"By God?"

"No, I don't think of any god. Why does there always have to be a god with people?"

"Who else would hold us accountable?"

"I suppose any number of overseers, or groups of overseers, or natural laws, or metaphysical arbiters. Perhaps the divinity of the universe will then make itself manifest."

"If you are talking about redemption, then you must be talking about God of the bible."

"I am not speaking of redemption. No, there is not redemption. For us there is no salvation or reclamation. People, they want redemption. They want salvation. So they speak of the reclamation of our souls. They speak of a great cleansing. That is wishful thinking."

"Then why should I care about unburdening myself? What is the purpose?"

"We ought to unburden ourselves so that we may die clean deaths. Our only hope is to be judged well in our deaths. Fairly but well. You see. After we die there is a darkness."

"How can you know about such a thing?"

"Because I lived it."

"A near-death experience?"

"Perhaps. It was when I was a young man, maybe a little older than you are now. This was before everything became so easy. Before automobiles and mechanized equipment all around us. Men engaged in honest work and received honest pay. I was working with a young horse. He was a spirited colt, this one. And one morning when I was leading him from the barn to the corral he was spooked. It could have been a bird or a mouse or a rabbit. Who knows. At any rate, he reared up and kicked me in the head. I was out. Gone. Everyone thought I was dying or maybe already dead. And I was. During this experience I was in the darkness I described. It was dizzying and terrifying, and I hadn't any footing. I was falling. And there was a sensation, a knowledge, that my life to that point was being accounted for. But I was spared. By some miracle of science or by some providence, I don't know. I woke up. I was alive again. So after the blackness?"

Henry nodded with a certain cautious understanding.

"Who is to say? You see, we are humans. Humans are born of some divine essence."

"By God?"

The man shrugged and shook his head.

"Then who?"

"Who is to say? We are humans, molded out of perfection. But we are not good. And it isn't just that we are bad, you see. We are an abomination."

"You must be speaking of God."

The man was visibly frustrated. "Why does everything have to be about God with people? Is there no other explanation? You see?"

"I don't know that I do. None of this makes any sense otherwise."

"However we came about, we are not good. We are not good. We treat each other with contempt and dishonesty. We hate ourselves and mistreat our bodies and the bodies of those we love. We are not loyal, and we are not kind. We act in the spirit of unceasing self-interest. You see? We are fine-tuned to this earth. This world, we are matched to it with such precision. But we are monsters, and we treat the world with the same contempt that we once reserved only for one another. And we expect redemption? The cleansing of our souls? A recognition of our innocence and our goodness?"

"Not everyone is evil."

The man waved him off. "Evil is yet another thing entirely. There is evil. Of course there is evil. But evil resides in a few of us only. Evil is not always to be spoken of. Some choose evil, and some are born with it. And it is unfortunate. But for those of us who have been cast into a darkness, there is no redemption."

"You said everyone is cast into the darkness."

"This is true. Everyone is cast into the darkness at some time or another. And we will be forced to come to terms with ourselves. We will fall and fall and fall after the accounting. And then, after some length of time, perhaps some of us are fortunate enough to find our feet. But this is not redemption. Do not think you can be redeemed."

"Is it luck?"

"I don't think so. The universe operates with something that seems to us like randomness, and at times we are on the unfortunate side of the universe's sense of order. Within this, however, there is always balance. Not on an individual level, nothing so specific. There is this randomness, but there is also balance. Always there is balance. I don't subscribe to chaos, necessarily, but who can really say? So the question is how one finds one's feet, how one makes his way through the darkness and can again stand."

"I guess if he's done more good things than bad."

"Yes, perhaps if he does more good than bad. But that is not the only factor in this accounting of our actions. You see, there are degrees of goodness and badness. Many degrees."

"What about you?"

"I am no different than anyone else."

"Surely you know how to make it through this reckoning safely."

The man looked away for a moment. "For some of us it is too late. There is no safety. We have acted in ways that can't possibly be reconciled. We have left ourselves with no options but to hope for mercy."

"God's mercy?"

"There you are again with your god. I don't know. No one knows, you see? No one knows. We can only hope for our misery to end. But we don't deserve it. We deserve nothing."

"What is the point of all this?"

"All this? All what?"

"Everything? What is it that we are trying to get? Where are we trying to go?"

"Where are you trying to go?"

"Jesus, I don't know. Goddamn." He felt like a child, a child asking stupid questions of a wise man who must find him ridiculous and tiresome. He put his head in his hand for a moment and then leaned back and closed his eyes and thought of his dead wife who was so beautiful and innocent and who he missed more than he would have thought possible.

The man said: "Maybe I was right, what I said earlier about clarity."

"Clarity?"

"Clarity and focus and a sense of purpose. And nothing more, nothing more. Wiser men, perhaps there is more for them. Men of esteem and society and letters and the world. Men of the world, what are they? Do they have clarity? Have they a sense of purpose, these men? Who can ever know?"

"Will clarity of purpose help me when it's time for my reckoning?"

"No. No. But it might help you until that time. Shouldn't we all strive for clarity?"

"It seems like nothing is clear to me."

The man stared unblinking at Henry. Some shriveled witch doctor, a shaman, or druid from a different era or even a different world altogether.

"You have suffered a great loss. I can see this."

Henry only nodded.

"Our suffering can help us achieve clarity, which is the most important thing in the world."

"More important than love and life and family?"

"Of course."

He shook his head.

The old man repeated: "Clarity is the most important thing in the world. Don't you see? Think about all the bad in the world. All of it."

"I'm plenty aware of the bad in the world."

"How much bad in the world is the product of some misalignment? Some misunderstanding or stilted communication? Or confusion? Think about the wars men have fought and the violence they have waged. Think about the massacres and suffering that occur only as a result of some unfortunate muddling of words or boundaries."

"What does any of that have to do with me?"

"What is it that you want?"

He thought for a moment, unsure if he could voice aloud his thoughts.

"I want more than anything to have my wife back."

"I see." The man did not question further for some time.

"She was murdered. And it was my fault." Henry could no longer control himself, was unable to hold back his tears. He did not sob loudly in that diner; rather, he wept the quiet cry of a beaten man with a broken soul.

"I see," the man said again. "I see."

"She's gone."

"Yes. Yes."

"I could have done something. I should have known."

"No, I don't think so." He placed a hand on the counter for emphasis. "We often think of things past with that sense of clarity I mentioned. Of course things seem clear later. We oughtn't to allow ourselves to think this way. It is a self-destructive way of thinking. Anyway, it's only an illusion that we might have control of our own death. Men and women, they are not the arbiters of this. They are not."

"What should I do?"

"I don't understand. Do about what?"

"I have to make it right."

"Make it right? There is nothing to do."

"She was innocent. She was beautiful."

"I'm sorry for your sadness."   The man motioned to the proprietor for more coffee for the two of them. The proprietor poured the coffee. The man asked her name.

Henry was silent for many seconds and then said Grace very quietly.

"What did you love most about her?"

Henry said nothing and sat motionless like a man defeated. The man gestured toward Henry's coffee, and Henry placed his hand around the mug but did not drink.

"I loved most that she loved me."

"Are you a difficult person to love?"

"Why do people keep asking me that question?"

"Well? Are you?"

"Maybe. But maybe no more difficult than anyone else. But."

"But what?"

"I don't know. I play the piano, and she was blind."

The man then understood. He closed his eyes and nodded, and he sighed heavily for the young man who was so profoundly lost. He could do little to help, but he shared Henry's sadness. For it is so painful to lose someone without a proper goodbye.

Henry said: "It's like we were put on the Earth for one another."

"And now she is gone. Of course. Of course. But there is no making it right. You see? You cannot change what is in the past, and you cannot force the future around your worldview, no matter how wide or narrow. This is not how it works. The future cares little for our agendas."

"Do you believe people can be made for one another?"

"I think there are certain relationships in the world that bring to the individuals such tremendous joy that it seems somehow preordained. And these people, even if these relationships are short-lived, they are so lucky. It is only fortune that brings us such love."

"It didn't just seem that way. It was that way."

The man had finished his coffee. He seemed prepared to say something further but stopped and pursed his lips. For a moment he ran his finger around the rim of the mug. Then he said: "I must go soon. Remember what I said about changing the past."

"I don't aim to change the past."

"There is no redemption, you see? Please remember there is no redemption. Not for your misery. Not for your misery and not for revenge. You cannot reclaim Grace. You must understand."

Henry did not answer.

The man sighed once more and placed some bills on the counter and nodded to the proprietor. He placed his hand on Henry's shoulder for a brief moment. Then he was gone.

Canto 7

Henry SAT ON THE SOFA in his grandmother's living room. She sat almost opposite him on a chair, the upholstery worn and faded, and the chair's wooden legs aged and scratched and weathered. He stared across the small coffee table at her grandson, whose eyes were black and whose lip was cut and bleeding.

"Your principal said this was out of character for you."

He shrugged and then leaned back into the sofa and looked away and shook his head, blinking back tears.

"This boy, he is two years older than you? A senior?"

Henry nodded, the gesture barely perceptible.

"Tell me about it," she said very softly. "Tell me how it started."

Without looking at her, he said in a wavering and gravelly voice: "His girlfriend was talking to me."

"Talking to you?"

"She walked over to me during lunch and sat down near me. She said her parents heard me play at Sammie's last weekend. She was just asking me questions about the restaurant and how I learned to play and that kind of thing."

"And her boyfriend came over and hit you?"

He nodded. "I didn't even see him. He came up from behind me and pushed me to the floor. I couldn't even hit him."

"Was the girl sorry at least for what happened?"

"I think so."

"Girls are a lot of trouble, aren't they?"

"The ones with boyfriends are."

"Good point."

Canto 8

GRACE ASKED: "What would you do if I disappeared?"

"Disappeared?"

"If something happened to me. If I died."

"What a terrible and ridiculous question to ask. Why would you say that?"

"Just curious."

They sat on the porch swing. The chains creaked with each sway. The swing's white paint was faded and chipped and flaky. Inside, Diana and her husband packed their belongings, readying for the move across to the mainland for his new job. Henry and Grace held hands as they gently arced back and forth.

"I don't want to think about it," he said.

She rested her head on his shoulder and closed her eyes.

Then he said: "I would be so sad that I wouldn't be able to eat or think or sleep. I would suffer a heartbreak so intense that I wouldn't be able to live. Even thinking about it makes me sad. Please, let's talk about something else."

She shrugged and smiled slyly. "Eh. You'd find someone else."

"There is no one else."

"There are a lot of girls in the world."

"But there's only one Grace."

"That's true," she said.

"There's no one else for me."

"I guess I'd better stay alive then."

"You'd better."

Part V

"The sound of rain was everywhere, but the wind had died and it fell straight down in parallel paths like ropes hanging from the sky. As I waited, I peered through the downpour, but no one came."

–James Hurst

The Heresy of Rain

BREWSTER COUNTY. The land was beautiful and desolate. It was Mexico and Texas. Hues of browns and grays all the way to the horizon. Dust of reds and yellows and a sky blue and deep and unwavering. There were mountains, the Chisos range. Brewster County was named after a War Secretary of the Republic of Texas, and the land is not for the faint of heart nor the faint of spirit. The mountains rose in the distance and in all their vastness rested entirely within this single county. A desert land that offered everything and nothing.

Henry looked at the small photo of Grace, whose corner was again wedged into his dash, and he reached into his shirt pocket and took out the matchbook and looked at it also for the thousandth time and put it back in his pocket. It was mid-afternoon, and he passed by a green and white road sign that said forty miles to Alpine. He drove on, and a short time later he was in the town, the only city in this immense county. After only a few minutes on the main road he drove by the Cattleman Grill. It was a small restaurant whose façade had the look of an old western saloon. Even at this early hour there were cars in the parking lot, pickup trucks and family cars alike. He continued on without stopping. Toward the edge of town he passed a park for mobile homes and recreational vehicles, but he drove on. Just a few miles outside of Alpine he saw a large sign advertising a motel, and he pulled into the parking lot and sat for a bit. It was a sprawling one-story complex with several different wings or buildings. Light tan stucco with orange-red Spanish tile roofing. Many of the doors were adorned with wreaths, and there were chairs and card tables and potted plants about the place, which gave the impression that many people called this place home.

Henry cut the engine and walked into the office and was met by a stern man with dark, weathered skin and a big black mustache and cowboy hat. The office was stale and uncomfortable, warm even, though it was a cool day. There was little by way of furniture or files in the room. Henry asked whether there was a room available, and the man said yes, a couple.

"What's the nightly rate?"

"Five a night."

"That include breakfast?"

"Do I look like a cook?"

"All right."

"Do you want a room or don't you?"

Henry gave the man enough cash to secure a room for two weeks and scribbled something undiscernible on the sign-in sheet. The man gave him a key marked 406 and pointed generally in the direction of the room.

Henry asked: "What's the best place for a meal around here?"

"The Cattleman makes a good supper. Sometimes the crowd is a little rough, especially on the weekends, but it's usually calm enough. There's a small café in town and a donut shop that serves a good cup of coffee."

"What about a supermarket?"

"I hope you don't aim to cook in your room. We don't allow burners or hotplates or anything like that."

"Of course not."

"We got public grills out on the premises if you want to barbeque."

"All right."

"Anyhow, there's a little grocer about two miles back the way you came and then a left on thirty-one. Look for a yellow sign."

"All right. Thanks. I'll give you plenty of notice if I plan to extend my stay."

"Sure. What are you in town for, anyhow?"

"Seeing the country."

The man snorted. "Whatever you say, cowboy."

Henry furrowed his brow but only nodded and then walked back outside and got his bag from the truck. He slung the bag over his shoulder and looked at the key again and then walked in the direction that the man pointed. The cool day was met by dozens of people outside. They congregated in central locations such as benches or picnic tables. Kids ran about with thin jackets but some with no shoes. Henry found room 406 and unlocked the door and entered. It was a small room with a double bed and a radio and an old dresser. There was a single lightbulb attached to the middle of the ceiling, and a thick string hung down. He pulled the string, and the light came on and revealed a tiny bathroom with a cracked mirror and a chipped and stained sink. He turned the sink's silver handle, and a few seconds later water spurted out of the faucet brown and then clear and clean. There was no air conditioner or heater. He tugged at the window, but it only rose a few inches. There was no fan in the room.

Henry took from his pocket the last of his money.

"Why the hell did I pay for two weeks? Goddamn."

He still had more than two hundred dollars, but he had no way of knowing how long he would be in Alpine or Brewster County or if Maddock was even in Texas anymore or dead or alive or if Grant Wisdom was near or a thousand miles away. He went outside and walked the grounds for a bit before climbing back into his truck. He sat in the truck for a moment and looked back toward the building that housed his room and saw an old woman sitting on a bench. Just sitting and staring. She didn't appear to be watching anything or anyone in particular. She was motionless with her hands resting on a knobby walking stick. Henry shook his head and started the truck and drove to the supermarket for soap and shave cream and to pass the time.

AT SUPPERTIME THE FOLLOWING DAY he drove over to the Cattleman Grill without any kind of plan. The evening turned cold when the sun went down. It was early February. The Chisos Mountains did not protect the valley from the wind. Rather, the mountains seemed to flush raging winds into the valley and then trap them against escape. If the owner of the supermarket was to be believed, dust storms in the region were deadly if ignored. He told stories of men and women driving into canyons or falling from mountain roads or bridges while trying to navigate through a terrible dust storm. He said the best thing to do is get the hell indoors and keep your ass there until visibility improves. Henry told the supermarket owner he would do just that in such a case.

It was dark by the time he arrived at the restaurant. Even so, he parked his truck far from the entrance, almost out of sight from the building. He had no idea what to expect. He took the matchbook out of his shirt pocket and looked at it for a bit. He had almost rubbed the lettering off the surface of the matchbook. He slid it back into his pocket.

The restaurant's interior was homey and warm. Good smells floated about, and most of the patrons were families or older couples. There was a bar off to the side of the place, but the only drinker was a man in a business suit. The barman chatted casually with the suited man. The restaurant's wood-paneled walls were adorned with an assortment of taxidermy animals and cattle skulls. There was a sixteen-point buck and two coyotes and several rabbits and a few does. There was an entire bobcat and a longhorn head and a mountain lion. There were also a few fish here and there. Henry ordered meatloaf and mashed potatoes and coffee. He ate his meal quietly and then asked for a few refills of coffee. After an hour he paid his check and smiled at the waitress and tipped his hat to the host and walked toward the door. He passed by the bar and stopped to ask the barman what beers he had on tap. The barman listed a few and said he'd be happy to let Henry try one on the house. Henry politely declined but said he'd be back in a day or two and might take him up on the offer. The barman said most evenings are pretty quiet, like on this particular night, but Fridays and Saturdays feature a livelier crowd after the families finish their supper and clear out.

"Ranch hands, cowboys, dart-throwers, card-players, and the like."

Henry said: "Is there a poker game on the weekend?"

The barman frowned and pursed his lips and looked from side to side and said sometimes they have a game going. "Depends on who's in town and whether anyone has the money to put up or whether folks are in the mood for poker."

"Sounds interesting."

The barman shrugged. "You never know. The guys who run the game, I haven't seen them for a few weeks. Hard to tell. But again, it's a livelier crowd on the weekends."

Henry thanked him again for the beer offer and said he'd hold him to it. Near the end of the bar there sat a glass bowl filled with matchbooks. They matched perfectly the one in Henry's shirt pocket. He fished one out of the bowl and smiled again at the barman. Then he left the Cattleman Grill and climbed into his truck and winced at the soreness and headed back toward the motel. It was only Monday.

Henry spent the better part of the next week holed up in his motel room or secreted away in the donut shop drinking coffee or taking short walks through Big Bend country. By the end of the week he was stir crazy. The weather had turned from cool to cold, with the temperature at night reaching freezing or below. He bought a small space heater from the hardware store for two dollars and set it up in his motel room without asking the permission of the mustached man in the office.

On Friday he went to the post office to change a few dollars for dimes. Then he went to the supermarket and bought a couple of sodas and some pretzels and put the groceries in the truck and then walked over to the payphone. It was just before six o'clock in the evening. He stacked up the dimes on the ledge and dialed the number and waited a few seconds. She answered after the third ring.

"Andrews Diner."

"Hey, Charlotte."

"Oh my God. Henry?"

"Yeah, it's me."

"Oh my God. Where are you?"

"I can't tell you that."

"Not even me?"

"Especially not you. I don't want to get you into any trouble."

"How are you feeling? Are your ribs better?"

"I'm feeling fine."

"I'm so happy to hear your voice, Henry. I've been worried."

"Good to hear yours too."

"It's been crazy at the diner. Jack can't find a dishwasher, and Suzanne took off with some truck driver, and—"

"Listen, Charlotte. Has anyone come to Andrews looking for me?"

"The other day Jack said some man came in looking for you."

"Do you know anything about him? What he looked like or where he's from?"

"Jack said the man said he was an old family friend of yours. Jack wasn't buying it, but the guy showed him a police badge. So Jack cut the attitude after that. Honestly, Jack is more bark than bite. Way more."

"A guy about my height but a little bigger, maybe fifty-five, sixty years old?"

"Hold on."

She was off the line for several seconds; Henry was instructed by the robotic voice to keep chucking dimes into the phone.

She came back: "Yeah, that's about right, he said. He also said I've got to get back to work. Will you call again?"

"Has that man talked to anyone else?"

"Jack mentioned to him that you'd been staying with the Whitmans for a while."

"All right."

"Are you in trouble?"

"I'm always in trouble."

"Will you call again?"

"I don't know, Charlotte. Be safe."

"Henry, please. Please call again."

"Maybe. You take care of yourself."

"Okay." He could hear her voice quavering.

"And don't marry Davey."

She snorted in defense of herself. "Not in a million years. Jack keeps yelling at me."

"Bye, Charlotte."

"Bye, Henry."

THE WEEKEND CAME AND WENT without any excitement at the Cattleman Grill. Henry moved toward the bar both Friday and Saturday nights but demurred. Each night, he took his supper in the dining area, asking the hostess to seat him along the back wall so he could see the entire place from his seat. He had in his waistband his handgun like some Reconstruction Era renegade looking for trouble in a boomtown tavern in the American West. A few men sat at the bar each evening, but there seemed to be no outlaws, no bandits, not any kind of criminal. By Saturday night at ten o'clock he was convinced there would be no showdown this weekend or maybe any weekend.

He eyed the bowl of matchbooks on his way out.

The Heresy of Rain

It was the middle of the following week. He walked into the restaurant for the third or fourth or fifth time and stood there with his hands in his pocket and looked around at the walls for the hundredth time.

"Something I can help you with?" It was the barman.

"No. I don't know. I don't know."

"I've seen you here a few times. The offer still stands."

"What offer is that?"

"Of a drink on me."

"Sure. Why not." Henry walked slowly to the bar and took one of the empty stools. He was the only patron. There would be few patrons on a Tuesday, even a Tuesday evening. He didn't recognize the music that played in the background. It was like bluegrass but a little twangier. Heavy on guitar. He saw the bar up close for the first time, really, and touched its pockmarks and scratches and scars.

The barman pushed the drink toward Henry, who cupped it with his right hand and thanked the barman but did not drink.

"Are you looking for someone? Waiting on someone?"

"Maybe. I'm not sure. I'm not sure I'm even in the right place."

"What led you here?"

"A series of choices, I guess."

"Were they the right choices?"

"I don't know. I was just recently certain I was in the right place, but now I'm not so sure."

"That's a tough spot to be in."

Henry finally took a sip of the whiskey. It was harsh, searing his throat. He winced and drew in a sharp breath. "You're right. It is a tough spot."

"How will you know whether you've ended up in the right place?"

"I guess I may never know. At some point I'll run out of money."

"That would be a bad thing all around, I'd guess."

"It sure would."

"Maybe the man you're waiting for will turn up."

"I didn't tell you whether I was looking for someone."

"Son, I've been serving men drinks all my adult life. More than thirty years. I served drinks when serving drinks wasn't allowed and even before that. I know when a man is married or when he is single. I can tell if a man has children. I know when a man is lying or telling the truth. I can see it in a man's eyes if he's killed another man. I can tell when a man is trying to hide. I know when a man has plenty of money or when he's come upon hard times. I can tell when a man is looking for someone else. And I can tell when a man knows he's being hunted."

"Is that right?"

"Right enough."

"Do any of those apply to me?"

"I'd say most of them do."

"Well. All right."

The barman said: "Maybe I can help you find the man you're waiting for."

"How do you know I'm waiting for a man? Maybe I'm waiting for a woman."

"You've been wearing the same trousers and shirt for more than a week, and you haven't shaved in several days. You hide in the shadows and eat quietly or not at all. You've got your eyes on the bar. If you're looking for a girl then I'm Butch goddamn Cassidy."

"I guess you've got me pretty well figured."

"Like I said, I've been at this a long time."

Henry finished off the whiskey and slid the glass a few inches with his fingers toward the barman. The barman took the glass and placed it in the sink behind the bar.

The barman slid a few wine glasses into the latticework above the sink and walked back toward Henry and leaned against his side of the bar.

"Look, son." The barman lowered his voice a bit. "I got a feeling I know the group of guys you're waiting on. You're not the first man to show up here looking to set things right. My advice to you is—"

"I don't recall asking for your advice."

"Well as far as I'm concerned, you're a guest of mine right now. You'd be wise to sit quietly for a minute and hear what I've got to say."

Henry looked away but did not object.

The barman continued: "Like I was saying, my advice to you is go home."

"That's not an option."

"It's a better option than tangling with outlaws and roughnecks and kneebreakers out here in the Wild West. Because that's what this is: the Wild West. There may be some nice families that live out here, and there's the national park and some ranches and so forth. But if you've got the idea that you're going to agitate a racketeer and avenge some past grievance and then the goddamn Lone Ranger or Jesus Christ himself is going to show up and help you out of a jam then you've got the wrong idea. There probably isn't a law enforcement officer within fifty miles of us right now. And Jesus resides elsewhere. Your savior is not here, however you figure him."

"I don't have that idea, necessarily. But I can't go home. I don't even know that I have a home. If this is the end of the road then so be it."

"What in the blue hell are you talking about, son?" The barman stood up straight and tossed a white towel over his shoulder.

"I don't care about living or dying. I'm past that. If I find the man I'm looking for then I'll settle things with him. If I don't find him then I guess I'll head out."

"What are you going to do if the law catches up with you first?"

"What makes you think the law's after me?"

"I told you I can tell everything about a man. Plus, you said going home's not an option. I suspect someone's after you. What if the law catches you before you find your man?"

"Then I guess I'd head out on that account as well."

The barman shook his head. "All right. I guess I hope for your sake and mine that you don't find what you're looking for in Brewster County, and you just head out."

"I suppose that's a possibility." Henry started to stand.

The barman leaned over and spoke quietly again: "Son, there's more to life than settling scores. Jesus, you think there's a man alive who doesn't wish he could right some long-ago wrong?"

"I'm looking to right a wrong that's still pretty fresh."

"You'll get yourself killed. You understand that?"

Henry shrugged. "All right."

"Don't be a goddamn fool. You think you can't go home? Then go to Mexico. You're just a half-day's drive away. Hell, I'll give you the gas money. Fill up and drive south. Far as I'm concerned, you were never here."

"Thanks for the offer. I think I'll wait around a bit longer."

The barman shook his head again and repeated: "Don't be a goddamn fool."

Henry said: "I'm afraid it's too late."

The Heresy of Rain

THE FOLLOWING DAY WAS COLD BUT STILL. The slate sky did not end, and it offered no wind. There was stillness everywhere. Henry stood on the motel grounds, several paces from the door of his room. He looked off to his left and saw at a distance the old woman sitting on her usual wooden bench. Still like a wax figure or mannequin. Henry took a few steps toward a bench closer to his door. Near him, small children played unsupervised. About a dozen kids playing soccer with an old, half-deflated brown basketball, made bald and shiny from years of use. It was the middle of the day. The children were not in school.

Henry looked to the bench near him. It was unoccupied save a newspaper. It was the Lubbock paper, and Henry sat on the bench—still somewhat gingerly for deference to his aching ribs—and took up the paper and read through it for boredom and turned to look at the ads on the lower fold of the back section. His eyes caught the words "jazz music," so he took a closer look. The ad was small, just four short lines. It declared blues pianist Octavian Pace would be at the Orange Club in Oklahoma City in two days. Henry had few possessions as a child or young man that meant anything to him. His Octavian Pace records were such possessions. He thought of his most recent purchase from the bookshop in Galveston. A record he never listened to, a record he'd almost forgotten.

He took a short breath and said to himself: "Well, shit. How about that."

He tore the ad from the paper and took the clipping and pocketed it and threw the rest of the paper in a garbage bin. Then he walked over to the motel office. The man with the mustache and cowboy hat was on duty. Henry cleared his throat to get the man's attention.

"You looking to go another week? Do some more sight-seeing around here?"

"I've still got a few days on my current deposit."

"All right. What can I help you with, then?"

"How far do you reckon it is from here to Oklahoma City?"

"Why in God's name would you drive to Oklahoma City?"

"I can ask someone else. Or buy a map, I guess." Henry began to turn toward the door.

"No, you're right. Not my business. I'd say six hundred miles, more or less. Probably more, but not by much."

"Thanks. I appreciate it."

"All right."

"If I decide to take a quick trip, I'll be back in plenty of time to pay for another week if I need to."

"Drive safe."

Henry nodded and left the office.

The Heresy of Rain

HE LEFT THE FOLLOWING MORNING for Oklahoma City. He had done some rough calculations on a notepad the night before. He figured gas alone would cost him almost fourteen dollars for the roundtrip. On his way out of Brewster County he filled up at a service station and bought some sodas and snacks. When he asked the clerk if they had any Oklahoma maps in stock the clerk asked him why in the goddamn hell would they have Oklahoma maps. Henry told the clerk he had a good point and took his leave. The weather was the same as it had been. The sky was an unchanging gray. It looked as if it could rain or snow at any second, but the sky did nothing. There was no wind. The morning was bitter cold. Henry was out of Brewster County by eight o'clock Thursday morning.

By suppertime he was near the Texas-Oklahoma border. The small town was Burkburnett, Texas. He stood in the parking lot of a service station that stood next to a small café, and he looked at the sky. It was the same gray sky he had left in Alpine. Still there was no wind. He thought again it could snow at any time. He bought gas for the truck and checked the oil and bought a Northern Texas/Oklahoma map inside. Then he walked over to the café and sat at the counter and ordered steak and eggs and coffee. He waited silently for his supper, sipping his coffee. There were a few other diners in the restaurant. After a few minutes he heard the door swing open, and he could see in the corner of his eye a few men enter the restaurant.

The waitress said: "Evenin, officers."

One of the men said: "Evenin, Doris."

"Do you all want to sit in a booth tonight?"

"That'll be fine, Doris."

After the men had been seated Henry chanced a look in their direction. It was four policemen in uniform. Henry looked the other way and saw through the window out to the parking lot. They had arrived in two patrol cars.

Henry's supper arrived, and he tried to eat quickly without appearing suspiciously hasty. One of the officers walked over to the counter to amend his order. He stood near Henry for a few seconds, waiting for Doris' attention. A big man, tall and burly. He caught Henry looking at him and said good evening to Henry. Henry nodded. His face grew warm.

The officer said to Henry: "Don't believe I've seen you in here before."

"I'm just passing through."

"Where you headed?"

Henry cleared his throat: "Oklahoma. There's a musician playing tomorrow. I thought I'd drive up and hear him play."

"Anyone I'd know of?"

"A blues pianist."

The officer shrugged. "I wouldn't know any of those. Can't say I'm a fan of Negro music, anyhow." When he said "negro" the final syllable was an "uh" sound. Nee-gruh music.

The officer got Doris' attention and added potatoes to his order and turned to join the rest of his party at the booth. He made it across to the booth but didn't sit down. He spoke quietly with his fellow officers while leaning on the table. Then he straightened up and walked back over to Henry. Henry was waiting for Doris to bring his check. He took deep breaths.

The officer stood next to Henry, far too close. He said: "Say, son. Is that your truck out there?"

"The black one?"

"Yes, the black one. It's the only truck in the lot. Is it yours?"

"It's mine."

"You been in a fight lately?"

"I reckon I have. Just a scuffle over some nonsense back home."

The office looked doubtful. "It appears you've experienced more than a scuffle, son. Looks like you've had your nose clean broke and half your head bashed in."

"Well. I reckon so." Henry picked up his coffee mug with a shaking hand and saw it was empty and placed it back on the counter. More deep breaths. Look him in the eye.

"How'd the other guy make out?"

"Can't say I did much damage. But he did spend the night in jail."

It was almost dark. Henry looked again at his truck in the lot. Flanked by the two patrol cars, his truck looked guilty and sad.

"Can you prove your ownership of that truck yonder?"

"Sure. The title's in the cab, officer."

"Go ahead and settle up with Doris. I'll wait here, and you can walk me out and show me the paperwork."

Doris placed the check in front of Henry. Henry took a dollar and slid it back toward Doris and tried to offer a smile. Doris did not look at him.

Henry said: "Can I ask what this is about?" He immediately regretted the question.

"How about you just show me the title, son?"

Henry saw the man's nameplate for the first time. It read OFFICER CLARK.

"All right. No problem, Officer Clark."

Henry lowered himself off the stool and cleared his throat again and walked toward the door. Officer Clark nodded toward the other officers and put up a hand as if to tell them he was okay on his own. Henry walked out and held the door open for Officer Clark and walked briskly to the truck, even though the physical stress of walking quickly was still painful. Clark asked him to slow down, but Henry ignored him and arrived at the truck a few seconds before the other man. Henry fumbled with the keys and unlocked the passengerside door and opened the glove compartment and reached under the cloth bag that held his gun and grabbed whatever was in there.

Clark asked Henry what the hurry was, and Henry said it was cold is all, and he was looking forward to the jazz show and wanted to make good time. He shuffled through maps and sweet roll wrappers and even the bill of sale before finding the title, faded and worn but clearly declaring Henry King the rightful owner of the truck.

Clark said: "All right. Can I see your license please?"

It was then that Henry realized he'd left his wallet inside. His heart beat like some pulsing, rhythmic drum. So fast and so loudly he was sure the officer could hear it. Even for the biting wind he was dizzy and hot.

"I reckon I left my wallet at the counter," he said. "I'll just run in and get it." He started back across the parking lot, but Officer Clark caught him by the elbow.

The officer said: "There's no need. I'll get it. That way you don't have to walk anymore than you need to. Have a seat here." Clark gestured to the rear of the truckbed where the tailgate should have been.

"All right." He sat.

"Can I trust you not to drive off while I'm in there just a quick second? I don't need to take your keys for a bit, do I?"

"I haven't got anything to hide, Officer."

The large, uniformed man nodded seriously and turned and headed back for the diner. Henry watched as Clark quickly made it through the glass door and took the wallet from the stool where Henry had stupidly left it then exited to the parking lot again. As he ambled more slowly back to the truck he opened the wallet and took out Henry's ID. Henry almost objected, almost hollered that Clark's actions amounted to an illegal search, but he wasn't even sure of the matter. Perhaps he'd given the man permission. Nervous and anxious and breathing hard again, he couldn't remember the events of the past two minutes.

Clark got back to the truck where Henry was still sitting and took a long look at both the title and the driver's license and then stepped back to look at Henry's license plate and then nodded and shrugged.

He said: "Well, I guess it checks out, then. There was a black Ford reported stolen a few days ago. Stolen from a guy who lives here in Burkburnett. I don't reckon this is the one."

"I bought this truck a few months ago."

"The title says you purchased it way down in Galveston."

"Yes sir."

"And you say you're on your way to Oklahoma?"

"Yes sir."

"Where, exactly?"

Henry paused for just a beat then said Wichita.

"Any particular reason you've got you a whole wad of cash?"

Clark's meddling and pushiness was really starting to aggravate Henry.

Henry said: "Christmas gift from my grandmother."

"Hmm. All right." He handed Henry's papers back over and nodded once toward Henry and told Henry to drive safely and stay out of scraps with men who could obviously whoop his ass.

Henry said yes sir one more time and stood and watched Officer Clark re-enter the café. Henry could see from out in the dark night the entire well-lit café. Clark walked back over to his booth and sat down. Henry watched as Doris balanced several plates and served the group. Then

The Heresy of Rain

Henry walked around to the driverside and climbed in and then leaned over and shoved everything back into the glovebox and took his map of Northern Texas and Oklahoma and tried to read it in the dark and asked himself: why didn't he take the map inside where it was light?

He looked into his rearview mirror before backing out and could again see into the restaurant. Officer Clark was back on his feet, at the cash register now, near where Henry was seated a few minutes before. Clark was talking on a phone whose cord ran behind the counter toward the register. Clark talked for a few seconds more and then peered into the dark evening toward Henry's truck. Then he motioned to his fellow officers, who began to rise. Clark looked back toward the parking lot and then handed the phone to Doris and walked back to the booth where he retrieved his hat. By now, Henry had started the engine and was backing out. The officers hurried outside, but Henry did not wait around to see what had caused their quick exit. He was on the highway, rushing toward Central Oklahoma before the four officers were in their vehicles.

HE DROVE SLOWLY TOWARD OKLAHOMA CITY but still arrived well before midnight. He parked his truck at a motel and walked for a while, finally locating the Orange Club. He walked back to his truck and climbed inside. It was now after one in the morning. He cracked the windows open just a bit and slid over to the passengerside and leaned against the passenger door and draped his jacket over his shoulders and chest and went to sleep. Less than an hour later he was rattled out of his sleep by a man who stood outside his truck. The man was pounding on the window and saying loudly, "No sleeping in the parking lot; you want to sleep here then you get a room." Henry nodded and slid back over to the driverside and started the truck and drove away. After a few minutes he found a small park and pulled into the empty parking lot and went to sleep again.

He awoke mid-morning with a start. He did not remember immediately where he was, and he looked outside half-expecting to see the entire Oklahoma City Police Department surrounding his truck. There were no police officers. This day had dawned blue and clear. Cold but sharp. There were two women playing tennis in the small adjacent park. They wore sweatpants and jackets against the chill. A man was walking his small dog, and another man sat at a picnic table reading and drinking coffee, which steamed from the paper cup. Henry opened the glovebox and then closed it and then checked his wallet to confirm he still had his cash and then climbed out of the truck and locked the door. He flipped up his jacket collar against the wind. The man at the picnic table looked at him and nodded, and Henry nodded hello in return. He stretched and walked to the sidewalk and headed deeper into town to find something to eat.

After eating a late breakfast at a drugstore lunch counter Henry walked the streets of Oklahoma City until he came to the public library. He sat on the steps for a while and then stood and ran his hand through his hair and then went inside. He spent a few hours reading. Having struggled in school from boredom or inattentiveness or reluctance, he had never read for more than a few minutes at a time. He read about the history of Oklahoma music, central Oklahoma's surprisingly rich jazz and blues tradition.

Just before sundown he walked back to his truck and drove to the Orange Club. He parked almost a half mile from the club and walked along the street, and when he arrived at the front door thought perhaps he was terribly underdressed, but it was too late to do anything about it. He paid the two-dollar cover and entered the club. In some ways it reminded him of Sammie's. There was a kind of plushness to the place. Round tables, a bar, thick carpeting, wainscoting and some wood paneling. The Orange Club was a little rawer than Sammie's. Crystal and glass were replaced by this club's pewter and mahogany. It was classy but rustic. The bar was full already, so Henry found a two-seat hightop and climbed up and waited. The place was almost full. There were people in cowboy hats and bolo ties and fedoras with tweed jackets and blue jeans with bow ties and newsboy caps. Women wore pearls or opals or furs but also cocktail dresses with white boas or out-of-vogue straight, formless flapper dresses with translucent shawls. There were white people and black people and Hispanic people. There were elderly couples and middle-aged couples with their grown children and singles and university students. The waiter reminded him there was a two-drink minimum, so Henry ordered a whiskey and waited patiently for Octavian Pace to begin his first set. Toward the front of the room there was a trap set for the drummer and a fine looking black upright piano and a tall upright bass.

Finally, the Octavian Pace Rhythm Trio appeared to much applause and some whistling and hollering. The trio wasted no time. They played "Twelfth Street Rag" and "April in Paris" and "Oh, Lady Be Good" and "Summertime." And then they played half a dozen others. Henry recognized each jazz standard, of course, but it was a marvel the way the trio was able to put its own stamp on each number. Henry ordered another whiskey. The trio closed the first set with a hot arrangement of "Bicycle Built for Two," which Henry had never heard as a jazz number. The house loved it. The drummer and bassist were excellent musicians to be sure, but Henry's attention was focused on the pianist, Octavian Pace. Henry was seated at his back, perhaps twenty feet away. Because he was sitting at a hightop, he could watch Pace's hands. Pace played these triplet riffs up and down with his right hand, but instead of crossing under his thumb and forefinger he would play the majority of the riffs with his pinky and ring finger. This left his thumb and forefinger and middle finger free to change directions or dance about into different chords. The dexterity had a dizzying effect. Henry had never seen anything like it. He had heard Pace play on his albums but seeing his technique in person was hypnotic. There was a short intermission during which Pace and his combo members walked over to the bar and had a drink. The club's buzz did not dip or falter; the air was alive. Waiters dashed about with cocktails as if gliding on the floor. Henry ordered a third whiskey.

Whereas Octavian Pace's first set consisted mainly of traditional music, ragtime, and jazz standards, his second set was strictly the blues. He and his rhythm trio started the set with "Catfish Blues." The bassist's solo was a crowd favorite. He closed his eyes and moved his lips as if singing along with his bass. He cradled the mahogany instrument as if it were his child and swiveled it to time on its peg. The drummer had switched to highhat brushes, and Pace sat out for the entire three-minute solo. Then they performed "Mean Old World" and "Stormy Monday" and ten other blues numbers. They closed the evening with a medley of "Walking Blues" and "It Hurts Me Too." The trio received a rousing applause from the house, and people finished their drinks and paid their checks and finished their conversations and began filing out of the club. It was almost midnight. Henry waited until most people had left. Then he placed a five-dollar bill on the table and climbed down from his seat and moved slowly toward the bar. Octavian Pace was seated at the bar with his back to Henry. He wrapped up a short conversation with a few club patrons and turned toward his drink. Henry got the barman's attention and cleared his throat and said he'd like to buy Mr. Pace a drink.

"Kid, it's late. Get on out. We're about closed."

"Could you at least ask him if he'd let me buy him a drink?"

The barman shook his head and said: "I said beat it, kid. He doesn't have time."

Octavian Pace placed his glass on the bar and turned to Henry and shrugged and looked at the barman and said: "I've got a few minutes if this young man wants to buy me a drink." He looked at Henry again and said: "What do you think about a Tom Collins?"

"Sounds good to me."

Pace said to the barman: "Let's have a couple Tom Collins cocktails."

The barman sighed and rolled his eyes and went to mixing the drinks.

The Heresy of Rain

Henry sat next to Octavian Pace at the bar. Pace had close-cropped hair, and his skin was the color of jasper and his eyes deep and black and soulful. Henry said: "I sure appreciate it."

"Hell, I appreciate it. You're the one buying the drinks."

Henry smiled and said: "Look, I know you hear this all the time. But this is a rare treat for me. Back at home I've got your records worn out."

Pace said: "I'm grateful for your patronage." The barman placed the drinks in front of the two men. Henry's sloshed a bit. Pace said: "And I appreciate the cocktail."

Henry said: "Maybe this is a dumb question, I don't know. You probably get it often. But how do you play those riffs with your right hand? Just using your pinky and ring finger? I didn't realize you did that until tonight when I saw you play."

Octavian Pace just chuckled and took a sip of his drink.

Henry said: "I'm serious. I play piano myself, and I can't see how you run up and down the keyboard without crossing under with your thumb. I apologize if I'm asking you a silly question, but how do you have the control and muscle strength with your weak fingers?"

"I'll tell you. I wish I could say it's because I was born a piano virtuoso or because I've got uncommon dexterity." He laughed heartily. "The truth is, when I was fifteen I was playing baseball with my friends back in Montreal—"

"You grew up in Canada?"

Another big laugh. "You think we don't have jazz in Canada? Did you know Gil Evans is from Canada? And Jackie Washington? And Charlie Biddle and Maynard Ferguson and Oliver Jones? You've heard of these guys, right?"

"Yes, of course I have. I'm sorry."

"That's all right." He chuckled. "Anyhow, I was playing baseball with a big group of friends. I was the catcher that day. We had one catcher's mitt for lefties, and it was a goddamn piece of shit. Threadbare and colorless. Jesus, we may as well have been using an old oven mitt. Anyhow, I was catcher. And I reached out with my right hand to catch a pitch from Sal Winters, and old Deuce Ferris was batting. He's a lefty too. Old Deuce swung and missed, and on his follow-through he caught me square in the back of the glove. Fractured my middle finger and my forefinger and bruised the goddamn hell out of my thumb. The doctor, bless his soul, did a miracle for me. But my forefinger and middle finger were taped together for months, and my thumb was bruised to hell and useless."

"So you didn't have a choice but to learn a new way."

"You got it. My two little fingers had to pick up the slack."

Henry smiled and looked at his glass and took a slow sip, trying to drag out this experience, so he'd have something happy to remember when his heart started hurting again.

Pace turned back to Henry: "You said you play some piano?"

"Yes sir. Down at Galveston. At a restaurant called Sammie's."

"Sammie's?"

"Yeah, on the island."

Octavian Pace let out another wheezy belly laugh. "Oh my, oh my. Good old Sammie's near the seawall."

"You've been there?"

"Yes, I have. Played a couple nights at Sammie's, back I'd say, ten years ago or more. I enjoyed that club. Great acoustics. A joy to play. Those folks down on the Texas Coast like their jazz, don't they?"

"Yeah, they do. I was the house pianist until recently."

"No shit?"

"Yeah."

"But not anymore?"

"Right."

"Why the hell not?"

"Well, I'm laying low for a while."

"Huh. Laying low. You get yourself into trouble with the law?"

"Yeah, I think so."

"That's too bad. Why can't musicians stay out of trouble?"

"That's a good question."

"How about you step over there and show me a little of what you got?" Octavian said, motioning toward the piano.

"Now?" The club was just about empty. Waiters were bussing tables and sweeping floors and emptying ashtrays.

"You got somewhere else to be?"

"No, I'd just be a little nervous is all."

"Get on, now."

Henry put a few bills on the bar for the drinks and walked over to the majestic black upright on the dais. He'd never seen a piano with this sort of detailed artistry carved in, like relief sculpture done in black onyx. He stared at the instrument while the bassist and drummer stepped back a bit and joined Pace at the bar.

Henry sat on the bench and closed his eyes for a bit and ran his hand through his hair and took a deep breath. Then he played a vamp he'd composed a couple years before, a four-bar introduction repeated three times. Without having a chance to warm up and get a feel for the piano, the vamp gave him a chance to gather himself. And then he played about two minutes of "Body and Soul." He had his eyes closed still, and he rocked with the rhythm and shook his head soulfully. After a time, he brought his number to an end and looked up at Octavian Pace with embarrassment.

Henry said: "Sorry, I didn't mean to go so long."

Pace applauded slowly for a moment and then said: "Son, I believe you've got the blues. I can see why you had a steady gig down there."

Henry said thanks shyly and turned on the bench to face the other man.

Pace continued: "Did you write the vamp or just improv a bit to get a feel?"

"I wrote it; just a few bars I put together a couple years ago. I can use it for 'Body and Soul' or 'Crosscut Saw' or even 'Key to the Highway.'"

"Very nice. I like your phrasing, and where did you learn to play that left hand like that? I love how you thump it to keep time."

"I just practiced at my grandmother's house when I was a kid."

"Ha! Grandmother's house." A pause as Octavian Pace stared smirking at his new friend. "How about you meet me in Kansas City in a few weeks?"

"Kansas City?"

"I'll be stopped in Kansas City for about a week, maybe a little longer. I think I know a few guys who would be interested in talking to you. If not for recording then for some rhythm combo work."

"I don't think that would be a good idea."

"Because you're laying low?"

"Right."

"You must be in some real trouble."

"I think I am."

"Damn, but you can play."

"Some days better than others."

Octavian Pace said: "It's like that, isn't it? Some days are better than others."

"Seems that way."

Pace leaned forward a bit and nodded his head. Henry still sat a few yards away on the piano bench. Pace said: "Some days we just got it. Like it all comes together. And we wonder why every day isn't like that. You follow baseball any?"

"Sure."

"It's like a pitcher who has his best stuff on a given day. He's in the zone. Maybe he's always a good pitcher. Maybe he's a hall of famer. But some days he's got some extra zip or his knuckleball dances a little more than usual. It's the same with music. Some days it's a struggle, my left hand can't keep up, or I'm stumbling over riffs. Then there are those special days. It's like the universe has channeled everything toward me. Maybe it's the perfect weather and the perfect piano or the shirt I'm wearing or the time of day or what I had for breakfast or the woman I was with the night before. Who knows. But the universe has funneled all of this positive energy, this musical energy, to me and the light or energy of the universe just fires right through the tips of my fingers."

"I know what you mean."

"Wish every day could be like that."

"For you, it seems most are."

Pace chuckled. "Don't be so sure. I've just become skilled at covering my mistakes. Also, I've had some bad times, some real bad times. So on those days when I don't have my best fastball, I just think about those times. Friends I've lost, for instance. Or times when I didn't know where my next meal was coming from. It's amazing how you can summon up that sadness sometimes and just will yourself into playing with more soul."

"Yeah." Henry's face became gray and morose. Suddenly he was very tired.

"You know that kind of sadness?"

"I do."

"I'm sorry to hear that. And I hope you don't have to lay low for too much longer. I'd like to meet you again sometime."

"Well, I appreciate it. I'll keep the invitation in mind."

The Heresy of Rain

Henry stood from the bench and took a few steps toward the bar. The barman stood staring at Henry with his arms folded and his lips pursed like some insolent little boy who's been held late after school. Henry said: "Thanks for sharing the drink with me. And for talking to me."

The men shook hands, and Henry left the club and walked to his truck and climbed in and sat in the driver's seat and smiled to himself. Then he drove back to the small park where he'd slept the night before. The night was cold. He rolled the windows down just a few inches and closed his eyes for a few hours before heading back to the motel in Brewster County. Just before dawn he woke with a start after another dream. He rubbed his eyes and yawned and took up the map and figured a route back to Texas that wouldn't take him through Burkburnett. Within an hour he had a cup of coffee and a small box of doughnuts.

Just south of the Oklahoma-Texas border, Henry stopped at a filling station with a payphone and filled up and then got his dimes ready and made the call. It was mid-morning. The sun was rising toward its topmost point. Everything was awash in sunlight. It was very cold. It was a Saturday, so he knew she wouldn't be at the diner.

"Hello?"

"I'm glad you're home."

"Henry!" Charlotte sounded giddy. Like a small child.

"Can you meet me at the bridge today?"

"You're here?"

"I'm a few hours away. I'll pass through Andrews. No one can know I'm in town, though. All right? No one."

"I won't tell anyone."

"Can you get to the bridge a little after noon?"

"Yes. Yes, I'll be there."

"I can only stay for a bit. But I'd like to see you."

Three hours later he had sneaked his way into Andrews County near the Texas-New Mexico border. He parked in a clearing near the footbridge, his truck partially hidden in the trees and undergrowth. Henry could see the bridge from the spot where he parked the truck. Charlotte was already there. The sun was high and bright, but the air was still cold. She turned when she heard him approach, and she popped up and skittered back across the planks and jumped toward Henry, and they embraced.

Then he pulled away from her and saw she had tears in her eyes. She told him he looked much better than the last time she saw him, with the injuries from that night in the diner. She told him she missed him and thought she would never see him again. She told him she didn't have any friends. She told him all of her old friends were mad at her and refused to talk to her because in their eyes it was her fault Davey was arrested. She gripped his arm so tightly it hurt. Henry pulled her over to the middle of the bridge, and they sat on the edge with their legs dangling off like school children.

He said: "I came here to tell you everything. I can't stay long. And I can't take you with me when I leave. But I owe you the full story."

She stared off into the distance, across the creek and across the flat land and all the way to the horizon. She wore light tan pants and sneakers and had on a thick white and red jacket. Her sandy hair was pulled back.

She said: "I've heard some things already."

"I'm sure you have."

"I heard you did something bad at home down at the Coast and fled from the police. And then you left Andrews when you knew the law was about to catch up with you. I'm not sure I believe it, though. I also heard Mr. Whitman was covering for you and could have given you up but didn't."

"All right."

"Is any of it true?"

"It's all true, more or less."

"Henry." She tilted her head and closed her eyes in sorrow.

"But I came here to tell you the complete truth of it. I owe you an explanation. You were my friend, and I didn't tell you everything."

"Okay."

So Henry told her everything, from the beginning. He told her his mother abandoned him when he was only in the fourth grade and that his grandmother raised him from that point. He told her his father had died years before that, and it sent his mother over the edge. He told her he learned to play the piano and practiced and practiced and spent hours every day listening to records of the masters playing the blues and how he started playing at Sammie's. And how his grandmother died when he was sixteen. And how he dropped out of school to play piano at Sammie's full time. And he told her how he met Grace outside a small church in Galveston and that Grace was blind and that Grace loved to listen to him play and how he wrote songs for her that helped her sleep at night. Charlotte wiped her eyes, and Henry's eyes glassed over as he told Charlotte that he started playing cards in a back room at Sammie's. And he confessed to Charlotte that he ran up an incredible debt and he couldn't pay it, so some goons looted his home and killed Grace in the process even though she was helpless and innocent. Charlotte gripped Henry's arm tightly again as he said he used what little money he had left to buy a gun and the truck. He told her he tried to kill the gang's leader but ended up wounding a few guys instead and that the police chief is his godfather and that the police chief is doubtlessly searching for him and that he's the man who was in the diner that day not so long ago. And lastly, he told Charlotte how he's close to tracking down the man who killed Grace, and that's the last thing he needs to do. Then they both stared into the distance and didn't say anything for a long time.

Then she said: "You don't have to do it. You don't have to find him." She was pleading, pleading.

"Yes, I do."

"Why?"

"Because if I don't then who will?"

"Let the police find him."

"The police know where he is. He's not hiding. I am."

"Then let the police arrest him."

"They don't have enough evidence, or they would have by now."

"How do you know they haven't?"

"I just do."

She sighed heavily but did not let go of his arm, and she dropped her head and looked at the water below. Then she tucked a strand of hair behind her ear. And she asked him one more time to reconsider.

"I'm sorry," he said.

"You're still young. Why throw your life away?"

"My life's over. My godfather knows I shot those guys in Galveston. I'll never escape that."

"Run off to Mexico."

"You aren't the first person to suggest that."

"Then maybe you should consider it."

They were silent for a long time. They stared not at each other but into the distance. They both knew this was the last time they would speak to one another. A pair of doves left the ground from the underbrush near the creek and flitted about for a time and then engaged in a kind of ritual spiraling and then took off together toward the horizon and then disappeared as if into the ether.

"Charlotte, I can never love again. Don't you see? I don't know how to explain it. I don't know how to describe it to you. It's as if all my love, in the past and the future, was invested in Grace. And now it's gone. I don't know how else to explain it."

"You haven't given it enough time."

"I'm sorry."

"So now you'll leave?"

"Yes. I'll head out again soon."

"Where?"

"You know I'm not going to tell you."

"You think I'm going to follow you?"

"No. But I think you'd try to stop me somehow."

"You're right. I would."

He stood up and pulled her up with him, and they hugged there on the footbridge. The cold brown water trickled over rocks and then out of sight around the bend. The sun was still bright and fierce but not warm. He smoothed her hair and tucked the strand behind her ear and kissed her on the forehead and then thanked her for meeting him. She just bit her lip and nodded as the tears flooded her cheeks. He said again he was sorry and that he never meant for any of this to happen. She only nodded and cried.

Then he said softly in her ear: "Don't marry that son of a bitch, Davey."

She tried to laugh but couldn't and nodded again and said: "Don't worry. I won't marry that son of a bitch."

Then he cupped her face with one hand and stroked her cheek with the back of his fingers and then looked down and turned and left her there on the footbridge in the day's brightness. She stood sobbing and then sat with her legs dangling over the edge and cried bitterly with her elbows on her lap and her face in her hands. Henry still heard her crying when he got to his truck. Then he climbed in and closed his eyes for several seconds and sat still and then started the truck and headed back to Brewster County.

He drove on through the afternoon and approached Alpine, Texas just before dusk. The air was frigid, but the sky was alight. There were golds and reds and brilliant oranges against the Chisos Mountains, as if the horizon was ablaze, as if the mountains themselves formed the core of some heavenly forge or cauldron or oven, with the fire swirling out of the valley. Henry drove straight to the Cattleman Grill and eased into a parking spot and waited for almost an hour. There were just a few cars, all familiar to Henry by now. Nothing amiss. Nothing new. Nothing actionable. Henry began to think not for the first time that it was all just nothing. So he drove to the motel and counted his money and paid for another week and went to his room and slept like he was dead.

Canto 9

THE HOSPITAL WAS WHITE AND STERILE. It was all angles and sharpness. It bore with it no feeling and conveyed only a sense of harshness. It was overclean. It was not a place for dying. It was a place for death. Everything in the hospital was the result of meticulous planning and precise measurement. The beds and desks and triage stations and doors were all portioned against some unseen calibration. There was white. And where there wasn't white there was the uncaring glint of steel. It was a place for death.

On the hospital's second floor there was a small wing for those with respiratory ailments. This was a section reserved for the sickest of Galveston's numerous sufferers. Patients would go into such awful and violent fits of coughing that their very beds would shake and scrape along the floor. A nurse or some other hospital official would hurry to the miserable wretch and instead of comforting the patient would use her leg or hip to scoot the bed back to its original spot just inches this way or that, as if the bed were a coffee table or a dining chair. The patients of this wing could breathe only with the help of the oxygen pumped from green tanks through tubes and into their lungs via a rubber mask or cannula.

For a person concerned with dignity, this was no way to die.

This was no way to die.

Henry's grandmother's bed was along the far wall. In this large communal room there were six beds. Six women of varying ages dying amid a web of tubing like poor houseflies caught by a terrible spider and now waiting patiently and alertly to be put to death. Her bed was like all the others: a steel-framed twin with linens of only the most brilliant and blinding white. Between her bed and the bed of her neighbor there was a dock with large green tanks of oxygen. In the saddest way possible their breathing had synched, and they wheezed together in perfect unison.

At the foot of her bed there was a clipboard that held together a number of important and private documents. On the top page in large, thick black letters was PNEUM. Lung cancer had its designation, as did emphysema and all kinds of fibrosis and asthma and even the occasional anachronistic tuberculosis. In her late sixties Ellie Ballard was expected to make it another few hours or maybe a day and then that was it. The hospital would have an opening in the lung wing for another wheezer set to expire loudly within a short time, another poor soul diagnosed to rasp to death.

Henry sat on a sterile silver chair next to his grandmother's sterile bed. It had been more than ten years since his father's death, but he barely remembered that. In his mind this would be the first meaningful loss of his life. He sat very close to the bed with one hand on his grandmother's arm and the other holding up his head. He could not even voice his profound sadness. His grandmother tried to smile for him to show she was happy about meeting Jesus in just a little while. This was no comfort for a young man who was about to be all alone in the world.

She removed the mask and motioned for Henry to bring the cannula to her nose. She would be able to breathe like this for only a few minutes until she would again need the mask, but maybe that was the point.

"Listen, sweetheart."

"Don't talk. Save your strength."

"Save my strength? For what?"

"I don't know. I don't know."

"Listen to me while I can still talk."

"All right." The tears welled up in his eyes. He felt exposed and frightened. He was not ready for this. He was not ready for the world.

"There's a slip of paper in my jewelry box. Top compartment. It's blue. It's got your mother's address on it."

"I don't care about her."

"One day you might want to square things with her. Or you might need her help. Take the paper and don't lose it."

He nodded.

"Also. You take care of that piano."

"All right."

"I want you to remember me with your music, Henry. I'll be a batshit crazy angel flying about in heaven, dancing to my grandson's music."

"You shouldn't curse in here."

"Are they going to kick me out if I do?"

He smiled sadly and shook his head and wiped his eyes with his sleeve.

She said she loved him and don't ever forget that, and then she had a violent fit of coughing and rasping and asked him to return the mask.

A few hours later she was dead, and Henry was alone.

He walked around the island in a daze, thinking to himself that it wasn't fair. Perhaps at some point he realized this was not an issue of fairness but rather an issue of what is. Destiny has no favorites. She is steadfast and resolute. Perhaps she suffers with the miserable. Perhaps she aches with the wretched.

But she has no favorites.

Canto 10

It was springtime, and Henry led Grace into a small bungalow on 8th Street not far from the beach. It was not the prettiest house on a street with very few pretty houses. The neighborhood was not rundown and dilapidated, but it was a working-class neighborhood with houses that suited the working class.

"How many is this today?"

Henry gripped her hand firmly and gave her a playful tug.

He said: "This is the sixth. Or seventh?"

The real estate agent had already disappeared into the house and commenced with turning on the lights and chasing the roaches back into their dark corners.

"I'm exhausted," Grace said. "We've been visiting houses all day. Our wedding is in three weeks, and we don't even have a florist. And we're worried about buying a house?"

"There's got to be someplace for me to carry you after the wedding."

They stood just inside the door of the bungalow. The real estate agent was clopping around somewhere in a bedroom.

"Carry me anywhere. It doesn't matter to me as long as you're the one carrying me."

They took a few more steps, hand in hand. It appeared Grace had formed a word on her lips, but she said nothing. Merely, she let her shoulders rise and then fall with a sigh.

She asked: "What do you think?"

"What do *you* think?"

"What am I supposed to think? These are all the same. They smell the same, they feel the same."

"Yeah. They do smell the same and feel the same. They look more or less the same too."

"Then why are we are doing this?"

"Doing what? Looking for a house to buy?"

"Yeah. You have a house."

"It's my grandmother's house."

"And?"

"I thought you wanted to get a new house."

"I thought *you* wanted to get a new house."

He said: "It's home. To me, it's home. It's been home for years. I thought maybe you wanted to start fresh, get a place that's ours instead of mine."

"It can be ours," she said. "It should be ours."

He looked at her and smiled, though he knew she couldn't see him.

"Then I guess it's settled."

"It is."

They walked back through the door toward the street, Grace clinging tightly to Henry's arm and her head on his shoulder, and the whole of life beckoning and familiar.

Part VI

"I screamed above the pounding storm and threw my body to the earth above his. For a long time, it seemed forever, I lay there crying, sheltering my fallen scarlet ibis from the heresy of rain."

–James Hurst

The Heresy of Rain

HENRY SPENT HIS DAYS IDLING ABOUT in his motel room or reading the newspaper. Often he wore his jacket against the cold and strolled the grounds of the motel or the neighboring area. He would sometimes walk to the café in town or stand and stare at the church across the street from the motel. Always the woman sat on the same bench. He finally strolled over to where she was sitting, his head down and his hands in his pockets.

The woman was old. She was rough and worn with dark skin. She was the matron of everything but the mother of no one. Her black eyes were obsidian, and her silver hair was tied back with a thick turquoise ribbon. She was regal and dwarfish, with hardened hands that had touched the world and grasped every knowable sadness the world could possibly offer and with those hands overcame the world's sharpness and with her fingers smoothed over uncountable rough spots. Those hands bled, too, and her ancient heart had bled for a million souls both good and evil. For she was the dame of all enterprise, a woman ageless and expressionless who bore the burden of all humanity.

"I've seen you here for many days now," she said without judgment. She sat with both hands resting on top of a walking staff.

"I'm sorry."

"Sorry? Why should you be sorry for walking the grounds of a motel? There isn't any sorrow in that."

"I mean, I'm sorry for interrupting you, for—"

"Do you always apologize so much?"

"I suppose. I don't know."

"Why don't you sit for a few minutes?"

"All right. Thank you." He sat on the chipped and faded bench. He felt honored to share the seat with this woman he did not know.

"Anyhow, you aren't interrupting anything. This is nothing." She took one hand from the knob of her walking stick or staff and motioned widely. "The weather is cold, and the sky is slate. Yes? But it is nothing. Certainly, it is nothing subject to interruption."

Across the street at the church people began exiting through the wide doors. The service had ended, and soon worshipers would mill about. The people were dressed proudly, the men and boys in their good brown pants and their starched-white dress shirts but no tie or jacket, and the women and girls in their gray woolen dresses and black sweaters. Some held bibles or pocketbooks, and some of the men and older boys separated themselves slightly from the larger group to roll and smoke a cigarette while the women chatted happily. Some of the young children, dark-skinned boys and girls with their big white smiles, made piles of leaves or played tag. Finally, everyone had exited the small building, and the preacher walked out, too, with his black-rimmed glasses and kind eyes.

Henry said: "Is that a catholic church?"

"No," said the old woman. "It is a nondenominational church. But there is no difference."

"Sure there is."

"A difference? No. No."

"What do you mean?"

"I mean, it doesn't matter. Are there fundamental differences between a catholic church and a protestant church? Sure, of course. Are there fundamental differences in the way they worship and pray and congregate and tithe and commune? I suppose." She shrugged to show how little it mattered.

"You think it doesn't matter?"

"I know it doesn't matter."

"All right," Henry said, "but do you mean it doesn't matter because people can reach heaven in different ways?"

"No. I mean it doesn't matter because there is no heaven."

"How can you be so certain of that?"

"Maybe because I am old and know more than one person should know. I've seen more than one person should see. Mostly I know there is no heaven because I know there is no hell."

Henry chuckled lightly and shook his head.

She said with no emotion: "I'm glad you find me funny. Good for you. People don't often find me funny."

"I'm sorry, it's just—"

"If you apologize one more time I will hit you with this stick."

"Why do you dislike apologies?"

"I don't dislike apologies. What an absurd notion. What I dislike is insincerity. Do you understand? When people say they are sorry as some sort of kneejerk reaction or apologize out of a feeling of discomfort or awkwardness, it is insincere. Sorrow is like love."

"How so?"

"Think about your life, young man. Your whole life. How many people have received your love? To how many people have you said, I love you?"

"Two."

"You see? You didn't hesitate. Why should sorrow be any different? You've said you are sorry to dozens or hundreds, probably. Shouldn't we be at least somewhat as selective when deciding who receives our sorrow as who receives our love?"

"I understand now."

"Good. Look at those people across the street. All of those beautiful people and their children. These are people who are uneducated and poor. They are so, so poor, with very few material possessions. But they are so happy. Right now, they are not thinking about whether their children will eat supper every night this week. The men are not thinking about how they will never be able to feed or clothe the children their wives are carrying in their bellies. The women are not thinking about how they will not be able to keep their homes warm tonight against the terrible cold."

"All right."

"But they are happy because they love one another. That is sincere love you see. Authentic. These are not people who apologize as some sort of societal nicety. You know why?"

"Why?"

"Because they understand the value of sincerity. They know they owe each other the truth." She glanced at Henry. "That is all we owe each other in this world."

"The truth?"

"Honesty and sincerity, yes. We owe each other so very little, but at least there is honesty. We must be honest with one another."

"If you believe we owe each other honesty and you believe there is no heaven or hell, then why don't you go over there and tell them?"

"That would be a despicable thing to do."

"How so?"

"Two reasons. One, they are very happy. To deprive someone of happiness for so senseless a reason is despicable. Two, they have not solicited my opinion."

"But it's fine to tell me there is no heaven or hell?"

"You are not happy. I have deprived you of nothing."

"I'm not sure I solicited your opinion."

She waved him off. "It's no matter."

After a few seconds he said: "If you believe there is no heaven or hell, then you must believe there is no god."

"Yes, there is no god."

"How can you be so sure of such a thing?"

She seemed to ignore him. "I believe in the tenacity of the human spirit."

"But not god?"

She was silent for a moment. Then she said: "People have been religious for more than two hundred thousand years. Religion predates human beings even. There is evidence, if you read about such things, that these beings who came before us buried their dead in epitaphic arrangements, as if there were some sort of tradition that preceded them and that the afterlife was important. Two hundred thousand years ago. And with each successive century, each passing millennium, religion became a more and more significant part of humanity. By the time human beings had suffered their way to the Neolithic Age—do you know what I mean by Neolithic?"

He shook his head no.

"I mean roughly ten thousand BC. Twelve thousand years ago."

"All right."

"So by this time, this new stone age, the world was a smattering of small kingdoms that we would call theocracies. Religion ruled the day. Then move forward another six or seven thousand years, and there are the Egyptians. Then the Greeks, the Romans, the Anglo-Saxons, the Vikings, and so forth."

"All right."

"Each of these civilizations was deeply rooted in religion, in gods of its own."

"Why is that a bad thing?"

"I'm not judging, young man. I don't claim to evaluate the goodness or badness of religion, just the rightness or wrongness. That is all."

"Fine."

"So this is my point: my point is that each of these civilizations, starting with the prehumans and all the way up to the New World and beyond, all of these people's religions have been disproved or abandoned. Religion is not transcendent the way people might like to think. It does not stand the test of time."

"So god does not stand the test of time?"

"Exactly. What makes those people across the street think they are more correct than some poor Egyptian or Nubian or Phoenician of long ago? There is no difference. In time their god will be disproven and abandoned as well as all the others. The very notion of god is an insult to nature."

"I'm not so sure."

She glanced at him in such a way that dared him to challenge her thesis.

He said: "What if someone is finally right? So dozens or hundreds of civilizations have been wrong about god for thousands of years. That doesn't make these people wrong." He tilted his head to indicate the gatherers across the way.

She said: "Consider my forebears."

He cocked his head and raised an eyebrow.

"My ancestors. A whole hodgepodge of Mexicans and Native Americans or Indians and so forth. They worshipped whatever invisible force was beneficial or convenient. We did rain dances and ghost dances and sun dances and dances that were rites of passage and prayed over bison and elk and wolves and sacrificed our babies and sacrificed our enemies and sacrificed our warriors and built temples and longhouses and burial sites. This has all been abandoned by right-thinking people."

"But it's still a part of your tradition. Your heritage."

"There's nothing wrong with tradition. It is true we shouldn't forget where we come from. That's fine, even important. But we should not cling to beliefs just because we've always held them dear. How ridiculous would it be if I were to go into the middle of the street and do a rain dance or start yammering some nonsensical chants about ghosts?"

"It would be pretty ridiculous."

"Because we've moved past it."

"Not everyone has."

"You are probably right. But there are also people in the world who live in mud huts and hunt with spears."

There was a reticent lull while the worshipers across the street began to make their way home in separate directions.

Henry said: "Then what is there?"

"What do you mean?"

"If there is no god and no heaven or hell, what is there?"

"There is nothing."

"Darkness?"

"No. Darkness is something. I am saying nothing."

"What do you mean when you say there is nothing?"

"I mean the world as you see it today, right now, is the result of millions or billions of years of particles whizzing about and clashing and forces working with or against each other and conflicts both microscopic and megascopic. Perhaps time and space are the same, as some scientists would like us to think. But whatever the case, here we are. We are no more or less than what we can see with our eyes. So when we die we close our eyes to nothing. There is no existence beyond this."

"You think our existence is owed entirely to science?"

"You make it seem too distasteful."

"I have a hard time thinking there is nothing controlling us."

"You want to be controlled?"

"Not controlled, exactly. Guided, maybe."

"Then what are you doing on this side of the street?" She looked at him and raised one eyebrow and curved her lips into something like a smile. "Ah, well. It's too late today anyhow. The churchgoers seem to have disappeared until next week."

"So that's it? There's nothing at all? What happens when we die?"

"Nothing happens. We die."

"You believe there's no reclamation or redemption or salvation?"

"We are free to pursue those things while we are alive."

He slumped his shoulders a bit and rested against the arm of the bench. "But what is the point, then?"

"The point of what?"

"The point of life? What does it matter? The meaning of life?"

"The meaning of life. I think that's an odd way of framing the concept. Perhaps we should, in the spirit of clarity, put it this way: what is the purpose of our lives? Each of our lives individually."

The Heresy of Rain

"Fine. What is the purpose of our lives?"

"The preservation of humanity."

"That's it?"

She chuckled lightly and closed her eyes for a moment. "That's no small thing. Our collective purpose is to allow for those who come after us a fighting chance. Progress, perhaps. We should endeavor to contribute something positive to the world, to humanity."

"But not everyone does that. Not everyone cares. What about people who do bad things? People who sin."

"This is an unfortunate by-product of absolute freedom, yes? Perhaps it's the most unfortunate thing about our reality. We are free to do good things but also free to do bad things."

"Then you do believe in good and bad."

"Of course I do. I also believe in music. I believe in poetry. I believe in beauty and art and love. I believe in family. I believe in science. And I believe in horses. I believe in the stars and the wind and history and cats and dogs. I believe in compassion. In second chances and benefits of the doubt. And love. And also, laughing. I believe in laughing. Too, I believe in sacrifice. Sacrifice and redemption. And storytelling. And contribution. Fire and ice. I also believe in honor and charity. I believe in peace, I believe in scholarship, and I believe in family and truth and humility and justice. Perhaps I believe in justice above all. What is there if there is no justice?"

Henry was silent.

She said: "As long as there is justice the world is safe."

Henry said very quietly: "I agree."

"You agree? I thought we would be at odds all afternoon and have to take this up again tomorrow until we find common ground."

He offered a faint smile.

"Young man, here is the truth of things: we have each other, and that is all we have. Don't let my lack of piety suggest to you that I believe in anarchy. Far from it. I said earlier that we owe each other honesty and sincerity. Can we agree there as well?"

He nodded.

"Good. In the end it is up to each of us to decide our purpose. We should each live a life of purpose. We should be kind to one another, and we should live with purpose."

"Let me ask you something else."

"Go ahead."

Henry sighed heavily and stared toward the horizonless sky and then looked at the old woman. He asked her: "Do you believe in karma?"

"You mean a cosmic force that balances the universe? A star-crossed aura that tallies our good deeds and our bad deeds so that we are accordingly punished or rewarded on a carnal or spectral level?"

"Something like that, I guess."

"No, absolutely not. Karma is a thing that exists in people's imagination and in their worldview that is ruled by fairness and equality."

"Something about that doesn't seem right."

"That karma doesn't exist?"

"Right."

"But again, what seems doesn't matter. Only what is matters."

Henry shook his head and peered into the colorless sky.

She said: "Allow me to tell you a quick story about some people I once knew. I grew up not far from here. We had nothing to speak of, just like the people who now live in this area. Nothing. I had three brothers and two sisters, and our neighbors were also overcrowded and underfed and so were their neighbors and so on. The neighborhood, if you can call it that, was entrenched in poverty. One of my younger brothers—and this is the truth; I'm not making this up—one of my younger brothers once threw a five-dollar bill in the garbage because he thought it was trash. He'd never seen currency before. Can you believe that? The sort of penury that drives children to discard money because they don't know what money is? It's true. He was in town looking for food, begging, digging through waste bins. He saw some papers skipping down the street in the wind, and he picked them up. Some of it was trash, but one of the items was a five-dollar bill. Weeks later he saw a picture of a five-dollar bill in a magazine my mother had found and was using to teach us to read English. He told my mother about it, and she began to cry. My father asked what was the matter, and she told him Junior found money but threw it away. My father beat my brother until his own hand was chaffed. Then he apologized a hundred times to my brother and started to cry and went behind our house and moaned to God aloud, asking for forgiveness for beating my brother and asking for God to deliver us from such wretched indigence."

The Heresy of Rain

"That's a hell of a terrible thing. Was your father afraid that karma would somehow come back and punish him for beating your brother?"

"No, of course not. That wasn't my story about karma. That was just an anecdote to illustrate how poor we were."

"All right."

"So it was extreme poverty everywhere. There was a family that lived across the street from us, a little ways down but very close. The children in my family were friendly with the children in this other family. But this was the poorest family in the area. I never saw any of the children wearing shoes. They often ate whatever weeds they could harvest behind their house. They never even dreamed of electricity or running water, even when these things became commonplace. Their clothes were filthy. Much of the time the boys went without shirts. They just ran about in tattered pants. There were nine children in this family. Nine. You've never seen such a destitute group of people. But here is the important part of the story. Every Christmas, this penniless family with the derelict house and the shoeless feet would somehow put together enough resources to bake a few cakes. They were simple yellow cakes made from cornmeal and goat's milk and molasses and maybe an egg. More a tasteless cornbread than cake. They would gather these children and form a little delivery cadre and bring cakes to the neighboring families. It was the most incredible demonstration of generosity I've seen in my life. Not only this, but something else. I can remember a dozen or more occasions during my childhood when the mother and father of this poor family ordered their children to help someone else rebuild a home blown down by a strong wind or search for a lost goat or plant a garden. So my point is this: the terribly impoverished family was always willing to sacrifice what little it had to help others. It was an amazing display of altruism. Certainly, these people were prime candidates for karmic reward. Do you know what happened?"

"What happened?"

"They all died in a fire. It was the day after Christmas. I was eleven years old. To this day it is my single worst memory. It haunts me. There have been times when I wished myself dead, so I wouldn't be forced to endure the memory any longer. The day after Christmas, very early in the morning. Everything was so dry with no rain or moisture for so long. But it was very cold. These people had built a small fire in their fireplace so that they might stay warm during the night. Their house—just like all of our houses—was drafty and poorly built. All wood. No brick or cement or anything. A dirt floor almost throughout. A cinder must have escaped the fireplace while they were asleep. It was the screams that woke us so early in the morning, before dawn. Such painful shrieking. The torture of being burned alive. A few of the children made it outside, but they were already dead. Human torches. Babies aflame. Eleven innocent and loving people. Not only killed by some fluke, but killed in the worst way possible, the most painful way possible. Karma is for the lucky. For the unlucky there is only grief and pain and misery."

"That's a terrible fate for those folks, but that's only one example."

"It's the only example I need. Anyway, history is full of examples like this. Good people meeting terrible ends and bad people seemingly rewarded at every turn. We've enough of a sample size, I believe."

"So you think there's no light at the end of the tunnel? Even in death?"

"Especially in death."

"But what's the point if we die and enter into eternal darkness? If there is nothing?"

She was silent for a moment, thinking. Then she said: "You might say the point is your legacy. We are born, then we live for a while, then we die. But during all of this we have an opportunity to contribute to the world. Listen, this is important. If you leave this bench and decide I'm an age-addled old woman who does ghost dances, please remember this at least: remember to act not always in the spirit of self-interest but in the spirit of contribution. Yes?"

"That's a tall order. Aren't we all guided by self-interest?"

"Perhaps. We are guided by an instinct to survive, certainly. But we should try as much as we can to be givers of second chances and benefits of the doubt."

There was a long silence. Then Henry said: "I don't know. It seems like it would be easier to flounder my way through life and let God sort it all out in the end."

"Eh, maybe. But no one ever guaranteed life would be easy. And don't forget: you are free to believe in your god. After all, what do I know?"

With that, she touched him on the knee and then struggled to stand but finally made it up. The matron of everything gave Henry a soft smile and then walked slowly back to her room.

The Heresy of Rain

IT WAS SATURDAY EVENING, ALMOST DUSK. Henry drove to Cattleman Grill and parked his truck in the shadows of a tree. The parking lot was full. And there were many vehicles he'd not seen in his many visits to the restaurant over the weeks he had lived at the motel. Among the cars and trucks and motorcycles not regular to the restaurant was the sedan Henry had followed in Galveston all of those months ago, the very car that led him from the bait shop to the tavern. He eased his truck out of the parking lot and drove back to the motel. He took his bag and his meager belongings from his room and set them in the passenger seat of his truck. Then he took his remaining money from his pocket and counted the bills. He had one hundred fifty dollars. He went to the motel office for an envelope and stuffed one hundred forty dollars into the envelope and ten dollars back in his pocket. Then he locked his truck and left it at the motel and walked across the street to the small church.

The church was empty and silent. It was a modest wood building painted white. Henry tried the door facing the street, but it was locked. Henry could tell just from tugging at the door that it was locked with a simple hook. Anyone who wanted to pull the door down or kick in the door could do so with little effort. He walked on the gravel and weeds to the side of the building and found a mail slot on the side door. He stood near the door and looked around. There was no sign of anyone, nor were there any vehicles. He put his hand on a window and peered through the glass, but all he saw was darkness within. He sighed heavily and lifted open the creaking metal flap and slid the envelope through the slot. Then he waited a few seconds and started back toward the motel and his waiting truck. He had almost reached the road when he heard someone call him.

"Wait."

Henry turned and saw in the twilight the church pastor. The kind-looking man with the thick-rimmed glasses. Henry put his hands in his pockets and turned and stood. The pastor walked toward him.

"You just put this envelope in the mail?"

Henry nodded and said yes and cleared his throat and then looked down.

"Who are you?"

"My name is Henry. I've been staying at the motel across the street."

"I thought I recognized you."

Henry shrugged but did not reply.

"I wanted to thank you for the offering," said the pastor.

"Sure."

The pastor walked to Henry and offered his hand. Henry shook the man's hand. The pastor said: "My name is Tomas Soto. Most of the folks in the church call me Reverend Tom or just Tom."

"All right. It's good to meet you."

Tom held up the envelope. "This is a lot of money, Henry."

"I figured you all could use it."

"Of course we could use it. I'm just curious about why you gave it to us."

"I don't know. I don't think I'll have any use for it."

"You're sure?"

"I'm sure."

"Perhaps you'd like to attend the service in the morning."

"Well. Maybe. But I doubt it. I guess I'd rather folks not know where the money came from."

"Henry, the people who are members of this church, they have very little. This money, even divided equally among all my regular church attendees, will go a long way. It will be more helpful than you know."

"I thought it might be useful."

"Forgive me for overstepping, but I'm curious. People don't often slide"—he flipped through the bills for a few seconds—"a hundred forty dollars through the mail slot and walk off into the night. In fact, nobody slips a hundred forty dollars through the mail slot and walks off into the night."

"I've been living at that motel for a few weeks. I've watched your congregation come and go. I understand most people around here don't have much. Like I said, I don't think I'll have any use for it."

"Would you come in for a cup of tea with me? I've been working on tomorrow's message, and I've got a bit of writer's block. Perhaps I could discuss generosity."

"No, I've got to head out. But thanks."

Then the reverend looked pensive. He said: "This may seem off-putting, but I have to ask. Did you come by this money honestly?"

"Honestly?"

"I'm sorry for asking. I mean was this money the result of a theft or the sale of contraband or something of the sort?"

Henry smiled and chuckled in spite of himself and the situation. He said: "Yes sir. I came by it honestly. I worked a few months as a dishwasher at a diner in Andrews County."

The pastor put up his hands apologetically. "All right, I'm glad to hear that. Thanks for soothing my silly concerns."

"I guess it's not really silly. Do people often steal money and turn around and give it to a church?"

"You'd be surprised of the things people will do to assuage their guilt. The human mind is a funny thing. I think you'd agree that rationalization is one of the great faults of the human condition. There are certainly people who justify their bad behavior by sharing the booty with God, as if that absolves them from the bad behavior."

"What if someone does something bad and gives the entire booty to God? A theft or something. Let's say a guy steals a thousand dollars from a bank and puts the entire amount into an envelope and slips it through the mail slot?" Henry gestured toward the slot on the church's side door. "The bank hardly notices the money is missing, but that thousand dollars is life-changing for a few families who belong to the church."

Tom smiled. "That's the Robin Hood principle, no?"

"I guess so."

The pastor adjusted his glasses and folded his arms in the cold. "It's not one man's responsibility to try to right the world's inequalities. Would such an act be beneficial for a church, especially one such as mine? Sure, of course. But one of the basic tenets of Christianity—and I would submit the whole of religion—is that stealing is a sin. I could not possibly condone such an act."

"But you wouldn't know. My question is, would God be angry with the man for stealing?"

"Who knows? One might suggest that the whole arrangement is part of God's plan. Perhaps he has guided the tender-hearted and altruistic thief toward the errand for the well-being of his people?"

Henry smiled and shook his head. "Maybe so. Like I said, I thought you all could use the money."

"Henry, I thank you. You're right: my congregation has very little. But the people have great faith. Strong, unwavering faith. They will see this money as a windfall. I will tell my church members it was an anonymous donation, and we'll decide as a church how to spend it. It's a tremendous gift. Only about fifteen to twenty families attend regularly."

"I'm happy to help."

"God bless you, Henry."

Henry stood but did not turn. He put his hands in his pockets and looked down. Reverend Tom asked if something else was on his mind.

Henry asked: "What does God think about revenge? Does the bible say anything about it?"

"The bible addresses the concept of revenge many times, dozens."

"How does God feel about it?"

"God tells us to leave judgment up to him. He tells us 'never to avenge ourselves, but leave it to the wrath of God.' It seems pretty clear. He also tells us to make sure 'no one repays anyone evil for evil' and 'blessed are the merciful.'" Reverend Tom slid the envelope into his pocket and crossed his arms authoritatively.

"How is that possible? How can God create people and give them free will and then hold it against them when they want to right the wrongs that have been committed against them?"

"I agree that sometimes it seems unfair."

"It doesn't make any sense to me."

"It isn't supposed to make sense, particularly. That's what faith is. Adherence to a doctrine based on trust and based on conviction."

"Does God think it's fun to see people miserable? Does he enjoy watching people try to follow his ancient, outdated rules only to fail and then grovel at his feet? Does he sit about and thrash all the poor unlucky bastards in the world again and again and then allow the evil and the wicked to thrive? Why are kind and blameless and beautiful people relentlessly broken? Why do good people die and bad people live?"

Reverend Tom sighed and looked down and opened his palms in a gesture of concession. Then he said: "I don't know."

"That's it? You don't know?" Henry scoffed.

The Heresy of Rain

"Faith doesn't always make sense, and it isn't always easy. You're right: often the poor and suffering people of the world seem to endure indignity after indignity. And often it seems as though those who most deserve God's wrath are showered with good fortune. We must remind ourselves—and God is very clear about this—that 'the meek shall inherit the earth.'"

The men stared at each other, hardly visible to one another in the evening dark. Henry shrugged and took a deep breath and tried to smile. "It was nice to meet you, Reverend Tom. Good luck getting that sermon written."

"Oh, I think I'll be all right."

They shook hands again, and Reverend Tom smiled faintly and nodded with his eyes sad and tired. He walked back to the side door and gave Henry a little wave and re-entered the church to finish his sermon.

Henry walked back across the street to his truck. He climbed into the driver's seat and took a deep breath and looked at the motel before pulling out and heading over to the Cattleman Grill. The lights along the exterior of the motel had switched on. In one of the rooms the curtain was drawn open a bit, and someone stood watching Henry from her room. It was the old woman with the silver hair. She nodded toward Henry and drew the curtain shut and disappeared.

Henry drove from the motel to Cattleman Grill. It was just a few minutes, but by the time he reached the restaurant it was dark. He backed into the only parking spot available on the far side of the lot. The new vehicles, the cars and trucks and motorcycles he recognized from Galveston, were still there. He cut the engine and rolled down the window and sat. After months of imagining this very scenario he was now unsure what to do. He took the cloth sack from the glove box and emptied the contents on the passenger seat. He did this without taking an eye off the restaurant's door. There was his .38 special and three bullets. He slid two of the bullets into the chamber and put the third in his jacket pocket. He took his eye from the restaurant for a moment to lean over and close the glovebox. Something caught his eye, and he reached to the back of the glovebox and pulled out the lapel pin Charlotte had given him. He turned it over a few times in his fingers and smiled to himself. A silver treble clef. He looked for a long time at the photo of Grace he had wedged into the dash. Then he took the photo from the dash and affixed the lapel pin to the bottom corner of the photo and looked at it again and then put the photograph with the pin into his other jacket pocket.

The evening was very cold. Soon after the sun went down the clouds began to drift about the sky, obscuring the moon from time to time. After a time a very light rain began to fall. Henry opened the truckdoor and stood beside the vehicle for a few minutes in that light rain, a rain almost so fine as mist or fog. He left the truckdoor open and stood behind it like some archer against a rampart. But he had no target. There were no men in the parking lot or standing on the restaurant's deep covered porch. A family exited the restaurant. Two parents and three little girls. Henry had seen the family before, twice at the restaurant. He climbed back into the truck and winced at the soreness he just now felt for the first time in days, and he suspected it was true what people said about feeling aches in their bones when it rained. The family was parked at the front of the lot, near the restaurant's door, and once the parents and their three daughters had tumbled into their sedan and pulled away into the night Henry opened the truckdoor again and eased back down to his spot behind the door, once again an archer or some sniper at war.

Then the restaurant's door opened again. It was two men who walked out and stood on the porch. They lit cigarettes and chatted loudly and laughed loudly. Henry creeped quietly through the drizzle until he was within twenty feet of the men. He did not recognize one of the two men. The other was Maddock. Just then the door opened, and another family exited the restaurant and headed for its car. Henry began retreating to his truck, but this family, too, had parked on the other side of the lot. As these people got in their car and left the premises, Henry began sneaking back toward the porch. Then the man Henry did not recognize went back into the Cattleman Grill, and Maddock walked toward his car. Henry heard Maddock tell the other man he was getting cigarettes from the car and would join the others inside shortly. Henry took a few deliberate steps toward Maddock, who was close to his vehicle. Maddock opened the car door and leaned into the car. As he stood straight again a car pulled into the restaurant, illuminating Henry in full. Maddock saw Henry standing there, his gun at the ready, in that ill-timed spotlight.

Maddock cursed loudly and got into his car because there was nowhere else to go. The car that had just arrived—an unwitting hindrance against Henry's plan—obscured Henry's line of sight. The rain picked up as Maddock started his engine and maneuvered his way out of the lot and onto the highway. Henry cursed loudly and ran back to his truck.

Henry climbed into the truck and started after Maddock, who drove wildly in the light rain. Maddock drove at first on the highway and then after a couple of miles took an exit toward the mountains and the national park. It was very dark now, and the land drank the water thirstily. Soon Maddock and his pursuant were in the wilderness. Small puddles and rivulets formed at the base of the Chisos Mountains. The rain was not much, but the land was eager for water. And Henry followed Maddock closely. There was no light. Maddock weaved from trail to trail, sometimes driving on no trail at all, just slaloming between trees and boulders. He fled from Henry with maniacal abandon. Henry slowed a bit because of the slick and muddy ground but also because of the trees. In the Chihuahuan Desert there were junipers and piñon and honey mesquite. If he waited long enough Maddock would run into a tree. Henry didn't know the land very well, but he knew there would be no patrol or rangers there at this hour. Maddock fishtailed on a gravel trail but regained control. Henry followed steadily behind. His gun was on the passenger seat. He bore no expression. There were no emotions. He followed his prey like some unrepentant and reconciled predator of the night. He saw in his rearview mirror a flash of light that might have been lightning or a reflection of some kind. He continued behind his quarry, content now to keep a distance at a safer speed.

The roads and trails grew steeper, though, and Henry followed Maddock toward the area he knew as Saguaro Falls. Here there were few trees, but the area was dotted with rocks and boulders. And the rain was light but steady, so it was a difficult climb even in a truck. After some time Maddock's car began to fishtail again, this time wildly. The car's front passengerside glanced off a small tree and spun about before coming to rest in a bed of juniper. Henry pulled to within twenty feet and stopped the truck but did not move otherwise. Maddock climbed out of his wrecked car and looked back toward Henry, whose headlights illuminated him. Maddock was a scrawny cornered animal, a rodent peering over his shoulder. Henry calmly took the pistol and left the truck and began walking toward Maddock. Maddock held only his knife and nothing else. He scrambled up the embankment toward the top of Saguaro Falls. Henry followed with resolute coolness. The rain still fell but more lightly now. The night air was cold.

It was only minutes before Henry reached the crest of the incline. Maddock stood at the edge of the cliff. Several yards to their south a stream rushed by and then launched itself over the cliff into the water nearly two hundred feet below. Maddock faced the precipice, holding his knife in his right hand. For a long time he said nothing, just breathing heavily. Henry also said nothing. There was only the sound of the rain and somewhere in the night a chattering coyote that was also cold and wet.

Maddock turned slowly to face Henry. He looked down at his knife. He could have thrown his knife at Henry; maybe he would have wounded him. But he only looked at it in his hand as if he were considering some great stratagem, as if in staring at his weapon the gods would deliver with the rain a new concept so novel it would be his savior. But there were no such gods and there was no such stratagem. So Maddock only laughed. He laughed into the deep relentless night a coarse and vulgar cackle not of this world. Not of this world at all. There was no joy in this.

There was only justice.

There was only justice.

Henry stood his ground, not twenty feet from Maddock, who now stared at Henry with a leering smile. He had nowhere to go. He looked again at his knife, and then he dropped it to the ground, finally coming to terms with the weapon's uselessness.

Maddock shrugged. "So it's come to this, Henry? I'm standing on the edge of a goddamn cliff, and you've got a gun."

Henry stared at Maddock for many moments, expressionless. Lifeless. "I suppose so," he finally said.

The rain was lighter still now. Clouds began to part above.

Maddock dropped his hands to his side. "What is there to say? I don't know what to say to you. Perhaps it was always destined to be this way. What do you think? I have to admit I didn't see it coming." A pause. Maddock shook his head and looked to the ground, and maybe he smiled in spite of it all or because of it all. "Surely there is something you want to say to me."

"There is nothing to say, Maddock. There is nothing."

"Do you want me to apologize?"

"No." Henry stared at him. Then he said: "I only want you to die. I need you to die."

"Fair." Maddock took a step from the edge of the falls toward Henry. The gravel crunched under Maddock's thick-soled boots.

Henry held up the gun and pulled back the hammer. "Stop."

"Fine." Maddock put up his hands, palms facing Henry.

"Do you understand what you've done? Do you understand why we're here at the edge of the earth, you there, and me here with a loaded gun?"

"What I've done? Henry, I've only done my job."

"Your job? A job is a teacher or a police officer. A waitress is a job. A soldier, a doctor, a librarian, a carpenter, a pilot, a nurse: these are all jobs. These are jobs, Maddock. What you have done is no job."

Maddock laughed again but not so wildly. "Fine. If you say so. But there's also the loan shark, the hitman, the smuggler, the thief, and the money launderer. Let's be fair. Your worldview is very narrow. There exist all about us people and institutions that carry on in the darkness, apart from everything else."

"The existence of a thing does not justify the thing. And I don't care about fairness."

"Then what are you doing here, Henry? If fairness isn't your concern what is this all about?"

"This is about justice."

"What's the difference?"

"Fairness is making sure children have the same amount of lemonade. Fairness is making sure no one has to wait in line at the bank longer than anyone else. Fairness is making sure customers at the service station get an honorable deal on car repairs. Fairness is the fish and game commission setting limits, so we can all get food on the table."

"What is justice, then, if not the same?" Maddock held his arms up in question.

"Justice is about balance. Justice is the carrying out of a punishment for an act, a crime someone has committed."

"So it's an eye for an eye? Is that it?"

"That's part of it. But there's more." In the distance the coyote prattled on while Saguaro Falls roared below. Spray from the falls glittered the night sky. The clouds continued to part as the moon tried to drive herself into the night. "There's more," Henry repeated. "Justice is about making adjustments in the greater scheme. I know that now. It's about balance, sure, and sometimes about revenge as well. But it's mostly about a kind of stability that exists in the universe. Understand?"

"I understand you've lost your mind."

"Then I'll make it simpler: you killed my wife, Maddock. You killed her. She was innocent, and you strangled her. You beat her. You murdered my wife."

"Do you think I wanted that to happen? Do you think I got up that morning and said to myself, what harmless woman can I kill today? She was in the wrong place at the wrong time."

"She was a woman, an innocent woman in her own home! She was beautiful and generous and kind."

"I was taking orders, Henry. Doing what my boss told me to do. Just my job." Maddock screamed this at the sky, his voice cracking and echoing this way and that. "And I wasn't even in the house when it happened. I was waiting in a car on the street."

"That doesn't matter. And I've already said: what you did is no job. It was murder."

"I'm sorry your wife had to die, King. Is it not murder if you shoot me here in the wilderness?"

"It would be justifiable."

Maddock said: "Then what's the difference? Do you believe it wasn't your fault she died? That at the very least you didn't play a part?"

"That isn't the point. I didn't kill her. You did."

"Because of your debts, King! Because of your carelessness. Because of your self-destruction. Do you think God will care that you've attempted to achieve this cosmic stability, as you say? You are just as far past redemption as I am."

"There is no redemption for you or me or anyone."

"There could have been."

"No. No. There could not have been. True, I am guilty. You are guilty, and I am guilty. But there was never hope for us. If I were to let you leave right now the demons of hell would escape and gnash their teeth and ferret you out of whatever hiding spot you've claimed. They would torture you past recognition. They would flay you and feast on your skin and howl with laughter in the face of your agony. And then they would turn to me and pin me down and smother me to within a second of death and then let me breathe only to smother me again, and they would do this for all eternity because it's what I deserve. Maddock, neither you nor I deserve redemption. But in the spirit of justice I am going to kill you."

"You've changed, Henry. Something has happened. You were once a cardplaying musician. A nice enough guy. Sometimes a little snooty, but nice enough, I guess."

"I've changed. What a ridiculous thing to say. What man wouldn't change after his wife's death?"

Maddock started at Henry, but something caught his attention, some light or shadow or sound over Henry's shoulder below the falls and beyond the spot where Maddock's car rested in the junipers. Henry dared not turn. The moon continued her surge. The rain had almost stopped completely.

Maddock smiled again his fiendish grin. The grin of a dead man. Or the grin of a man who no longer cares about right or wrong.

"Henry, I'm happy to leave this world. I'll let you deal with the hassle."

Still facing Henry, Maddock took one step backward to the edge of the falls, the rocks and rushing water below. He held out his arms like some gaudy and chuckling Christ. He began to lean back. Henry took a quick stride toward Maddock and not willing to allow Maddock to die on his own terms fired twice. Both shots found Maddock's chest, and his breast opened up with spouts of blood as he fell backward. Henry was close now and saw in that semidarkness Maddock's eyes become white with terror and pain in his last second. He fell back and down below to the water and boulders, having already died. Henry rushed to the edge of the cliff and watched Maddock's body disappear toward the water. He did not hear the splash or Maddock's bones crack against the rocks for the roar of the falls. He knelt there at that spot and said Grace, Grace, Grace, and wept for his fallen wife. He looked at his gun and fingered the trigger and the grip and touched the muzzle to his head and felt the gun's heat and smelled the gun's sulfur. He knelt there at the edge of the falls for some time, hearing the roar of the gun again and again and again as it echoed from canyon to mountain and back again and then beyond.

He was wet even though the rain had stopped, and now he truly felt the chill air. He did not know if he could find his way back to his truck nor once in his truck back to town. He did not know if he wanted to or if he even cared. He rose from his spot at the edge of the precipice and heard in the darkness someone approaching. He took his final bullet from his pocket and loaded it into the chamber and with the revolver in his hand fingered the action and the trigger and waited in the dark.

"Henry!"

"Jesus Christ," Henry said in exasperation. He was trapped against the falls.

"Henry?"

Henry said nothing as a form began to take shape. He could hear the labored breathing and the crunching of the boots before he saw Grant Wisdom appear at the top of the incline near the falls.

"Stop, Grant. Stop there."

Panting and cold and wet, Wisdom stopped several yards from Henry and put his hands up where Henry could see them. Wisdom's gun was holstered. Henry held his own weapon in front of him.

"Henry."

"I guess you found me, Chief."

The sky was undecided, the clouds drifting about the moon and casting shadows all around. The rain threatened to continue.

"Henry, put the gun down."

Henry ignored his godfather. "Maddock's dead."

Wisdom sighed and dropped his head a bit and looked downward. Then he raised his head and looked at Henry through the darkness.

"Did he fall?"

"He tried to fall."

"Tried?"

"I shot him before he had a chance to kill himself. His body is down there below. He'll have two gunshot wounds in his chest."

"Why didn't you just let him fall, Henry?"

Henry didn't answer for some time. He stared through the darkness and listened to the sounds of the wilderness, the rushing water and the yapping coyotes.

Then he said: "Because I couldn't let him go out his way."

"What difference does it make?"

"It makes all the difference. All the difference."

Wisdom looked around, trying to make sense of the situation.

"I'll stand here in the cold and talk to you as long as you want, Henry. But I need you to lower the gun."

Henry lowered the gun to his side. And he said: "Grace is dead."

"I know, son. She died months ago."

"Goddamn. Goddamn. I miss her so much."

The Heresy of Rain

Wisdom looked on as his godson began to cry in the night on some godforsaken cliff in the desert. "I know you do, Henry. I know you do. I wish I could make the pain go away."

"The pain will never go away. It will always be with me. Always."

"That isn't true." Spits of water began to fall again. Clouds moved to cover the moon. Wisdom continued: "You're still young. In time, the pain will be less. Every day it'll get better."

"How do you know? How can you possibly know a thing like that?"

Wisdom had no answer.

Henry said: "We aren't guaranteed anything. We aren't promised upon our births that life will be easy or that we will find love or that our hearts will be mended. There is no rule governing the subsiding of our pain and misery. There is nothing. Nothing at all. There is life, and there is pain, and there is death. A man is not rewarded for his good deeds. There is no destiny that assures us things will go our way next time."

"Surely you don't believe that, Henry."

"What is the other possibility?"

"Salvation. Redemption. Rehabilitation. Reclamation."

"Where is the evidence of this?" Henry was screaming in the night now, competing with the rushing water and rocks below and the rain and the coyotes.

"The evidence?"

"The evidence, Chief. Can you show me redemption?"

"I don't understand, son."

"I can show you misery. Heartbreak. Sadness. Pain. I can show you all of these things. They are real. Maddock's body is below somewhere, beat all to hell and shot up and probably half-eaten by now. Do you think his soul has been reclaimed?"

"I don't know. I can't speak to his relationship with God."

"There's where you're wrong, Grant. There are no relationships with God."

"Why don't you walk with me to my car, and we can get out of the cold and rain and talk a while?"

"Don't be ridiculous."

"Henry, be reasonable."

"Reasonable? What about my life strikes you as reasonable?"

"I know you've been through a lot—"

"You're wasting your time, Grant. This is no time for father-son talks. The time for that was long ago. It's no matter, though."

"I'm sorry."

Henry smiled softly and shook his head. "Someone told me not so long ago that we should reserve our sorrow and that we should apologize only when we are truly sorry."

"Well, I am truly sorry."

"What are you sorry for?" Henry wiped his eyes with his soaked shirtsleeve.

"I'm sorry I wasn't around more. I'm sorry you got into trouble with Maddock's gang. I'm sorry you lost your wife. I'm sorry I couldn't keep you from shooting up that tavern on the island. I'm sorry I couldn't catch up to you sooner. It would have spared a lot of pain, I think."

"Whose pain? Mine? My pain is inconsolable. Maybe if you'd have caught up with me sooner your life would be easier. But not mine."

"Well, then maybe that's it. I don't know. I know I've failed you, and I've failed myself. When I agreed to be your godfather I agreed to be your spiritual guide. Your father and I were best friends. Henry, we were inseparable. I failed you, I failed myself, and I failed your father."

"It doesn't matter."

"Sure it matters. I've followed you from down at the coast up to Central Texas and then all the way to Andrews County, and then I lost you. I realized I was following the wrong guy, so I found Maddock and tailed him all the way out to these godforsaken mountains. I've withheld information from the authorities to protect you. I thought maybe if I could track you down before things got further out of hand I could make a difference. I should have allowed the Rangers or the Federal Bureau to catch up with you. You'd be in jail, but at least there would be hope."

"There's never been hope."

"But you played such wonderful music, Henry."

"Music?"

"Have you forgotten? The whole island, all of Galveston, misses you. Not a day goes by that someone doesn't ask about you. People love you. Those folks love you, and they loved Grace."

"Music doesn't matter anymore."

Wisdom could only stare through the light rain and darkness and puffs of breath at Henry, and he shook his head sadly and shrugged and didn't know what do to.

The Heresy of Rain

Henry looked away from his godfather and then down at his gun, and he raised his right arm and put the gun's muzzle at his temple and pulled back the hammer and tightened his trigger finger.

"Henry, don't do that. Just keep talking to me. Please." Wisdom took a couple of steps toward Henry and placed his right hand at his hip.

"Stop! Do not move any closer."

"Henry, put down the gun."

"This is the end. I'm sorry you caught up to me. I truly am."

"Henry."

"I am irredeemable. I don't know if I have a soul, but I know if I do it is black as night. No god will have me, nor will any devil. I will drift about the land for eternity, my soul black and unreclaimed and my heart heavy with sadness. There is too much pain. And no one knows how to make it right. It's a dark world, and I can't stand it any longer. I miss Grace so much. I'm sorry, Chief Wisdom. I really am."

There was a deafening pistol report. It pierced the air and boomed over the night's noises close and far. Grant Wisdom smelled his acrid gun and felt its heat. He brought his revolver back down to his side and then dropped it steaming to the gravel and rocks and strode quickly the few yards to Henry, who was on the ground, all angular and ungainly and dying. A blossom of red spread outward on his soaked shirt. The rain fell. The air was cold and biting and would not stop. The police chief gathered up his godson in his arms.

He said, "I couldn't let you do it, Henry." He began to weep for the sorrow of it all.

Henry closed his eyes and did not open them again.

And the rainshower continued on, while the chief cradled his dead godson. And while the waterfall pounded the rocks below, tolling its lamentation, the moon began again to shine sadly above, by and by, the rainfall like her tears and the clouds still about her but now shielding her, perhaps, from the sorrow below.

Canto 11

THE MOURNERS HAD ALL CLEARED OUT. Henry was alone with his grandmother, whose grave was new and whose sole legacy stood before her. Only a boy, really, he stared at the earth and wondered quietly why people we love, those who deserve our affection, have to die. And he wondered why people we hate, those who deserve our enmity, are allowed to live. He reasoned God must have something to do with it, or maybe some folks just have terrible luck. Then he shook his head free of such thoughts and wiped his eyes and turned toward the gate and the street beyond. He had promised her he would take care of the piano, and that's what he aimed to do.

Canto 12

GRACE AND HENRY STOOD TOGETHER in the center of a cleared-out spot on the floor. They had been married for less than an hour. He had been nervous about a first dance, but she insisted. He suspected she was nervous too but wanted to show everyone she could do it. They were gathered with their guests in the smallest of the convention center's three ballrooms. Even this room was too large, really. Sammie's was catering the affair, and the servers were getting things ready off to the side. The small crowd of onlookers and well-wishers gave the newlyweds a wide berth. Henry stood with his left hand in Grace's right hand and his other hand behind her head, and he pulled her ear to his mouth.

He said very quietly: "Are you sure you want to do this?"

"Of course," she replied just as quietly.

"All right, then."

"Just like we practiced, Henry."

"Just like we practiced. Except I'm going to close my eyes."

"What?"

"So you won't be alone."

"Henry."

"I love you, sweetheart."

"I know you do."

And then the music started, and they danced together in the early summer evening, together, together, and then. And then the rain began, and they were glad they had chosen to hold the reception indoors.

Everyone said she was a beautiful bride.

And she was.

Epilogue

THE GODDESS OF MUSIC does not help the blind to see. She does not help the deaf to hear. She does not help the mangled to walk. She does not help the broken to be whole.

She does not.

She gives voice to the collective soul, that the soul may be elevated and that the soul may be blessed once more.

She is transformative. She is transformative and exalting.

She grieves our griefs and cries our tears.

And then she lifts our heads and calls out that we may listen, once again renewed.

Acknowledgments

Thanks to…
Mom for reminding me of the high road.
Dad for reminding me of the value of introspection.
Sophie, Luke, and Oliver for reminding me not to take myself too seriously.
Kelly, Mike, and Magnolia for always having my back.
Stephanie for your friendship, patience, and kindness.
The editors at April Gloaming for their vision and great taste.

Author Bio

Zac Mooney is a bookseller with a shop in Southeast Texas, which gives him plenty of time to write. Also, he is a mediocre amateur blues pianist. He does not take requests.